A COLD WIND

ALSO BY C. J. BRIGHTLEY

Erdemen Honor:
The King's Sword
Honor's Heir

A Long-Forgotten Song:
Things Unseen

A Cold Wind

C. J. Brightley

Egia, LLC

ISBN 978-0-9891915-1-7

Published in the United Sates of America by Egia, LLC.

www.cjbrightley.com

Cover design by Ivan Zanchetta

For Stephen

ONE

RIONA

L ani came running to me when I was folding sheets with Sayen out in the courtyard. "Ria, come see him, if you want to see him alive. Saraid says he won't last the afternoon."

She's much younger than I am, my cousin, though we could hardly be more different. She was fourteen then, and even the prospect of a hero's death couldn't sober her for too long. She'd been assigned to bring the dying soldier his meals, though he'd eaten none of them yet. He'd spent the last day and a half out of his mind with fever.

I followed her through the halls to the door of his room. Saraid rolled her eyes at Lani and me when we entered. "Have you no decency? The man's dying." She was trying, mostly unsuccessfully, to spoon honeyed wine between his lips.

I'd never seen a Dari before, and I stepped closer for a better look. His skin was very dark, the color of olives, with the same rich greenish undertone. His face was different from Tuyet faces, with a straighter jaw and a slightly narrower nose, all hard flat planes rather than the long elegant curves of a masculine Tuyet face. Not my conception of beauty, but not as monstrous as I'd expected.

His lips were open, and he gasped slightly with each quick breath. Sweat beaded on his forehead. When Saraid spooned the wine into his mouth, he swallowed convulsively, but choked on it and struggled for a long moment before the next breath. Regardless of looks, I pitied him.

Saraid sat back and her shoulders slumped. "I don't know what else to do." She sounded totally defeated. She rubbed her hands hard over her face and closed her eyes a moment.

"He still lives. You can't give up now." I'm no healer and I really had no idea if he had a chance, but I guess I thought that while he breathed, there was hope.

"He's taken two, maybe three good swallows. Since yesterday, mind. The fever's only gotten worse. I've never seen a fever so hot, not in anyone that lived. Here, feel." She put my hand on his forehead, slippery with sweat. It was burning hot, and he twitched at my touch, eyes fluttering open briefly before closing again.

I jerked back in surprise. "His eyes are green!" Green as grass, glittering with fever and oddly bright against his dark skin.

She snapped, "Yes, and you're standing there not working. Get on with you, and let the man die in peace."

I scurried out, not hurt in the least. Saraid is very kind-hearted; that's why she became a healer. Her anger was born of worry and frustration, not a quick temper.

I finished my work that night wondering whether the soldier had lived through the day. Saraid sent Lani to the kitchen to fetch her dinner because she didn't want to leave him. I brought it to her instead, because I wanted another look at the soldier. Saraid looked tired, and she nodded when I asked if I could tend him for a bit so she could rest.

The usurper Taisto was a vicious man. He had a smooth tongue and a pretty face, but we all knew Tibi and his wife and Anath the cook had nothing to do with the plot against the prince. They were in Taisto's way, so he eliminated them. Until the prince and his soldier friend arrived, we'd all thought we might be next. But where could we go? Asking to leave would only draw attention, and Taisto's attention was deadly. Anyone who removed him was already someone I was glad to serve.

If anything, the soldier was worse than before, his breaths quick and shallow. He shook with fever, his hands clenching restlessly at times. He choked and gasped when I spooned wine into him and finally I gave it up, though I did wipe his face with a damp cloth to cool the fever.

His eyes opened sometimes for a minute or two, but he wasn't really aware of anything. Each time I flinched away because the brilliant green was startling and a little eerie. I felt guilty for it though. A man deserves compassion in his last hours, especially a man like him, who'd done so much for Erdem. I pitied him, and I wondered what it would be like when the quick fevered breaths slowed and stopped.

He was shirtless, with only a thin sheet to cover him sometimes, and despite the strange, ugly tone of his skin, I couldn't help admiring a little. I thought if he were Tuyet, he'd be beyond gorgeous, lean and hard and richly muscled. A soldier, not a nobleman, but I was hardly one to be looking at noblemen anyway. He had scars, and I wondered what their stories were. An old one, a long faint line across his ribs on the left, a newer circle on his chest below his collarbone, a larger ragged oval on his back at the bottom of one shoulder. A fresh scar on his right arm near his shoulder that nearly disappeared under a bandage for a newer wound. And others. I wondered if he'd received them all in the king's service.

Most would have come in the time of the old king. It saddened me to think of a man so brave serving such a coward. The old king was a disgrace to his royal name, but we'd waited for the day when his son the young prince would take the throne. No one had been more anxious than those of us in the palace who saw the prince's potential. Not that we'd hurried along the king's death, of course, but we had hoped, both for ourselves and for Erdem, that the prince would be different than his father. Somehow it encouraged me that this brave soldier had also believed in him.

Saraid and I changed the sheets when she returned. The sheets were almost dripping with sweat, and she said the dampness would chill him and worsen the fever. He didn't awaken as we rolled him carefully to one side and then the other while we wrestled with the fabric beneath him. He moaned once, when we first rolled him to his right side, a low quiet sound that made me cringe.

I helped her change the bandage on his shoulder. It covered an ugly gash, but the wound wasn't infected. Someone had stitched it, and done a good job of it too, though it hadn't had much time to heal. Saraid said the fever was from Taisto's poisoned blade, which had scratched his arm. I wondered how he'd gotten the wound on his shoulder, and whether that was why he'd moaned. Whether it hurt even through the fever, or whether he was hurt in other ways.

I asked if I should come back in the morning, but she said no. She didn't expect him to last the night. But I could send Lani with her breakfast and one for the soldier if by some chance he was still alive.

Lani was nearly bursting with excitement at lunch the next day. "I saw him! He lives, and I took him to the prince's office. He's nice, Ria. I felt so bad. I was so excited I walked too fast, and I think he nearly fainted." She's always in trouble for walking too fast and even running in the palace, but she has a willing heart and does her duties quickly and well. She sounded a little upset.

"I hope you slowed down." I can barely keep up with her sometimes and I haven't been nearly killed by poison.

"Of course I did. He ate some breakfast too."

I didn't see him until the next morning, when Lani took me with her to bring him his breakfast. We were very quiet and didn't wake him. He slept on his back, one long muscular arm over his face shielding his eyes from the morning light. His breathing was easier, but even sleeping he looked drawn, tired, a slight catch remaining in each breath. Still, it was amazing he was alive at all. I wondered if it was scandalous of me to be so curious about him. Probably it was.

I saw him in the hallway the day before the coronation. We were busy preparing for it, and I'd scarcely thought about him at all for two days. He was tremendously tall, shoulders broader than I'd realized, and I squeaked out a polite greeting as I curtsied and scurried out of his way. He inclined his head more courteously than he probably should have, since I was only a serving girl. He didn't recognize me, of course, and it startled me that I wished he had.

I looked after him as he walked down the hall, but he didn't turn around. Despite his color, he wasn't really a bad looking man. As ill as he had been so recently, and probably still felt, his strides were long and easy and he moved with a taut grace most men could only envy. Not handsome, certainly, but his deeds more than made up for that.

Kemen Sendoa. We had received instructions to treat him as the most honored guest ever to grace the palace. It was hardly surprising. By the wild rumors sweeping the palace and out through the city, he'd saved the prince's life many times over, negotiated a temporary peace treaty with Rikuto, and almost single-handedly regained the crown for the young prince Hakan Ithel. The poison that had almost killed him was meant for the prince, but Sendoa had taken the blade instead. Of course, it was something of an accident and hardly much of a wound aside from the poison, but the rumors and the king's regard left no doubt of his courage or his faithful service. There were even whispers that he'd been offered the crown, but had rejected it in favor of the prince. True or not, it only added to his air of mystery.

Isn't every girl fascinated by heroism and mystery? I wasn't the only one, even within the palace, who watched him a little more closely than was strictly necessary at the banquet following the coronation. He smiled more than I imagined was usual for him; he didn't have the lines of smiles in his face. His teeth stood out very white against his dark skin. I thought he should smile more often; it softened his serious, intense look. He didn't eat as much as I would have expected for a man of his size, and I wondered if he was still ill. He looked tired. It wouldn't have surprised me.

When I refilled his wine glass, I let my sleeve brush his shoulder slightly. He smiled and nodded his thanks, not really paying attention. My mother would have been scandalized, of course. Good girls like me don't do such things, especially not with honored guests of the king. I didn't really mean anything by it, nothing scandalous. I just wanted to see his green eyes again. I'd heard green eyes in Dari are about as common as grey eyes in Tuyets; roughly a quarter of the population has them. But never having seen a Dari at all before, I thought they were fascinating. Eerie, but fascinating nonetheless.

In the next weeks, I saw him sometimes in the mornings, in the grey dawn when only a few of the servants were awake. I passed him in the hallways and saw him in the courtyard where he exercised. The first time I stopped and stared, my mouth open in awe. The kicks and flips, the pure and perfect energy, were breathtaking. It was beautiful in a wild and furious way, the same way a running horse or a thunderstorm is beautiful.

He finished a set of moves and rested a moment, leaning over to put his hands on his knees. He must have seen me out of the corner of his eye, for he suddenly straightened, his eyes on me. My ears burning, I curtsied, but I couldn't help sneaking a glance back at him again as I hurried away. He smiled slightly and inclined his head, but I wasn't foolish enough to think it was more than courtesy.

After that I was careful to watch him, the few times I did, from the windows. Though later I felt more for him, I can honestly say that then it was still purely curiosity, and I was terribly embarrassed to imagine that he might have thought I felt more. He gave no sign of anything more than proper courtesy when he saw me next, and I was glad he hadn't misinterpreted my interest.

AFTER THE CORONATION, we fell back into something resembling the routine of the palace. Things were changing a lot. The young king Hakan Ithel had Noriso, the palace administrator, rehire many of the servants who had been let go during Vidar's and then Taisto's brief reigns. I was lucky not to lose my position too during that time, but Noriso knew I had nowhere to go and no family to help me. I was grateful to him for it.

To tell the truth, I should have been married by then. My mother had arranged it; I was to be married at the age of seventeen to a small fabric merchant in Stonehaven. I didn't mind him, and he liked me enough I think, but it was a marriage of convenience. I'd already been working in the palace for a few years by that time. When my mother died, we were going to go through with it, because he still needed an heir and it isn't good for a woman to be alone and unprotected.

A month before the wedding, he came to me and begged leave to break the engagement. He'd met a woman, and they were in love. I released him, though I didn't have to since the papers had been signed already. But what is the use of being married to a man who pines for someone else? There is no security and certainly no joy in that, and I wouldn't, couldn't, have expected him to remain faithful to me forever. Instead, he was happy and she was happy and I was quietly disappointed but far from heartbroken. It was better for me too, at least as long as I kept my job.

But the months and then years wore on and I had no other suitors. I didn't have a way to meet men, working as I did in the palace, a closed environment where everyone knows everyone else. It breeds deep friendships and lasting enmity, but once you've figured out where you stand with everyone, it's set for years. Vidar and Taisto had shaken that up, but it quickly settled down again.

There were no particularly good prospects in the few new people Noriso hired, though there were some who might become friends. I didn't have anyone to take care of the arrangements for me, though Lani's mother tried a few times.

It's an odd business, this way that men and women dance around each other. They want our bodies and we want their protection and really, deep inside, I think what we all want most is friendship and understanding. But how do you find that amid the awkwardness and the halting words?

Not long before the king Hakan Ithel was crowned, I met a man in the market. I was twenty-six then, well past the age at which most girls are married, though I hadn't given up hope. His name was Riulono, and he was a footman in the house of Lord Kalyano. He smiled at me as he wove through the crowd, and I blushed and pretended I hadn't noticed. I saw him again when Lord Kalyano attended a banquet at the palace. With the other footmen, he stayed in the servants' quarters, laughing and waiting for their masters to finish. He smiled at me, and I smiled at him. He had curly golden hair and laughing eyes, and I didn't mind when he swept his eyes over me and smiled a little more. It made my heart beat a little faster to think I'd pleased a man. I, mousey little Riona, pleased a man! He noticed me, and I appreciated it more than even I had expected. He sent a letter of intent, properly worded and polite. I didn't have parents to handle it for me, so I answered it myself.

Riulono made me laugh, and he was dashingly handsome. It bothered me a bit that the one time he'd come to visit, bringing a bouquet of bright daisies from the market, he spent almost as much time looking at Tanith and Sinta as he did looking at me. But I wasn't sure what I could expect. I was twenty-six, after all, and hardly the most eligible woman in Stonehaven. I was used to being invisible. He scattered compliments around with careless generosity.

Once I met him in the market for the afternoon on my off day. He smiled and kissed me on the cheek, told me I was beautiful. He smelled of ale, soap, horse sweat, and leather, masculine smells that made my breath come a little short. He bought me grilled tomatoes and peppers on a skewer for lunch, and sticky rice with sweet beans afterward, and took me on a tour all around the most exciting part of the market, the jewelry stands. The jewels glittered with brilliant color in the sunlight. Sayen said later he should have bought me something, even if it was small, but I didn't expect him to; a footman isn't rich, and jewels are frivolous anyway.

We sat on the edge of one of the wells and he pointed out people he'd seen before. That man was a thief, but not very good; he'd been thrown in prison a hundred times. That girl was a harlot. I glanced at him sideways as he said it, and he didn't seem especially offended. I know some girls rent their bodies, I can even understand why they might be so desperate, but I guess I'd expected to hear a bit of scorn in his voice. I wondered if he'd paid the street women visits of his own. Probably not. He was handsome enough he wouldn't have to pay for that.

Lani's mother Ena and father Joka had already begun tentative negotiations with several prospects for her, though she wouldn't be wed for some years yet. She was intimidated by it, and I couldn't blame her. It frustrated me that I had no advice to give her - aside from the obvious, of course.

"It'll be fine. He can't be that bad."

"Your mother loves you, she won't make you marry someone you hate."

"You might like each other."

But Lani wasn't yet interested in men, aside from a general curiosity, so the idea of being attracted to one was far from her mind. She wasn't exactly unaware of men's needs, she just wasn't yet ready to have any desire of her own.

I wished I could say the same. I wished for a girl-friend closer to my own age I could talk to, and I did have a few, but they were all married or betrothed. I laughed when Sinta and Tanith teased me about Riulono, but the truth is I wished desperately for a husband, to feel loved, needed, protected. It's not good to be alone.

NOT LONG AFTER the coronation, the young king Hakan Ithel sent Sendoa to speak to the Rikutan king. The whispers ran about the palace like fire. The Rikutan king had specifically requested Sendoa, because his brother, an army officer, had spoken so highly of him. It was unheard of to appoint a man of war as an ambassador, but the king's trust in his friend was absolute. His official title became Ambassador and General Kemen Sendoa.

Two

Kemen

The day after the coronation, I wandered about the palace almost in a daze. I saw a few servants. The girl who had led me to Hakan's office gave me a bright smile as she hurried down a hallway and asked if I wanted anything. I shook my head, bemused and pleased by her friendly courtesy.

Finally I found myself in the kitchen, a great room with several open fireplaces, three ovens, dozens of strings of dried vegetables hanging all about my head, and so much other food that I was nearly overwhelmed by the smells. I had to duck my head quite far to see under the strings of onions and peppers, and I would have turned around but a cheerful voice rang out in greeting.

I answered, "I'm sorry, I think I'm in the wrong place."

"Nonsense. Come in, come in."

I bent down to find the source of the voice and finally made my way through the confusion to a man kneading some kind of dough at a table, with a woman and a younger girl behind him scurrying about, taking things in and out of the ovens. A young boy was chopping peppers close by. The onions and peppers were above the man's head, but I couldn't stand without catching my hair in them, and he motioned me to sit at the table across from him.

His eyes widened when he saw me more clearly, but he smiled very kindly. He had a generous round face with deep lines from smiling and white hair that ringed his head already. The whiteness and the baldness may have come a bit young, for he didn't look older than fifty. He began talking almost immediately.

"Are you the soldier Kemen Sendoa?"

"Aye." I nodded.

"I'm Joran. I thank you for your care of the prince. The king Hakan Ithel is a good boy, a good man now I suppose, and we were so worried for him. You know that Tibi and Torna and our own Anath had nothing to do with it, don't you?"

I nodded, assuming he meant the assassination attempt that Taisto had blamed on Hakan's tutor and the others. They'd been executed for it on Taisto's orders.

"He's well loved here. Far be it from me to criticize a king, but I will say that we look forward to serving under the king Hakan Ithel as a more pleasant experience than we've had yet in the palace. You have our gratitude, more than I can say. Here, Luko, bring me that meat pie."

The boy brought a steaming pie and Joran cut out a large slice, then quickly arranged some cheese and fruit on the side of the plate. "You look hungry. Eat while you rest." He slid the plate over to me with a smile.

"Do I?"

He bobbed his head in quick apology. "Forgive me for the insult, sir, if it is insulted you feel. The king has given orders that you're to be accorded every honor, as the most favored guest the castle has ever seen, and from what I've heard you've had a hard enough time of it in your service to him. Take it as thanks from us. We love him too." His voice had an odd inflection, and I wondered what part of the country he was from. He'd clearly been in Stonehaven for years, and I couldn't place the accent.

I shrugged and ate with a will. I'd thought I was full, but with the fever fading, I was already hungry again. The man talked all the while, though I hardly carried my end of the conversation. When I finished the pie, he pushed another plate in front of me, this time of tangy vegetables. Then another plate of pie, this one a fruit pie with cream and honey on top. Then pastries and fresh berries. Finally I forced myself to stop. I don't like the heavy slow feeling when I eat too much. The boy took away my dirty plates to wash with eyes wide with awe.

Joran asked, "Did you have enough?"

I nodded. The kitchen was warm and pleasant, but in a few minutes more, I bid them farewell, with many thanks for the excellent food.

I found Hakan in the courtyard behind the castle. He was speaking to one of the grooms, and I didn't want to interrupt them.

I leaned on the fence to watch the horses in the small corral outside the stable while I waited for him to finish. The sun was warm on my shoulders and the late spring breeze carried the scent of horses, flowers, and thick rich grass. I felt absolutely happy, more at peace with the world than I had been in years.

There was a foal nursing from a fat healthy mare in the far corner of the corral, and one of the barncats jumped onto the fence not far from me. I held very still.

Though I have a way with horses and dogs, cats are sometimes afraid of me.

The cat balanced on the top rail of the fence and walked toward me with perfect confidence. She, a mother still nursing, rubbed against me, the tip of her tail tickling my nose. Her fur was warm and dusty, black and brown mixed haphazardly. Her little white paws were the size of my fingertips. I wondered if that's what it's like to have a woman, a creature inexpressibly beautiful and delicate, with an entirely different sort of power.

Hakan stood beside me. "Kemen?" He hesitated. "Have you ever been with a woman?"

I wondered whether I had been speaking aloud. "Why?"

He looked out at the corral as he spoke. "I'll need a queen, and someday an heir. My mother was a commoner, but I don't know how my father met her. How can a prince, or a king, court a commoner?"

"If you only want an heir, it should be easy enough." Too easy. Most women would be only too eager.

He shook his head, as I had expected. "My father and mother had no love between them. I won't do that to my child. But how can I know whether a woman cares for me or for my crown?" The cat turned about and rubbed her head against his shoulder, purring loudly, and he rubbed her absently.

Finally I said, "I'll think on it. But in this I may not be able to serve you, Hakan."

He nodded. "I know. But I respect your judgment."

I raised my eyebrows but did not answer him. Of all things I was unqualified for, advice on women was probably foremost. Hakan would have been better served to go ask a stableboy.

THOUGH I'D EXPECTED to go to Rikuto soon after the coronation, it was nearly two weeks before I left. Hakan was busy with the work of ruling, and the palace soon took on a very different feel. Taisto had dismissed great numbers of servants, and Hakan enlisted the aid of the palace administrator to rehire the appropriate number.

Of course, Taisto's men in the kitchen had already been dismissed. Hakan would have preferred to arrest them for poisoning Vidar, but we were unable to find proof so long after the deed. The king's guards, who had been awaiting trial in the dank stone cells of the palace prison, were released and given an official commendation for their loyalty. They were pale, hungry, and badly needed washing, but after a hot bath, a new set of clothes, and a week of rest and rich food, they were as eager to serve as ever.

I was honored to meet Siri Andar, the commander who had sent the message to Hakan about Taisto's treachery. He was a man of thin and wiry build, smaller than most soldiers. His golden hair was liberally sprinkled with silvery grey, but his sparkling gaze and quick smile made him seem younger than he probably was. I knew immediately he was in deadly earnest in his promise to die for his men, though I might have suspected another man of bravado or posturing. He seemed to look on every man even five years his junior as a son to be protected and guided. When I met him, I bowed low before him because he deserved that honor. He returned the bow with more respect than was strictly proper, for he was my senior both in age and rank.

Though Hakan spoke with me about many of the changes he made, I didn't understand everything he did. He changed the way the taxes were collected; he said that the old way was rife with corruption. I'd heard a few complaints, but since I'd mostly kept to myself, I didn't know exactly how it worked, and had no experience of it myself. I'd never been taxed; I owned no land and no business.

Hakan said the new way would be better. It would give the king's treasury the same amount or even more without taking nearly so much from the pockets of the commoners. He said the only people who would be angry with him would be the nobility, but he didn't mind that much because the changes would benefit merchants and enable them to make more money on their trading. Eventually the greater trade would appease the nobility because they would be able to buy more luxurious silks and dates, nuts and expensive porcelain from Ophrano and Rikuto at better prices. I hoped he was right; antagonizing the nobility at the start of a reign is a risky thing.

He had grand plans to start a series of schools for common children throughout the country. The classes would be similar to those taught at the beginning of our education in the army, but instead of military tactics and strategy he wanted the children to study agriculture and trade. He was also very interested in developing strategies that would take better advantage of the crossbow, for it gave archers different capabilities than the longbow or the shorter bow of the suvari archers. It didn't require as much training, for one thing, and that meant that even kedani and suvari who weren't in the archery squads might be armed with crossbows to be used at need.

The day before I left, Hakan asked me to meet with him in his working office. We spoke about what he wanted from Rikuto and what he was willing to give. He had a good idea of what Tafari might demand most firmly and where he would be more flexible.

Finally he leaned forward, his voice very quiet. "I hope you will forgive me, Kemen. I've assigned you an assistant who will serve you as both scribe and advisor on this trip. He has some experience in diplomacy and can give you guidance. You hold my authority, but I believe he can help you. He's been to Rikuto often and lived several years in Enkotan in his early service. In order to have him best serve you, and Erdem's interests, I found it necessary to tell him about your difficulty reading."

I nodded. It was unavoidable, I could see that clearly enough. Yet still it stung, and my jaw was tight with shame when the man was brought in to meet me.

Farin Driniamo was perhaps two or three years younger than I was, a bit soft in his middle already. He had smooth pudgy hands and a round face, but his eyes were shrewd and brightly intelligent. He would serve as my chief assistant, but I was also assigned five couriers, several younger scribes to serve under Driniamo, and an escort of fifty suvari. That night Driniamo and I reviewed the agreements Taisto had signed with Tafari, and I saw better how calculating Taisto had been and how tightly he'd been squeezing Tafari.

Though Hakan gave me a carriage in keeping with my official authority, I preferred to ride. The rocking of the carriage made my stomach turn, and it made me uneasy to not see the road ahead of me. Besides, the summer was far too glorious to traverse with windows shuttered. Driniamo was not a particularly good rider, but he took pains to speak to me and suffered from saddle sores in his attempt to remain by my side. I suppose it was a form of honor, for I was the authority of the group, and if I rode, then it was unfitting for him to remain in the carriage.

He liked to talk and I found him tedious at times, but he was a pleasant companion for the most part. With many apologies for his presumption, he offered sound advice about Rikutan court etiquette and negotiation techniques. How to demand more than is possible, so when you compromise you gain more than you might have expected. The priorities that the old king Hakan Emyr had held and what was likely to have changed for Tafari since Driniamo had last been to the Rikutan court.

It was odd to discuss such things with him. At times, I was impressed by his perception and shrewdness, at times almost disgusted by the inherent duplicity of diplomacy, and at times profoundly grateful that Erdem was served so well. Most often, I felt unequal to the task. Diplomacy was far from my humble experience. For his part, Driniamo gave no indication that he thought less of me for my inability to read. I was more grateful for that than he probably realized.

Our travel to the border took nearly two weeks, for the carriage did not make the trip with the speed that suvari alone would have. We crossed the border on the Lobar Road pass, but we didn't meet any Rikutan border guards until we were nearly out of the mountains.

We had no trouble. Tafari had already told them to expect a diplomatic envoy sometime, and they gave us an honor escort to the capital. That part of the journey took another week. The Rikutan countryside provided ample interest while we rode. The weather on that side of the mountains is much hotter and drier, and that year it had been especially difficult.

I saw few farmers, but those I saw looked thin and weary. When I asked one of the Rikutan officers how the people in the country fared, he scowled and said that in some of the outlying areas, the roads had become nearly impassable for common folk, because Tarvil bandits and raiders had become so numerous. The crown had spent so much money on buying food from Erdem it could no longer support an army sufficient to protect the populace. Of course, many of the bandits were Rikutans driven to desperation by failing crops and failing markets, unable to travel and trade as they had before.

Once we reached Enkotan, we were escorted directly to the palace. I'd never seen it before, and I tried to get a glimpse of everything as we drew closer. We arrived late in the afternoon with the sun setting behind us, but the angle of our approach up a slight slope meant we didn't see the palace in all its glory, at least at first.

We were received with all due courtesy and respect. The Erdemen suvari were escorted to their quarters, which I later heard were quite adequate, though not luxurious. I dismounted and handed the reins to a groom, but before I had fully taken in the Rikutan palace, I was greeted by a man who introduced himself with a graceful bow as Virkama Niramsokai, the king's seneschal. He was a sober man, simply dressed given his rank, with light brown hair, pale blue eyes, and a careful, thoughtful air about him. He asked whether I would prefer to rest before seeing the king. I declined, though I did take his offer of a chance for a quick wash to make myself presentable.

The palace was beautiful and ancient, built within a hundred years of our own in Stonehaven, and I would have enjoyed the chance to examine it more closely, for Rikutan design is much different than Erdemen design. However, Niramsokai himself escorted me immediately to a guest room of deep red and gold. Driniamo's room was next door. I washed quickly and opened the door to find Niramsokai still waiting for me. He bowed respectfully and took me to the king's throne room, Driniamo following behind me.

Three

Riona

Riulono came to see me again. Tanith called me to the servant's entrance where she had left him outside inspecting his jaunty footman's cap for any specks of dust. "Ria, your catch is here to see you."

"He's not a fish, Tanith."

"He is! He has no soul. I like him, Ria, he's handsome and funny, but he's cold. Be careful. He's not your kind of man."

Tanith had the worst taste in men I'd ever seen; her advice was barely worth hearing, much less following.

Riulono didn't seem to care about her opinion of him. He winked at her and then laughed easily when she rolled her eyes. "Beautiful Riona, dearest, could you spare a moment for me? I have something to show you." He was nearly grinning.

I showed him to a table in the kitchen and sat across from him. I wasn't entirely sure I wanted to be alone with him yet. Joran was there, and he made me feel safe.

"Ria, darling, I have something for you." He was proud, white teeth flashing in another quick grin. "I found it at the market last week, but I couldn't get away until now. Here." He pulled a small wooden box from his pocket and gave it to me, leaning forward in anticipation.

I wish I could describe what I felt. Hope, anticipation, quite a bit of fear. I opened the box tentatively. Inside the box was a fine golden necklace, several thin chains linked together. They glittered in the sunlight streaming through the window.

"Do you like it?" he watched my face.

I smiled and nodded.

"I got a deal. It was only twelve golden eagles." He shrugged carelessly. Sinta rolled her eyes as she passed behind his back. It was quite a bit of money for a servant, even a footman in a noble house.

He leaned forward again, elbows on the table. "I could get the papers next week. Marry me, Riona."

I licked my lips, my heart racing.

"Here, I'll put it on you." He stood and walked around behind me. He fiddled with the clasp a moment, with one quiet oath under his breath. "Here."

I bent my head forward and he let his fingers linger on my neck, one hand trailing down much lower than it needed to.

He bent to speak into my ear. "Tell me, Ria, dear. Shall I get the papers?"

I tensed as he ran his hand down my arm. "Can I think about it?"

He let out a quick breath and straightened. "What's to think about? Darling, take all the time you want, so long as it isn't more than a week. I'm getting impatient." He grinned wickedly. "Am I competing with anyone for your affections?"

22

"No." My answer was quiet, and I glanced at Joran who was working steadily two tables away. I wondered if he could hear.

"Then I suppose you'll see reason soon enough. I can wait." He grinned and leaned down to kiss my cheek. "You're beautiful. The gold matches your hair. I need to go, Kally wants me back soon. I know my own way out." He whistled as he left.

Kally. Everyone else called him Lord Kalyano. It was another thing that bothered me. Riulono wasn't as respectful as I thought he should be. Not to Lord Kalyano. Not to me. I fingered the chain on my neck.

Joran slid into the chair across from me, frowning. "Ria, are you really going to do it?"

I shrugged. I didn't know. I didn't know if I should. He made me feel desired. A woman needs a man, at least in Stonehaven. I wanted children. I wanted a family, and I was tired of being alone. And Riulono was right; he had no competition.

Joran's soft face frowned more and he scraped at a spot on the table with one fingernail. "You can do better."

I raised my eyebrows. "Joran, I'm twenty-six. How many other men have you seen in here courting me?"

He shrugged a little uncomfortably. "You don't love him, do you?" His eyes flicked to my face and then away.

I hesitated. "Not everyone has the luxury of love."

I didn't really know if he loved me, or if I loved him. It was a lot of money for a footman to spend on a necklace. I wanted to believe that meant something, but sometimes when I thought about how he spoke to me, I felt a crushing weight on my chest. I felt trapped. Hemmed in.

FOUR

KEMEN

I'd expected to feel nervous at meeting the Rikutan king, but surprisingly I felt very calm. It was as though I knew already the meeting would go well.

The throne room was beautiful, a fitting tribute to an ancient and great culture. The floor was paved in white marble, with stark geometric inlays of black granite, and the walls were hung with red tapestries, tall and narrow to accentuate the vaulted ceiling. The throne itself was of dark wood inlaid with gold, surrounded by a red carpet with gold accents on the edges. I bowed respectfully when I entered and again as I approached the throne.

The king Ashmu Tafari was perhaps forty-five years old. The resemblance to his brother Zuzay was clear, the corners of his mouth turning up similarly though his eyes were more tired. A king has a difficult job, and I would not have traded places with him for anything. He stood to greet me and strode down the steps to clasp my elbow, as a warrior would have. The gesture surprised me, for it was an unusually warm way to begin negotiations, but I suppose he wanted to make his gratitude clear.

The audience was very short, only an invitation to a banquet that night in our honor. Niramsokai called a manservant to conduct me back to my room and stayed to confer with the king. As I left, out of the corner of my eye I saw Niramsokai standing by the king, his head inclined respectfully; their eyes were on me. I wondered what they thought, and hoped Hakan was right to send me.

A servant offered to attend me before the banquet, but I preferred to prepare alone. I had a bath to wash away the sweat and dirt of the road and dressed in the court clothes Hakan had provided for me. The fabrics were luxurious; thick, fine wool breeches of a dark grey-green, a brilliant white silk shirt, and a dark green tunic with a supple dark leather belt. When I saw myself in the mirror, I couldn't help smiling to think how strange it was, that I, a foundling and a soldier, should be representing the Erdemen king in a foreign court. In all my years of hard training, I had not prepared, had not even thought to prepare, for this challenge.

I looked out the window at the city sprawled below the palace, and wondered how things were different there. In the sunset, the distant houses looked golden and warm, but there were too few cookfires burning and too few shouts of children's laughter in the streets. I hoped our agreement would change that.

Tafari welcomed me to the banquet that night with an apology. "I would offer you better fare, more in keeping with the honor I wish to accord you, but I fear this is all we have available. The king exists as a servant of his people, and as such does not enjoy luxuries unavailable to the people."

This was not entirely true, for clearly the palace was more luxuriously appointed than a farmer's hovel, but the principle was valid and well observed. Each dish was elaborately prepared, but there weren't as many dishes as at Hakan's coronation banquet, nor was the amount of food so generous, although it was more than sufficient. I liked Tafari and how he honored his country and my status as Hakan's ambassador without throwing away Rikuto's scarce resources. If Zuzay had told him to ask for me, Zuzay had also read my preferences aright.

We began in earnest the next morning. To my surprise, the king himself was the principal negotiator, with his seneschal Niramsokai and a scribe to assist him. We spoke in Kumar, for Tafari was more than fluent. I suppose it serves almost as a common language across our kingdoms, for the soldiers and kings of many nations speak it. Common, or what we call Common, is really only spoken on the west side of the mountains, in Erdem, Ophrano, the Senga tribes, and many of the Tarvil.

Driniamo listened quietly by my side. Very occasionally, he would lean close to whisper a bit of advice or something from an old agreement that he thought might be helpful, but mostly he left me to it. Tafari was clear and direct but much better accustomed to diplomacy than I was, and I could tell he was aware of my inexperience. I stood firm where Hakan had told me I should and was quick to agree where I knew it would cost Erdem little. There is nothing to be gained by needlessly antagonizing a potential ally, and an ally he was.

One of the most important things Hakan had hoped for was the repair and security of the major roads between Erdem and Rikuto. He wanted the roads enlarged and made more secure, for though Tarvil raiders would no longer be paid by Taisto, they were yet a menace to unguarded travelers and traders. Throughout the day, Tafari was more than gracious and acceded to most of my requests. His own were much as Hakan and I had expected and prepared for, and I was glad to be able to promise our cooperation.

To my utter surprise, we finished the day with much of the final agreement decided upon, though it was not yet written. We were treated to a banquet again that night, with music and a demonstration of traditional Rikutan dancing. Tafari was in good spirits, for our arrangement promised great improvements for his country. Zuzay Tafari arrived that afternoon in time for the meal and festivities.

The banquet was more than pleasant. Though I was among strangers and acquaintances, I felt as though I were among friends. Both the king and his brother took pains to make me feel welcome. Driniamo told me later that though Tafari was always gracious, that evening showed his great pleasure in the day's agreements.

Afterwards Driniamo spent several hours writing a tentative copy of the agreement, speaking to me all the while to confirm the details. Of course, the next morning we changed many of the finer points, but Tafari was pleased with the outline and we signed the final agreement before noon.

I practiced signing my name that night. I'd done it before, but it had been years since then and I'd never done it often, only for the highest orders for the army. I swallowed my pride, though it stuck in my throat, and asked Driniamo to help me. I wouldn't shame myself or Hakan by ruining the agreement with a faulty signing.

He spelled my name and wrote each letter individually for me, but then showed me a good form for the final signature, a smoother and more practiced hand, the letters running down the page like water. It was easier to imitate the casual signature than to form the letters into precise words, and this reassured me. Driniamo was tactful enough to hide even the slightest hint of mockery. When we finally signed the binding agreement the next day, my signature, at least to my unpracticed eyes, looked nearly as fluid as Tafari's.

We were set to depart on the morrow, after a greater banquet than before.

Before the celebration, Tafari himself took me on a walk through his garden. It was a wondrous place, and I could tell he loved it, for he told me far more than most would ever want to know about each plant and flower. The garden was a beautiful example of Rikutan style and design. The pathways were laid out in perfect arcs intersecting with arrow straight paths, all of which were covered in tiny pebbles of pure white or deep grey. Each flower and tree was pruned to perfection. There were glittering pools of still water, their floors paved in cobalt blue tile. Every detail was arranged in an exacting symmetry that must have been stunning from the top of the tower. Off to the west side, well separated, there was a section of the garden left a little more free, the pools unpaved but still carefully tended. It was a peaceful place that the king clearly enjoyed. I imagined it a retreat from the cares of his office, and considered it an honor that he shared it with me.

I saw a girl some distance away as we walked. She was sitting on a bench with a book before her, though she was not reading. Instead she was carefully braiding some flowers into a small circlet, which she eventually put on the head of a small dog laying next to her. I tried not to stare at her, though I was intrigued, but we passed close by her twice as we followed a curving path through the garden.

Finally I asked, "Who is that girl?"

He glanced at me quickly. "That is my daughter, Kveta."

I cannot tell what spirit of audacity prompted me to ask it, but I did. "How old is she?"

His eyes narrowed slightly. "She is seventeen."

Well into the age of eligibility then.

"Why?" He stopped and turned to look me square in the face.

I inclined my head to show him my respect. "She is very beautiful." In fact I'd been unable to see her face, but her form was pleasing and I liked the quiet laugh I heard once.

"Aye, she is." He studied me closely. "If you were another man, I might ask you not to notice so closely."

I swallowed. A father has every right to be protective, but I would not jeopardize my mission for something so foolish. Again, the spirit of audacity took my tongue, as well as a stroke of genius, which I cannot normally claim. "I notice not for myself, Your Highness, but as the envoy of a king."

He blinked in surprise.

"The king Hakan Ithel is young, wise, and kindhearted. Yet he has no queen."

He smiled suddenly and resumed walking. "You have a smooth tongue, but a good heart behind it. Tell me about this king Hakan Ithel. Not as a king. As a man. Tell me that."

"He is calm of temper, not easily angered. He is patient, though he wasn't always so, and very hard working. He likes to sing. He likes history and the stories of the heroes of old." What else? What can a man say when evaluating the heart of a friend? What was my right to say and where should I keep silent?

We walked in silence for several minutes, and finally, almost before I realized it, we had reached the bench where the girl was sitting.

She jumped up and curtsied to her father and to me before embracing him with a smile. He smiled at her, and it warmed me to see their love. I wanted that kind of love, if I ever had a daughter. I studied her face a moment. She had wide blue eyes and blond hair, common enough in Tuyets. Her face was bright and kind. If she'd dressed differently, she might have been any commoner but for her eyes, which showed a light of educated intelligence I thought would please Hakan. Her eyes on me were curious but showed little of the fear I expected.

"Kveta, this is Ambassador Kemen Sendoa. He is the representative from the new king Hakan Ithel in Erdem."

She curtsied again, her eyes on me.

"Ambassador, you have the honor of meeting my daughter, Her Royal Highness Kveta Aranila Tafari."

I bowed deeply and as gracefully as I knew how. In a moment, he'd drawn me away. It was not fitting for a common warrior, even one acting as an ambassador, to speak at length with a princess.

We walked in silence a moment before he finally spoke. "Surely you do not ask for the hand of a princess yet. Your king has not even met her. Besides, I will not give my daughter as a pawn."

Nor would he send her to be rejected by Hakan. That would reflect badly on them both.

"No, Your Royal Highness." I thought a moment. "I merely beg your leave for the king to write letters to the princess. If, after some time, the two desire to meet, Erdem would be honored to receive your daughter as a guest."

He glanced at me. "Only letters?"

"That's all I ask. Maybe in time His Royal Highness Hakan Ithel will ask more."

He nodded. "You may convey to your king that she will receive his letters."

The banquet that evening was more extravagant than the ones before. My favorite part was the dancing demonstration. The dancers were like flowers in their bright silk tunics, tight waist sashes, and wide skirts for the ladies, flowing pants for the men. Most of the words to the songs and narration were Rikutan High Tongue, and I could understand only parts of it, but Zuzay, sitting next to me, gave me a running commentary. On my other side was the king, and beside him was the princess. She looked across him at me sometimes; when I glanced up and caught her eye, she flushed and looked down at her plate.

The next morning, when we were nearly ready to leave, the seneschal knocked on my door. "His Royal Highness requests your presence."

He had a very odd look on his face, and I followed him curiously to one of the small offices. When I entered, Tafari was standing behind his desk, and his daughter was standing beside him. He too had a strange expression.

"Yesterday I said that my daughter would receive your king's letters. I neglected to ask my daughter her thoughts on this arrangement, and in this she has the right to an opinion. Upon her request, I have changed my mind." His eyes were very steady on my face, sharply observant.

My jaw tightened with frustration, the sting of insult, but I bowed deeply. "As you wish. His Royal Highness would not wish to displease the princess."

The girl turned quickly to look at her father, her eyes wide, and he smiled tautly.

"My daughter has instead requested that she be allowed to accompany you back to Erdem to meet the king Hakan Ithel for herself."

It was a test, and apparently I'd passed it, though I am unsure exactly what he had expected me to say or do.

He continued, "I have given my consent, and would request your forbearance while her retinue is made ready."

I bowed again. "Yes, Your Royal Highness. Your daughter is more than welcome."

The girl smiled at her father and then directly at me. Though Hakan might be very angry with me, I was wholeheartedly glad that she was coming.

THE PRINCESS KVETA Tafari rode in her own carriage and I didn't see her much the first day. I wondered if she'd repented of her decision, but I heard no word from her until that night. I didn't know whether I should say something to her or pay my respects, or whether it would be improper, and I decided against it. The suvari were eating quietly and I prepared to sit with them, when one of her men came asking for me.

Her tent was luxurious, at least to me, and she sat inside on a little folding chair behind a small table. The lamps made the space seem cozy and bright, white and red and gold on the fabric walls.

"Come. Would you eat with me?" She licked her lips nervously, and I bowed low before her. She was very young and very frightened, but she held her head with the pride I expected of a princess.

"As you wish." I sat across from her, wishing my legs weren't quite so long. My height is less of a problem when I'm at a normal table, but traveling furniture makes me look even more ridiculous than usual. I kept my eyes down on the table for the most part because I did not wish to frighten her further.

One of her women put plates of food in front of us, and I waited until the princess Kveta began before I took a bite. I glanced up to see her staring at me and biting her lip. "What shall I call you?"

"You may call me Kemen." I should have introduced myself to her again without prompting.

She chewed her lip for a moment, and I wished I knew how to tell her that she didn't have to be nervous. "My uncle spoke very well of Hakan Ithel."

"Your uncle Zuzay Tafari?"

She nodded.

"That was good of him." I tried to make my voice soft, appropriate for speaking with a lady.

"He also spoke well of you. I wouldn't have been so bold if he hadn't." The words came out in a rush, and she blushed.

I bowed my head. "I'm honored by your trust." My eyes caught hers as I looked up.

She smiled nervously but with a bit of gentle humor. "You needn't be so formal. My father is the serious one." She hesitated. "What is he like? The king Hakan Ithel, I mean."

How does one describe a friend? I thought, and I suppose I thought too long, because she prompted me.

"Is he serious? Funny? Tall? Thoughtless or deliberate?" Now she was holding back a smile.

"He is tall for a Tuyet, but quite thin. Near your age."

She nodded, smiling slightly.

"More humorous than I am, but quite serious when he needs to be." Her eyes on me made me nervous. "He's thoughtful." I paused as I thought some more. "Sensitive?" It was a question, because I wasn't sure it was the

33

right word, but she nodded more confidently now. "He sings well."

"Is he a good swordsman?"

I hesitated. "Good enough." That was true, if a bit generous.

She smiled delightedly. "You mean he's not especially good."

I kept my eyes lowered so that I wouldn't laugh. A soldier doesn't laugh in the presence of a princess. It isn't respectful. "He's good enough for a king."

"But not a soldier?"

I licked my lips, thinking she was probably mocking me. I didn't really mind. It wasn't unkindly done. "A soldier has different duties. Hakan is very good at his, but a king does not need his sword often."

I reached for my glass of wine and took a sip. It was Rikutan wine, of course, dry and strong. I glanced up at her when I put the glass down. Her eyes were full on my face and she leaned forward to put one hand on mine for a moment. I almost lost my breath, not from desire, though she was pretty enough, but simply from shock. I could count the number of times I'd been touched by a woman on my fingers, all serving girls brushing by in a tavern or an inn. Never by a princess, and never deliberately. If Tuyet men shrink from my dark skin, how much more do Tuyet women? A Tuyet princess? Her hand was smooth and milky white, and perhaps she saw my shock, for she suddenly clasped her hands together.

"Kemen. Maybe I'm being stupid. I do that sometimes. But my uncle Zuzay and my father spoke so highly of you, I would like to count you as a friend."

I stared at her in surprise before lowering my eyes. She stumbled on nervously but gaining a bit of confidence.

"If the king likes me, and I like him, then Erdem might someday be my home. I will have need of friends. I don't know what the people would think of me being Rikutan."

"If you become queen, I'll be at your command. As I am now, provided it does no harm to Erdem." I took a sip of wine. Protection. Of course. She would have it without need of this.

She sighed quickly in frustration, and I glanced up at her. "I didn't mean your sword. I really did mean friendship. I would be alone. Friends and family make a place home. If Erdem is to be my home, I'll enjoy it more with friends. If I don't stay, I'd still be honored by your friendship. My uncle is difficult to impress, but you did it. That's high commendation." She smiled shyly.

I bowed my head again. "I'm honored." I knew I was repeating myself, but I couldn't think of anything else to say. I suppose my world is a very small one in some ways. Honor. Courage. Duty. I don't know how to move beyond those to other virtues.

She frowned a little. "You don't yet know that my friendship is worth anything."

I blinked in surprise. I had meant it in reference to her position, not her character, but now she smiled more easily and leaned forward again.

"Father would think I'm being terribly bold, and maybe I am, but I trust you'll take this the way I mean it. If I stay, if I like your king and he likes me, then I'll have to get along with the nobility. But nobles are fickle and slippery and clever as snakes. I'm not like that, and I don't know how to pretend I fit in. I never learned the trick of it. I can't imagine Zuzay would have liked your king so much if he were like that either, nor would you serve him so readily. I'd like to know I can call you a friend, not for your sword, but because I'll want a few friends I can trust to be honest."

I sat back, smiling slightly. If she hadn't been a woman, she might have been a soldier. She had the same clear gaze and apparent disregard of slippery words.

She must not have been able to read me, for she suddenly looked down. "I'm sorry, I only thought," she sighed and flushed.

"You needn't apologize. It isn't every day a common soldier is honored by the friendship of a princess."

"You're not a common soldier!"

I raised my eyebrows.

"You're the king's representative."

I wanted to laugh but managed to restrain myself to a smile. "As of five weeks ago. I was a common soldier, and I was retired for injury five years ago. I serve at the king's pleasure, based on our friendship and what service I was able to offer as he sought to regain his crown."

"All the better then. You earned your position of trust."

"I remain a common soldier all the same. Retired, at that. The king Hakan Ithel is more than fair in his rule, and honors me more than perhaps he should."

"Why did you jump when I touched your hand?" She was studying me curiously.

I licked my lips, but my mouth was suddenly dry. It seemed like an unfair question to spring on me.

"It didn't bother you, did it?"

I shook my head, still trying vainly to think of something to say.

"I've heard that things are different in Erdem. Did I do something wrong? I hope it didn't mean something scandalous."

I shook my head again. "No. No, it means nothing." That at least was true.

"Then why did you jump so?" She was still staring at me. I thought that she and Hakan would get on exceedingly well. They both had an interrogator's endless supply of questions.

I don't know what possessed me. Thirty-four years of frustration. Her curiosity. Her kindness. The strong Rikutan wine. To this day I cannot say. "Put out your hand."

She stretched out her hand beside her plate, flat on the rich red silk covering the table. I put mine beside it.

"Do you see the color?"

She nodded, but she still did not seem to understand.

"White is the color of beauty, of purity, of light, of good clean things. Dark skin, like mine, is the color of ugliness, of dirt, of danger. A Tuyet does not touch a Dari, unless the Tuyet is a soldier and I've proven my worth to him already. Even then, most prefer not to, though they don't say it to my face. Do you see the scars on my hand? This one is from a knife in training. This from a battle, I don't remember it. This small one from someone's tooth. This from a sword fight. This from a rock in a wrestling match. Look at your hand. There are no scars, are there?"

She shook her head, eyes wide.

"My hand is common, a soldier's hand. Yours is royal and beautiful. You shouldn't dirty it by touching mine. Do you see my eyes?"

She was very quiet, but met my eyes unflinchingly.

"They're green, green as grass. Blue is normal. Grey is beautiful. For Dari, ugly as we are, brown is normal. The color of dirt. Only an unfortunate few have demon eyes, like mine." My tongue seemed to have a will of its own. "You took me by surprise. Excuse me." I stood

37

abruptly and walked out before she uttered a word, her mouth hanging open.

I still cannot believe I said it all. I hadn't raised my voice, but the words themselves appalled me. I couldn't believe I'd said them, and to her of all people. I thought even at the time it must have been the wine, though I didn't feel drunk. I hadn't had much, but I would like to blame the wine. In fact I hadn't eaten much at all, I'd been so ill at ease. I paced through the camp quickly, and I suppose I looked none too friendly, for none of the men said a word to me.

It was only a few minutes before I heard steps behind me. I stopped and waited. She deserved an apology. My words had been unfair. It was not her fault that I was stupidly irritated with Tuyet attitudes. With my own inability to blend in. With loneliness.

I suppose in some ways I even agree with the Tuyets. My skin is ugly; I only wished I wasn't judged for it.

If I'd grown up among Dari, would I think the same way? Would I think dark skin beautiful, and Tuyet skin the color of fish bellies? Perhaps. Who can tell? I live in a Tuyet world, and I cannot tell how it has shaped me.

"Ambassador, Her Royal Highness Kveta Tafari wishes to speak with you." His voice was quiet, respectful. Subdued.

I followed him back to her tent and entered. I dropped to one knee immediately and bowed my head. "I most humbly beg..."

She interrupted me impatiently. "Stop it! Stand up."

I looked up at her. She had tears in her eyes and she had to crane her neck to look up at me when I stood. "Sit." She sat across from me at the table again, her face flushed and unhappy.

I closed my eyes as I bowed my head. "I'm sorry to—"

Again she interrupted. "Stop! I don't want your apology."

Then there was nothing I could do. Her father would be furious. Hakan would be baffled and justifiably angry. My jaw clenched in frustration and anger at myself. I would give her a moment, then try once more, and then, if that failed, I imagined she would demand that we turn the convoy around.

I kept my head bowed in case she could see the apology in the set of my shoulders. How should I begin? I hate words. They are always the cause of my biggest failures. Think. Think hard, before you ruin it again.

"Give me your hand." Her voice was very small and quiet, and I looked up at her in shock. "Give me your hand."

I swallowed and put my hand flat on the table. I could feel it trembling slightly, but thankfully it wasn't visible. She looked at me and very deliberately clasped my hand between her two small ones. They were soft and cool, very smooth and white. "Kemen, I don't mind the scars on your hands. I don't mind your green eyes. I don't think dark skin makes you dirty. If anyone tells you differently, he's a fool, and a man like you ought to know better than to listen to him!"

I would have pulled my hand back, but she held it tightly.

"I have one question."

I nodded, but she had already continued. "Does the king Hakan Ithel treat you differently because you are Dari?"

I shook my head, my throat unaccountably tight. "No, he's been more than just."

"I don't want to know if he is just. In your opinion. I want to know if he treats you differently."

I suppose there is a difference, but I had not meant it. "No."

"I have a request. Only one, and then I'll let you go." She smiled a little now, though there were still tears in her eyes, her lashes damp.

I nodded, feeling terribly stupid and awkward.

"If we're going to be friends, you can't think of yourself as less than I am."

I don't know that I have ever thought I am less than other men, and often I know that in some ways I am more. But never has that *more* been *better*, has it been anything important. Men are given different roles in life. I fill mine, but I could not fill Hakan's role. He could not fill mine, but time proved him an excellent king, intelligent, wise, just, and generous. But my role was not the equal of a princess's role, and it would be foolish of me to pretend it was. And women are on an entirely different plane of beauty and delicacy that I could never really comprehend, much less reach.

We stared at each other for a long moment before I managed a smile and bowed my head again. My heart was warm toward her, but I had no way of showing it. I've never been good at those things.

I said only, "I am honored by your friendship. If we would be friends, I beg that you accept me as I am, with all my many failings. You may see my courtesy as one of those failings, in which case I humbly beg your forbearance."

She smiled. "Only for now."

Five

Riona

Ambassador and General Sendoa was gone for more than a month. A few days before he returned, a courier arrived with a message that flung the whole palace into an uproar. Sendoa was returning with a peace treaty, a trade agreement, and the daughter of the Rikutan king as a guest. She wanted to meet our king. That was bold, I thought, but then I've never been a princess, so maybe it wasn't so bold for someone of her status.

We were busy until they arrived, preparing a banquet and airing out all the guest rooms that hadn't been properly cleaned since the king had returned. We cleaned everything. We washed sheets and tablecloths and dishes. We prepared food. We scrubbed the floors and the windows, dusted the paintings and shook out the tapestries and rugs. By the time they arrived, we were exhausted, but we didn't mind the work too much. We were glad to have the king back.

When the group entered the palace courtyard, I was lucky enough to be assigned to make sure the travelers were refreshed and made welcome. Well, lucky is perhaps a bit misleading. I did have some choice in my duties, since I'd been there so long and supervised several younger girls. I wanted to see the travelers, especially the Rikutan princess.

It was a stirring sight, one to make any Erdemen proud. Ambassador and General Sendoa cut a striking figure at the head of the column, with the suvari behind him laughing and triumphant. Even then, when perhaps he most deserved it, he wasn't one to call attention to himself or to his accomplishments. He bowed low to the king, who greeted them in the courtyard, and helped the princess from her carriage. He introduced her to the king, just a quick meeting before the banquet that night, and escorted her into the palace. The men waited respectfully as her entourage followed her, but I heard them laughing as the door closed behind us.

Noriso met Sendoa and the princess and I followed them to the room that had been chosen for her. I'd helped prepare it, and I smiled to see her admiring look. I wondered what her room in Rikuto looked like, whether this felt a little like home or entirely strange. She was young, seventeen or so, and pretty, though not a remarkable beauty. I liked her quick smile and the kind look in her eyes. Sendoa bowed to her on his way out, and I wondered what it would be like to have a man bow like that to me. I wasn't jealous, because I didn't have any claim to him, but I did wonder.

I liked the princess immediately. Her Common was good, and her accent sounded delicate and sweet. She had a lilt to her voice, as if she wasn't quite sure she'd spoken correctly, and she watched my face each time she spoke to see if she'd mangled the words or grammar.

I helped her wash for the banquet that night and answered her questions as best I could. Her women hovered about, but she let me brush her hair and fluff the pillows on the bed. She had some time and wanted to rest before the festivities, which was entirely understandable. She looked a little tired, and I couldn't blame her. In all my life I'd scarcely been out of Stonehaven, and the thought of traveling for nearly three weeks to a foreign land was overwhelming.

Noriso said I might be the princess's Erdemen maid, for a while at least. He asked me to wait outside her room while she slept in case she needed anything, so I stood in the hallway. I couldn't sit, of course, there was no chair, and you can't just stretch out your legs on the floor of a palace hall. I was shifting uncomfortably from one foot to the other after some two hours when Sendoa himself walked by. I dropped into a curtsey.

To my surprise, he stopped in front of me. "What are you doing?" His voice was softer than I'd expected, low and a little rough around the edges.

"Waiting, sir."

"Do you need the princess Kveta for something?"

"No, sir. She's resting, and I'm to help her get ready for the banquet when she calls for me." I glanced up to see disconcerting green eyes on my face.

He raised his eyebrows slightly. "Must you stand while you wait?"

I stumbled over my tongue. "I can't sit on the floor, and, well," I didn't finish.

He strode off down the hall and returned in a moment carrying a chair. It was one I'd never sit in, red velvet and dark carved wood, a beautiful antique easily a hundred years old. I stared up at him in shock.

"Is there something wrong?"

"No, sir. I can't sit on that chair. But thank you all the same." I rushed through the words blushing uncomfortably. Why was he even talking to me? Surely he had more important things to do.

"Why not?"

My voice felt squeaky. "Servants don't sit in the good chairs, sir."

His mouth twitched into a slight smile. "If anyone questions you, say I told you to sit. Today at least no one will argue with me." He turned to go and I breathed a sigh of relief. He made me feel odd, edgy. His eyes were too intense. Too green, too bright, and too perceptive. Then he turned and looked back at me. "Have I met you before?"

The heat rushed to my face again and I stared at my shoes. "I watched you in the courtyard." That's what happens to girls who do scandalous things; they are later embarrassed about it and have to regret it. I wished the floor would swallow me.

He stood a moment more, and finally said, "You were familiar then too. Had we not met before that?"

I shook my head, keeping my eyes down in respect.

I think he was as surprised as I was when he persisted. "Would you look up a moment? I'd like to see your face."

I raised my eyes, and he swallowed.

"Forgive me for asking it of you. I know I'm not much to look at."

I think my mouth nearly dropped open in surprise, for that was not what I expected at all. I might have been bold enough to question him, but he spoke first.

"I have seen you before. Have you always worked in the palace?"

"Since I was fifteen, sir. I helped Saraid, the healer, when you were ill. Perhaps you remember me from then?"

A muscle twitched in his jaw, and I wondered if my answer had upset him in some way. But he said only, "Then I'm grateful for your care. I would have thanked you earlier, had I known." He bowed solemnly. Men of his status do not bow to commoners, and certainly not to servants. It isn't done, and it made me terribly uncomfortable. Maybe he saw something of that in my expression, for when he straightened he smiled slightly and strode quickly away.

I did sit, because I was tired and his name would allow it, but I don't know how comfortable I was. I thought I'd seen a little sadness in his smile, but then I thought maybe I'd imagined it. I wondered if I'd done something wrong, stepped out of my place.

"You can't, Ria!" Lani was outraged. "He makes me ill! Didn't you see he practically undressed Sinta with his eyes last week? It's obscene!"

I sighed. Dinner was not going well. Ena and Joka had invited me over again. Ena knew how much I was struggling with the decision, and I'd finally, tentatively, decided that I would tell Riulono yes. Yes, I would sign the papers. Yes, because I wanted children. Yes, because I wanted to belong to someone.

Joka harrumphed and scowled at his plate. Ena put one hand on my arm, as if it was a comforting gesture. It felt more like the sympathy after someone you love dies, which didn't encourage me at all. But only Lani gave me her opinion openly.

"Ria, you can't." She was pleading. "It's not worth it. If you want children that much, there are plenty on the street. You could love them."

"What do you know of the street foxes, Lani?" It felt like an unfair attack. I wasn't a bad person because I wanted my own children, was I? To feel the life growing within me, to see my features mixed with a husband's beauty in their faces?

She puffed out her cheeks and huffed. Joka frowned at her. "Lani, Ria is a grown woman. Leave her be." Then even more gravely, to me, "I don't think it's a good idea, Ria. Just because he's handsome."

"It's not because he's handsome! It's because..." I stopped and tried to say it kindly, so it didn't sound like a complaint or an accusation. "You all belong. You're a family. You have each other. I don't have anyone. You're lovely to me, but..." I blinked back tears and stared at my hands clenched together in my lap.

"Ria." Ena stood and moved around behind my chair to embrace me, wrapping her arms around my shoulders as if she were my mother. I leaned back and closed my eyes, trying not to cry. "I understand, Ria. I do. Be careful with him, that's all."

"I'll think about it. I haven't decided yet." It was almost true. I had decided, but I was willing to change my mind.

"Good." Joka let out a sigh of relief that was almost comical. "Good, Ria. Think about it hard. No one can make you as happy or as miserable as your husband or wife. No one. Better to be lonely than married to the wrong person."

LANI FOUND ME in my room a few nights later. She was grumpy, nearly slamming the door behind herself. She's not normally so ill-tempered, so I merely waited, and finally she sniffled a little.

"Now Da wants to talk to Aku Parvisano about me."

"You don't like him?"

"No. He smells funny and he walks with his fat gut sticking out."

I almost laughed. "He does. A little. But what would make you happy, Lani?"

"I don't know. I don't want to get married yet. And Da just wants him because he's 'a step up' for me. He doesn't want me to have to work as much as Ma does. I'd rather do that than be married to Parvisano, though." She played with the hem of her apron.

"It won't be for years yet. Don't worry."

"He'll just be older and fatter by then!" She scowled ferociously. "Just because you'd settle for someone with one foot in the grave doesn't mean I want to."

Tears sprung in my eyes and I turned away. My hands were shaking, and I clasped them together.

"I'm sorry, Ria. I didn't mean it."

Riulono didn't have one foot in the grave; he was young, and handsome. But the desperation she touched was real.

"I didn't mean it, Ria." She came up behind me and wrapped her arms around my waist. "He's not so bad. I guess. He isn't fat and he smells alright." The reluctance in her voice was so obvious even she couldn't pretend she didn't hear it. "He's..." she sighed. "I just think you deserve better."

I took a deep breath and let it out slowly, making sure my voice was steady before I said anything. "I don't have a lot of choices, Lani."

I'd have been grateful if Parvisano liked me. He might not have been handsome, but he'd seemed kind, and that's more than many women get in a husband.

RIULONO SENT ME a message asking me to meet him behind Harl's fruit stall at the market. Despite my lingering doubt, I said I would. Lani didn't know, of course.

I was early. Harl gave me a slice of moonfruit to eat while I waited, so I didn't look so foolish. The noise of the market swelled around me, voices in a dozen accents and a few foreign tongues. A Dari sold grilled lamb across the market, and I watched him with interest. He was new among the vendors, and I hadn't gotten a look at him the one other time I'd seen him. He wasn't as tall as General Sendoa, nor as... I hesitated. What was General Sendoa? *Alive.* Vigorously alive.

I jumped at a touch on my back.

"Morning, darling. Eager to see me?" Riulono grinned and tried to kiss me.

I turned my head, and his lips slid across my cheek, catching a few stray hairs. He smelled of ale, and it wasn't even midday. His hand tightened on my arm as I tried to twist away.

"What's wrong?" he frowned and pulled on my arm.

"Stop! You're hurting me." I was more irritated than scared.

"Don't like that?" He pushed me away and spat on the ground. "I had something for you, but I lost it." He laughed a bit too roughly, and Harl looked back at us.

I took a half-step backwards. "It's fine. I'm sorry, I need to go."

His face darkened. "It was a joke. Here it is." He smiled again, teeth glittering, and I suddenly felt afraid. He pulled some papers from his coat. "I got the papers, Ria darling. Good fruit man here can be our witness."

Harl glanced at me again, and he kept one hand on his knife.

"I told you I wasn't ready yet." I swallowed hard, my heart thudding raggedly as he pushed close to me and twisted my arm so that I gasped.

"Come now, what's to question?"

"Let me go, 'Lono." I jerked my wrist back.

He let me go but stepped in closer as I stepped away again.

"I'm not going to marry you. You can have the necklace back." I fumbled with the clasp behind my neck. I was afraid for a moment he would hit me, but he only trailed one finger down my cheek.

"Darling, dear little fool. You don't want to do this. There isn't someone else, is there?"

General Sendoa's face came to mind, the way he bowed so solemnly, but I shook my head. No. There was no one else.

Better no one than the wrong person, though.

Better alone than him.

"No." My voice was shaking. "No, 'Lono. I'm sorry."

He spat, grabbing the necklace and thrusting it into his pocket carelessly.

I cried in my room that night. I'd been willing to pretend I didn't see that he stared after every woman that walked by. Willing to tolerate his arrogance. Perhaps he had reason to be arrogant. He was handsome, dashing, funny. Sometimes. When he wasn't cruel.

Perhaps he was right. No one else might want me.

I could have tolerated many things for the sake of marriage. I wanted a man, wanted to be protected. I wanted children, babes to hold, laughing children to call me Mama, to nestle close, to kiss me sloppily on the cheek, to come running to me with their scraped knees. I would have settled, tried to find a measure of happiness with him. With love, with patience, perhaps we could have had a good life.

But the thought of his careless cruelty turned my stomach. I couldn't live with that. I couldn't live with the way he twisted my arm, the way his eyes flashed when I said it hurt.

He enjoyed it.

I TOLD LANI first, because she would never have forgiven me if I hadn't. But then Joran and Ena and Joka and soon nearly everyone knew. Both their sympathy and congratulations felt like salt on the wound, and I wished everyone would just pretend it had never happened. But my heart felt lighter, uncaged, and even the disappointment of being alone again felt less lonely somehow.

"DON'T YOU LIKE General Sendoa?" Lani's eyes were wide as she turned to me.

"Hold still." She turned back around. I brushed her hair and began the braid over again. I did her hair because she said I didn't pull as much as her mother did.

"Well, don't you?"

"Of course I do, silly goose. Doesn't everyone? He's a hero."

"I mean more than that. He's not much older than you are."

"Lani, he's the Minister of Military Affairs and the ambassador to Rikuto. He's a personal friend of the king. I'm a *maid*. You know better than that. You'd best not get any crazy ideas."

"I don't think he'd mind that. Besides, don't you think he's nice, at least? I think he has a nice smile."

I rolled my eyes. "You think everyone who smiles is nice."

"Not Riulono."

"Fine. Except Riulono. I'm sure General Sendoa is quite nice, but I don't see how that has anything to do with me."

"Well, isn't it time you started looking again? I don't see how you could do any better."

This time I did snap at her. "Nalani, I don't need you to lecture me on my marriage prospects! You're fourteen!" She deflated a little and I finished her braid in silence. "Now go on, I'll see you at lunch." I swatted her bottom as she went out, as if she were still a child, and she laughed and ran off.

That day, Avusta, was the day I led the girls scrubbing the floors. I had four to help me, all younger of course. We filled buckets with soap and water in the cool morning darkness. Tanith, Sinta, and Anthea were to do the Great Hall together, and Sayen and I would start at the door to the courtyard and work our way toward the Great Hall. Then we'd move to the next set of hallways. It's a never ending job, but we try to rotate it among the women so no one has to do it every week. Sayen was the oldest of the girls under me, but Sinta was quite responsible, most of the time anyway, and would keep the other two in line if necessary.

Sayen was twenty-one and pregnant with her first child. She and her husband Eko were happy together. He worked as a scribe and they hadn't been married long. I'd offered to transfer her to the kitchen, which is easier work, but she said standing so much hurt her back and the smells made her sick. She was a sweet girl, and I enjoyed working with her, though I sometimes felt a pang of envy.

We worked for some time. We'd started at the door to the courtyard since I wanted to finish before everyone woke for the day. We sang sometimes, quietly, but mostly we worked in silence. Scrubbing floors is tiring work, and though I don't really mind it, it doesn't leave much breath for chatting. Not that we had much to say. When you work with someone every day, you run out of conversation topics.

We'd finished the two connecting rooms and nearly finished the hallway when the door to the courtyard opened. I sat back in surprise and Sayen scowled slightly.

I should have known it would be Sendoa who strode through, dirty boots leaving a distinct path half-way down the hallway. Aside from servants, no one but him is up that early. He stopped suddenly when he caught sight of Sayen and me on our knees, rags in hand. Sayen, with her customary good humor, stopped scowling and smiled as we ducked our heads in respect.

"Sorry." He turned on his heel and retreated back the way he had come.

Sayen and I looked at each other.

"I'll do it." She sighed.

"No, I will. You keep on here."

But she scooted over anyway and I shrugged. It didn't really matter, either way we'd both have to work until we finished. The door opened again and we looked up.

Sendoa had his boots in hand, noticeably cleaner, and stood barefooted on the doorframe. "I just washed my feet too, they're not dirty." He padded around the muddy trail and put his boots at the far end of the hall. We were even more surprised when he returned and knelt near Sayen. "Do you have an extra rag?"

She shook her head, now thoroughly confused. "No, sir."

"Then may I use yours?"

We both stared at him in confusion. After a moment he repeated his question. "May I use yours?"

"Why, sir?" She glanced at me, as if I would be able to explain his behavior.

He raised his eyebrows slightly. "Because I muddied the floor you were cleaning." He reached out and took the rag from her hand and began to scrub the marble floor.

She watched him and then looked at me before trying unsuccessfully to stifle a giggle.

"What's funny?" Sendoa spoke without looking up.

"You don't need to do it, sir. It's a servant's job."

He glanced up and paused in his scrubbing. "I'm not royalty, you know. I'm not even nobility."

She said what I was thinking. "Sir, you're the king's ambassador to Rikuto! And commander of the army."

He looked back at the floor. "Minister of Military Affairs. All the same, I think I can manage to scrub a floor. If you can suffer my presence?" He glanced up, and at my wide-eyed nod bent to his task again.

I continued as well, though I watched him out of the corner of my eye. Sayen continued to kneel, unsure what she should do. He cleaned the long trail of muddy footprints, rinsing out the cloth periodically and pushing the bucket ahead of himself as he moved down the hall. Finally he wrung out the rag, stood, picked up the bucket and brought it back to her. Then he bowed slightly and was gone.

She looked at me with wide eyes. "What was that all about?"

I shrugged. "I don't know. I suppose he can do what he wants."

She bent over again. "If I have a son, I want him to be like that."

"Like how?"

"Cleaning up his own messes! Eko is lovely to me, but he can't see dirt until it grows legs." She smiled at the floor. "Besides, isn't he nice? Saraid said he searched her out and thanked her for her care while he was ill."

"He did?" I hadn't heard.

That was odd. Healing, staying with the sick and dying, is what healers do. It's their job, just like cleaning is one of my jobs. I don't expect gratitude. I don't do it out of the goodness of my heart. I don't resent it, and I try to have a cheerful attitude about it, but I do it to keep a roof over my head and food in my stomach, not for the joy of scrubbing floors. Saraid choose to become a healer because it fits her well and she had the opportunity, but it's also a job to her; a job she cares about, but a job all the same.

Six

Kemen

"Sir?" A girl peeked around the door shyly.

"Come in." It was quite early, and I was getting ready to exercise in the morning coolness. Only servants are up so early, servants and me. "What is it?"

She stood just inside the doorway as I pulled on my boots. "Could I talk to you a moment?"

"Aye." An odd request. It was the young girl I had first seen when I awakened from my fevered dreams after Hakan's duel with Taisto.

"My name is Lani." She bit her lip nervously, but she looked ready enough to smile. "I heard from Sayen that you said you're not a nobleman. Is that true?"

"Aye." I sat up and waited, wondering what she wanted.

"But you're not a commoner, are you?"

"I'm a soldier. But if you're asking about my birth, I'm common enough. I was a foundling."

"You were?" Her eyes widened. "You didn't ever know your mother and father?"

I shook my head.

"I'm sorry." She seemed genuinely aggrieved for me, and I shrugged.

"I suppose I don't know what I missed."

"Are you married?"

I blinked at the sudden change in topic. "No. I'm not." Would I spend every night alone if I were?

"Have you met my cousin Riona?"

I nearly laughed then. "I might have. I don't know many people's names in the palace yet."

"She's very pretty. She's nice, too. You should speak to her."

"You're a bit young to be a matchmaker. She didn't ask you to speak with me, did she?" Surely not. I couldn't imagine that this Riona was interested in me in the least.

"Of course not. She's far too shy for that." She grinned. "Now if you think badly of someone, it will only be of me, and I'm too young for you anyway. I think you'd make her happy. If you were younger I'd ask my father to speak to you on my behalf."

I hid a smile. "Thank you. I'd forgotten how ancient I am. I needed that reminder."

She looked stricken. "I didn't mean…"

This time I did smile. "I'm teasing you. I'm not offended. You'll make a younger man very happy someday."

She grinned at me. "You really should speak to her. You couldn't do better with any princess. She's twenty-six. Her parents died a long time ago, or they would do this for her. Well, they probably wouldn't aim so high as you, but I will. You should talk to her. If I'm too bold, and maybe I am, then she's too shy and quiet. She deserves better than scrubbing floors, but she'd never reach for it herself."

I liked the girl, not least for her persistence. "I'll speak to her if you point her out to me. But I won't promise to court her, nor could I promise she would receive my attentions even if I did."

"Of course. But I think she might." She grinned impishly and jumped up. She led me down the hallway and to a window that looked onto the courtyard. "There. Sayen is the pregnant one, and Riona is the one beside her, holding the bucket."

"I have spoken with her."

She looked up at me. "Really?"

"Not much. But I know her face. Thank you." She tripped away, and I wondered what, if anything, I would say to her cousin. I did like her enough, as far as I knew her, but that wasn't saying much.

Over the next days I watched Riona when I saw her, though I kept my glances well hidden. I wanted to see how she spoke with those she knew, how she treated them. She was kind and considerate, even-tempered. I have no tolerance for quick tempers. She had a good humor, smiling often with those she knew, but a humility that seemed quite genuine, a warm and sweet spirit.

WHAT DOES A WOMAN want from a suitor? I tried to address the question logically. A handsome face. There was little I could do about that. Tenderness. Concern. Stability. Humor? Perhaps fun? Fidelity, certainly. What else? How could I demonstrate these things? What is love, anyway? How does a woman perceive love? I supposed I wouldn't know until I spoke with her.

I found her scrubbing the floor in one of the back hallways, another girl not far away. "May I help?"

She looked up in surprise. "Why, sir?"

Phraa. I raised my eyebrows in what I hoped was a humorous look. "I haven't scrubbed many floors and would like a little more practice."

She frowned in confusion but handed over her rag. "As you wish, sir. I'll be back in a moment." She stood and disappeared down a hallway, returning in a few minutes with another rag, as well as an extra towel to fold under my knees. She knelt and began scrubbing again, not looking up. Now what?

"What else do you do in the palace, aside from the floors?"

"I work in the kitchen sometimes. I wash clothes." She glanced at me quickly, clearly a little uncomfortable. Finally she asked very quietly, "Do you need something, sir?"

Honesty. Still I hesitated. "I'd like to get to know you. Clearly you're busy. I hoped that by joining you in your work I might earn a bit of your time."

There was a long silence and I kept my eyes on the floor.

"I imagine Nalani prompted you to do so." Her voice was very quiet, almost brittle. "I'm sorry, sir. She's very young."

I wondered how badly I'd upset her, but I smiled, hoping she could see I wasn't irritated. "You don't think I am here only for her, do you? She gave me courage to act on my interest."

Again she was silent, though the slowing of her scrubbing showed that she had heard me. "I do not imagine you lack courage, sir. It is your interest I question."

I didn't really have an answer, so I scrubbed in silence for some time as we moved down the hall. The marble of the palace floors was beautiful. It was not bad work, though my ribs began to ache from the unusual posture. When we turned the corner to another room, I sat up for a minute to stretch.

"Sir, you don't need to continue. I'll tell Lani that you helped. Thank you. But more is unnecessary." She smiled, and I warmed to the kind light in her eyes.

"I believe you misunderstand me. My interest is real enough. How old is Lani? Thirteen? Fourteen?" She nodded. "You don't think I can be ordered about so easily by a fourteen year old, do you?"

"I suppose not." She looked down and blushed, which made me smile. Lani was right; Riona was quite pretty. The two cousins bore a passing resemblance, but it was already clear they were very different. When Riona wasn't looking I rubbed my ribs. They had been worse again since I'd been ill. I'd injured them before, cracked in training and cracked or broken in a few other skirmishes, but never so badly. I wondered how long it would be before they were fully healed.

As I bent to my work again she glanced at me. We worked in silence for quite some time, though I knew I should say something. Women make me tongue-tied in the best of times, and I was at a loss.

"What was it like in Rikuto?"

When I glanced up, she smiled shyly.

"I didn't see much of it, really. The people are very poor now, though it wasn't always so. Tafari is a good king, and did what he could for them, but they've had droughts and raids from the Tarvil for years. I think with the treaty it will be better for them."

She nodded.

"What do you remember of your parents?" I wondered if it was a bad question, one I did not yet have the right to ask.

59

But she smiled as she answered. "My mother was very generous with her time. She always had time to listen to me, and she helped everyone she knew. She spent a lot of time arranging my wedding before she died."

"You're married?" I tried to hide my shock. Had her husband died, then? Surely Lani wouldn't have encouraged me to speak with a married woman.

"No, we didn't actually marry. We signed the engagement papers before she died, but he met someone else. He asked to be released, and so we annulled it." She didn't sound bitter, but I wondered how badly it had stung her to be so blatantly rejected.

"I'm fortunate he was such a fool. I should thank him someday."

She giggled. "I wouldn't have thought you so bold, sir."

"Should I not be?" She looked up at me and I smiled, feeling awkward and shy. "I don't want to offend you."

"I'm not offended." She looked down. I wondered whether it was to avoid laughing at me.

"What else do you remember?" I've wondered before how I would be different if I had known my parents. Would I be more empathetic? More gentle? What if they had not been kind themselves? Would I be bitter, or would I learn from their failures?

"I don't remember my father much. He died when I was very young. He laughed a lot, I remember that. He was young when he died, only a few years older than I am now. I wish I'd known him better. He made my mother very happy."

"I'm sorry. It must have been difficult for her."

"It was. I realize that now, but she carried on with a grace I can only envy. She would have been my age, a little older, when he died. With me to care for, of course."

We worked in silence then. I racked my brain, but I had no idea what to say. What does a woman desire? Looks I did not have, and I certainly didn't have a smooth tongue. But perhaps a sincere heart would be enough, at least enough for her to judge me for whatever merits I might possess and not for my utter lack of superficial charms.

"Is it true you were a foundling?"

"Yes."

"So you were raised by the military? What was it like? Where did you live?"

I suppose I'd never questioned it, since I knew many other foundlings. "I lived with other boys and our guardians. When I was old enough, three or four, I started at a military school. Most of the boys were foundlings, or youngest sons of large families without enough money to feed them all." I sat up to stretch my ribs again.

"You don't have to scrub the floor. I'm used to it, but it does hurt your back at first." She smiled. "I'll still talk to you, if you wish."

"My back is fine." I bent to work again, but she stifled a laugh and I looked up.

"Are you showing off? It's hard work and takes some getting used to. I won't think less of you for not wanting to do it. It's a servant's job anyway." She was grinning, and I blinked.

"I don't think I am. Am I?" Women frighten me, not least because around them I hardly know my own mind.

She bit her lip. "I'm sorry if I offended you, sir. I was only trying to say that you needn't suffer to impress me. Your reputation speaks for itself." She looked solemn, almost upset.

"I'm not offended. My back is fine. It's my ribs that hurt, but not enough to make me stop. I'd rather stay and speak with you." I smiled, hoping she could see that I really wasn't offended, but she frowned.

"Your ribs? Why?"

It sounded foolish when I said it. "I broke them a few months ago. I was slow getting out of the way of a horse."

"It kicked you?" She sounded horrified. "That's why I don't like horses."

"Actually it stumbled. I was in the way."

She blinked. "Oh. Was the rider hurt? Why didn't he do something?"

It was my own fault. It's the way soldiers talk, minimizing things. "I'm sorry. I wasn't clear. It was in a skirmish."

"Is that a battle?" She had completely stopped working and was staring at me in interest.

"A small one, yes."

"Was it the battle against Rikuto in Senlik? The one that bought the king the support of the suvari and helped start negotiations with Rikuto?"

Her eyes were wide and I looked down. "It wasn't quite like that. It wasn't the Rikutan army, only a raiding party. The rumors have made it seem more than it was."

"How many of them were there?"

I licked my lips. "There were sixteen, but I didn't fight them all."

"But there was no one with you? What about the king?" She seemed curious rather than critical of him, but I was glad Hakan hadn't heard. It would have stung him.

"The townsmen would have fought for their daughters, but I'm glad it didn't come to that. Hakan was in training, and would have fought at need. We were fortunate there was no need. It isn't a king's place to cross swords with common raiders." In fact, he hadn't even carried a sword then; he'd been practicing with the wooden one I'd made for him.

"Of course not. But that leaves only you. So the rumors are true then, that you defeated the raiding party alone?"

I shrugged, feeling uncomfortable speaking of it. "Rumors have a way of growing at each telling. I don't know what you've heard." I bent again to work, though I hoped she was not offended by my reticence.

"You don't wish to speak of it?" she asked after a long silence.

When I looked at her, her expression was one of compassion rather than the irritation I'd almost expected.

"Battle is ugly. I'll answer your questions, but I'd prefer to speak with you on more pleasant topics."

SEVEN

RIONA

"**M**ay I help?" He ducked under a string of drying peppers hanging from the ceiling.

"You can cut up the potatoes." I
couldn't help smiling a little. I was making a piecrust,
trying to make sure it sealed properly.

"How small?"

"Like this."

He nodded quietly and set to work beside me. I
glanced at him from time to time. His hands were quick
and sure, the potato pieces all precise cubes.

Lani came in a rush some minutes later, when I was
still trying to think of something to say to him.

"Ria, His Highness wants tea with the princess in
the garden."

I nodded. "You can make the tray if you want."

She was fascinated by the Rikutan princess and took
every opportunity to serve her. She stood across the table

from Kemen and smiled up at him. "Sir, do you now work in the kitchen?"

"I do." He smiled slightly.

"You're quite good at cutting potatoes."

I glared at her. She had cheek to tease such an important man so impudently. Just because Noriso put up with it didn't mean that she should start with the king's officials. I'd thought she had better manners.

"I've had practice." He smiled a little more.

She cocked her head to one side. "Are you trying to impress Ria?"

"Lani!" My voice was sharp. I mouthed silently, *Stop it!*

He stared at the potatoes as if they were the most fascinating things he'd ever seen. Lani blushed, realizing that she'd gone too far. I think we were both a little shocked when he spoke very quietly, still studying the potatoes intently.

"No, I'm not that bold. I just want an excuse to be near her."

My mouth dropped open and Lani grinned at me. She arranged blueberries, raspberries, and slices of moonfruit on the tray in a graceful arc around some cheese. My face felt hot and red, and I pushed the pie away and pulled the next over.

"I'm finished with the potatoes. What else can I do?"

"Put them in that pot, please. The knives are dull. You could sharpen them." I kept my eyes on the table as I spoke.

Lani handed him the knife she was using to cut the bread. "Would you mind doing this one first?"

He took it from her and began to strop it expertly. She watched, but she couldn't keep silent for long.

"Do you have practice sharpening knives too?"

He nodded.

"What about cooking?"

His lips twitched into a smile. "I've cooked a little on campaigns. That doesn't mean I'm good at it."

Lani grinned. "What else are you not good at?"

"Talking." He studied the edge of the knife before handing it back to her handle first. "Careful."

"Thank you." She finished cutting the bread, put three roses on the side, dipped a little pot of honey for the bread, and tripped away with an impish grin.

I rolled my eyes. "I'm sorry, sir."

"Why?" He smiled almost shyly.

I blushed even more and pinched the edges of the piecrust.

"I don't mind her teasing."

I didn't know what to say. He stood in silence a moment.

"Would you like to go riding tomorrow?"

I glanced up at him. "I have to help prepare for the ambassador's arrival."

"What about the next day?"

I bit my lip. "I don't like horses much." It was a bit of an understatement. They frighten me. They've always seemed terribly dangerous, dumb as rocks, skittish, unpredictable, and armed with hooves and big teeth.

He seemed to hesitate. "We could walk instead."

When I raised my eyes again, he was staring at the floor.

"When?" I was nervous, blushing, unsure what to do.

He smiled. "Tomorrow, after Hakan's meeting with the ambassador."

The next day I served the tea during the meeting, and so I discovered that the reason he'd said *after* the meeting with the Rikutan ambassador was because he attended the meeting as well. While the king spoke with the ambassador, Kemen spoke with the military liaison. They had maps spread out nearly covering the table. I put the tray with fruit and honey-almond pastries near his elbow, and he glanced up with a quick thanks. Then he smiled, and it was more than he might have smiled at someone else. I ducked my head, feeling my face heat.

The meeting went long, and I was working in the kitchen when he found me. I was thankful we didn't see Lani on the way out. She would have said something to make me blush even more, and I was already feeling foolish enough. What kind of girl, at twenty-six, panics at the thought of a simple walk in a flower garden with a man?

I wanted him to like me, wanted him to think I was pretty. But I felt absurdly out of place. He was the king's dearest friend, a national hero, a distinguished and decorated soldier. I was a servant, and I would have been surprised if the king even knew my name or how long I'd served in the palace.

Our conversation was halting and absurdly polite. We were both nervous. He used his bootknife to cut a pink rose for me, searching intently to find the most perfect one.

I smiled at him over it. "You know the colors have different meanings?"

"I didn't know. What does pink mean?"

"Admiration or joy."

"What about white?"

"Purity."

He smiled and cut a white rose from another bush. I closed my eyes when I smelled it, and when I opened them he was smiling slightly, his eyes on my face. I blushed and looked down, hoping he didn't see how disconcerted I was. Partly because he was a man, and I wasn't used to any man's attentions, and partly, though

it shames me now to say it, because his eyes were so ee-
rily bright against his dark skin.

He cut another rose from a bush a little farther on, a
pale purple. "What does that one mean?"

I swallowed. "Enchantment. Captivation."

EIGHT

KEMEN

I folded sheets with her in the courtyard. The autumn was golden and perfect, and when she smiled, my heart sang. Everything was brighter with her. I swished clothes about in hot water over a fire with a long pole on laundry day. She showed me how to seal pie-crusts so the blueberries would stay in, how to stuff a pheasant with cheese and herbs, how to cook apples with spices, nuts, and butter so the smell was heavenly. The knowledge mattered little to me, but working beside her was joyous. I wanted to please her. When she smiled and nodded her thanks, my heart leaped. She and Sinta sang sometimes when they worked. She had a beautiful voice, full of sunlight and joy.

She was always very kind, but she was kind to everyone. That made it difficult to guess what she thought of me, whether my tentative hope was justified. I wished a thousand blessings on Lani for that awkward moment in the kitchen. Though I wasn't confident in guessing her intentions, she could not have been mistaken about mine. Riona smiled when I cut her that first rose, and after that I left her one every morning tucked in the handle of the door to her apartment. I asked the princess Kveta what the colors meant.

White for the purity of my love. Pink for joy and admiration. Peach for sincerity. Yellow for my delight in her. Pale purple for enchantment. A velvety cream for her perfection. After two months, when I'd become more bold, a dark red for love. Once, on a particularly adventurous day, I cut an orange rose and left it for her, a deep orange for passion and desire. When I saw her later, she flushed crimson and I stared at the floor, but I didn't regret it. She didn't tell me to take my attentions elsewhere, and I took that as a cautious, blushing consent. I scarcely slept that night for smiling.

I spent every moment I could with her, but I was busy with work for Hakan. Within a week of Hakan's coronation, Yoshiro Kepa, commander of the kedani on the northern border, had been tasked with addressing the growing difficulties with the Tarvil. The border settlers had been having trouble for over a year, but the persistent raids had greatly increased in the spring. Kepa's reports over the months had grown increasingly anxious, despite the reinforcements Hakan had sent and the letters of instruction and advice I dictated at Hakan's request.

"ARE YOU GOING riding?" Lani looked up at me wide-eyed and eager.

"Yes."

"Can I go to the stable with you?"

"Now?"

Lani nodded hopefully.

"Yes. Why?"

She followed me, half-running to keep up, though I slowed my steps for her. "I just want to see the horses. I can't go by myself. It's—" she hesitated. "Well, Mother doesn't trust the grooms."

"Ah. Come on then."

In the stable, she smiled with delight when I gave her some carrots and apples to feed to the horses. "Keep your hand flat. Don't make it so easy for her to bite off your fingers."

"Would she really?" Her eyes widened.

"Not on purpose. But she has big teeth, and she really likes apples."

"How does it feel to ride?"

"Have you never been?" I couldn't imagine it. I trained first for suvari service, so I'd learned early. I don't clearly remember not being able to ride.

"No."

"Do you want to?"

She looked up at me, eyes wide. "The king is waiting for you!"

"Not now. Tomorrow morning." I watched her face light up.

"Really?" She grinned. "I would love to! Should I come here?"

"At dawn."

She ran back inside the palace and I mounted Kanti, the beautiful grey mare that Hakan had assigned me. It was a gorgeous day for riding in early autumn, the sun warm but the wind carrying the chill of winter. At night it would be cold, but that afternoon the weather was crisp and bracing.

The next morning I was there before Lani, but I didn't have to wait long. I boosted her up first, then adjusted the stirrups to fit her. My long legs made mount-

71

ing in front of her awkward, but in a minute we were
more or less ready.

"It's so high!"

I took her around the corral and into a pasture at a
walk. "Do you want to try a trot?"

"Yes, sir."

"Don't put your feet so far into the stirrups. Your
shoes don't have heels, so you have to be careful not to
let your feet slip through. Just put the balls of your feet in
and keep your heels down." I waited while she adjusted
her feet.

"That's awkward. Everyone makes this look easy."

"You get used to it. When we start trotting, lift yourself up; don't ride all the bumps. Are you ready?" At her
nod I asked Kanti for a trot. She was a good riding horse,
with smooth gait changes and an even temper. Lani was
startled and I could feel her off beat as she tried to match
the rhythm. Around and around in a gentle trot. "Are
you ready for a canter?"

"I don't know." She sounded a little frightened.

"Hold on as tight as you want. It's easier than a
trot." Kanti shifted into a canter and Lani's grip on the
back of my tunic tightened. "How are you?"

"Fine!" The joy in her voice made me smile. We
crossed the pasture and circled back at a leisurely canter
before I slowed Kanti to a trot and then a walk.

"What about a gallop? Can we do that too?" She
sounded hopeful.

"If you want to."

"And jumping? Or should we not?"

"There's a stream at the northern end. We can jump
that. Hold on." Her grip tightened again as Kanti gal-
loped easily. The pasture had a gentle hill and when we
crested it Kanti pulled at the bit, wanting more freedom

to run. But Lani felt stiff and nervous behind me, so I didn't let the mare free as she wanted.

"Hold on." My warning was unnecessary as we approached and then cleared the stream easily. We circled the end of the pasture at a slow gallop and I turned Kanti toward the stable, with another easy jump back over the little stream.

"Thank you, sir. It was wonderful!" She was still grinning from the excitement.

As we approached the gate I saw Riona and another woman, and I heard Lani's unhappy sigh.

"What?"

"My mother. Riona too, but it's my mother I'm worried about. I didn't tell her I was going. I did all my chores early and I told Ria where I would be, but I knew Ma wouldn't let me come."

I wanted to laugh. As we neared the two figures by the gate I studied her mother's face. Not much older than I was, she looked genuinely worried, angry, relieved, and very embarrassed as we drew up. Beside her, Riona looked mostly amused, though she tried to keep a straight face.

"Nalani, get off that horse. I must apologize for my daughter, sir. She shouldn't have bothered you."

I dismounted and helped Lani down, and her mother continued apologizing for a moment. Lani thanked me quietly, her head down. Lani's mother curtsied deeply, probably more awed than she should have been by my suddenly exalted position as a friend of the young king.

"You needn't apologize for her. The fault is mine. She said she'd never been riding, and I asked her to go. Forgive me for not asking your permission."

She looked up at me in surprise.

I added, "I hope it didn't cause you any difficulties."

73

"No, sir."

"I hope you weren't worried. She was quite safe."

"Yes, sir." She ducked her head and I smiled.

"I'm grateful for her company. I would be proud to have a daughter like her." I hoped that would help with any worries about her daughter being alone with a man. "Excuse me." I bowed to her and led Kanti toward the stable.

I thought no more of the incident until I saw Lani that night in the hallway. I was leaving a meeting with Hakan, where we had been planning for the school he wanted to open.

"Thank you, sir." She bit her lip and grinned, and I couldn't help smiling back. "It was so much fun!"

Without warning she embraced me, arms about my waist and head barely coming to my chest. I patted her shoulders awkwardly, wondering what people would think if they saw us, but I couldn't help smiling back.

"My mother was so surprised at what you said she barely scolded me. Thank you, sir."

"Next time you should tell her where you are. She was worried about you. And call me Kemen."

She smiled. "Kemen, then. You're more fun than you look."

"Thank you, I think."

"You know what I mean! You should smile more often, so people see how nice you are."

I raised my eyebrows. "Maybe I'm not nice. Or maybe I don't want anyone to know."

She laughed. "That's silly. Of course you are."

It was strange to be so comfortable with her. There were twenty years between us, and we had nothing in common. Yet she had a special openness about her, a smiling warmth that wouldn't accept less in return. It

was an odd friendship we had, but one I always cher-
ished.

NINE

RIONA

In early Sensaasti, on a warm afternoon, we walked in the forest just outside the palace gate on the western side. It felt adventurous, but when I glanced up at him striding so confidently next to me, I felt a little foolish.

"What is it?" His voice was soft and low when he looked down at me.

"I haven't been out here in years." I wondered if he could sense my nerves somehow; he always seemed to see more than I meant to show.

"Do you always stay in the palace?"

"Except when I go to market."

He stopped suddenly and appeared to be listening intently. The leaves rustled in the slight breeze. He wore a faint smile and his eyes searched the branches. Finally he pointed. "There."

I couldn't see it at first.

"On the beech, just above the fork on the left side."

"What is it?" It was tiny, a delicate little bird with a spot of brilliant blue under its chin.

"A firza. They only sing in late summer." He still looked around until finally he smiled and looked down at me. "There's the nest. Do you want to see?"

I nodded.

At the base of the tree, he put out his hands and laced his fingers together. "I'll boost you up."

I bit my lip. It felt terribly awkward, but I put one hand on his shoulder, one on the tree trunk, and put my right foot in his hand. He straightened easily and then I was looking right into the nest. The chicks must have been nearly ready to fly, tiny bodies covered with a mixture of pale down and muted adult feathers. Their cries were nearly inaudible, mouths stretched wide. I nearly laughed with delight.

I was about to pick one up when I heard him say quietly, "Don't touch them."

"Why not?" I drew back my hand, but I still smiled to see them shrieking for food.

"The mother might abandon them." In a moment, he let me down with a quiet smile.

"How old are they?"

"Maybe a week. Firza chicks hatch late. Maybe it's why there are so few of them."

A FEW DAYS LATER, we stayed outside the gates until long after dark. I was nervous about it. Not that I feared for my safety; I didn't doubt him at all. It just felt a little scandalous to be out after dusk with a man.

"I want you to see the moon." His words had been simple, but his eyes held a shy hope. I'd nodded, blushing furiously.

We ate a picnic dinner on a hill to the west of the palace. The forest was just behind us, the palace grounds laid out before us like a painting. The wind was from the east, and the faint scent of late roses and lavender from the garden made everything seem warm and perfect.

"Now we wait."

"For the moon?"

He nodded. I heard the trilling call of some kind of bird behind us and looked at him.

"Palesinger." His answer was soft.

I glanced over my shoulder at the forest. The sun would be setting soon, though the trees blocked the best view, and the forest looked darker and a little frightening.

"What do you fear, Riona?" His eyes were kind.

I felt silly admitting it. "I've never been out here at night. The forest seems different."

He smiled quickly and put out his hand as if he would touch mine, but then drew it back again. "I meant in general. But you needn't fear the forest. So close to Stonehaven, it holds nothing more dangerous than men."

I smiled. "And you'll protect me?" I said it lightly to take the attention off my nerves, but he nodded.

"I will." His voice was quiet with no hint of either mockery or bravado.

There was a long silence, until he leaned back to stare at the sky. "Arctana, the stag, rises early this time of year. We should be able to see Ristan soon, over there. That's the point of his shoulder."

I lay back on the blanket. We might have been closer, but we both maintained a careful, cautious distance, too shy to shift toward each other. I half-wished he would take my hand. I almost reached for his once. Isn't that what men and women do when they're courting? Were we courting? I wasn't quite sure.

When I glanced at him, he was staring up into the brilliant sky, his expression unreadable. *Sir, what do you fear?* I wanted to ask. It was a good question because I wanted to know him. I couldn't really imagine him fearing anything, but everyone has fears, even the bravest hero. I didn't have the courage to ask it of him, so I settled for something less intimate, less prying.

"Were the stars different in Rikuto?"

"They're the same. Rikuto is east. To the north and south they're different. On the northern border, you see only the tops of Arctana's antlers, Sen and Forei. The best known constellation is Gevar, the Royal Crown. The line from Puran to Kal, in Gevar, points due north. To the south, in the desert where the Senga live, you tell north by the line of the string in Okcu's bow. Okcu is the Archer."

"It must be exciting to travel so many places."

He blinked and glanced at me. "I suppose." He hesitated, as if he wanted to say something else, but then looked back at the sky. The sunset was fading, and in the dimming light his profile looked strong and handsome.

When the moon rose, it lit the sky with silver brilliance. It rose behind the palace, and soon I saw why he'd chosen our vantage point. The light streamed toward us with such clarity that the palace was silhouetted, making sharp shadows on the gardens, and the tallest spire bisected the full moon. I stared in awe until I finally realized that his eyes were on my face.

"It's beautiful." My words were only a whisper. I half-expected some bit of flattery in response. That's what men do when they're courting a woman, isn't it? *Not as beautiful as you are.* Or *I hadn't noticed, I'm so captivated by you.*

He only a smiled a little. "I'm glad it pleases you."

We sat in silence for some time longer. It was magical, and I breathed in the warm air scented with roses and lavender and thought that life was nearly perfect. I wanted certainty, of course, but the evening had been beautiful.

When we finally rolled up the blanket and packed away the food, he slung the pack over his shoulder and started off. I followed close behind him in the woods. Though the moon was bright, the trees were thick and it was very dark in their shadows. I could barely see the white of his shirt, much less the path in front of me. He walked so quietly it was as if he was a creature of the forest himself, and I had great trouble following the sounds of his steps. I felt my heart beating faster with the small sounds of the woods around us. Once I stumbled over a root and let out a small cry.

"Are you hurt?" His voice was quiet, steady, and startlingly near, and I felt my face flush.

"No, I only tripped. I'm fine." I heard him step away.

He spoke quietly at intervals. "Careful. There's a branch over the path."

"It's steep here."

"This is where we stepped over the stream." He seemed to hesitate. "I can lift you over if you want."

I felt presumptuous to ask it, but I couldn't even see the rocks we'd stepped on earlier. "If you don't mind."

He lifted me with one arm behind my knees and the other behind my shoulders, and stepped into the water. It was hardly the graceful, romantic thing I would have imagined it; I was stiff and nervous and he was painfully proper. I'm not as light as a feather, but he made me feel so, the hard muscles of one arm next to my cheek. It was only a few steps across, and he set me on my feet again.

"Thank you." It wasn't much farther to the palace, and he escorted me to the door of my apartment. "It was a lovely night, sir. Thank you." I looked down at his boots. They were wet nearly to his knees. I bit my lip and looked up at him.

He smiled. "Sleep well, Riona." He bowed and then was off down the hall.

I BARELY HEARD the knock, but I knew it was Lani. It was after dinner several days after Kemen and I saw the moon, when I was preparing for bed. Her father had taken her when he went to speak to Frin Pireyu about a possible engagement. I knew it was unwise to take Lani. Her father wasn't a bad man, nor unkind, but he was painfully oblivious to a girl's fears.

Lani had never met Pireyu, but she knew he was much older than she was, a small time merchant who sold Senga cloth and imported spices. The prospect of travel south excited her, but she was nervous about him. He was more affluent than the younger men her father was also considering, and it would be a good match for the family, a step up in the world. But the age difference only made her more nervous.

When I opened the door, she rushed in and threw herself into my arms without a word.

"That bad, was it?" I rubbed her back. She was trembling, shaking her head and brushing at her eyes.

"Dog! He's a filthy dog! He said…" she sniffed furiously.

There was another knock on my door and she stiffened. "Ma. I don't want to talk to them, Ria! Don't make me."

"I won't, I won't. Let me answer it though."

81

She moved away, just out of sight. I opened the door, but it was not my aunt Ena or my uncle Joka. It was Kemen.

"I came to see if…" he stopped. "What's wrong?"

I'd completely forgotten. In the kitchen that afternoon he'd said that a storm was coming. He'd asked if I wanted to go to the highest tower of the palace to see the sunset because it would be especially beautiful. "Not now. I'm sorry." My voice trembled a little. I'd been looking forward to it all afternoon, but Lani needed me.

He nodded, hesitated, and then turned away.

"I'm sorry, Ria. I can go." Lani said quietly, her eyes red.

He must have heard her, because he turned back with a slight questioning frown. She stepped around the door and tried to slip past him.

"Lani, what's wrong?" His voice was so kind that she began to cry.

He glanced at me and pulled her into my apartment with a gentle hand on her sleeve, sitting her down at the table and kneeling to face her. She was sniffling and half-choking on angry tears.

"He's a dog! He made Pa tell him all about the dowry, down to the last kinds of cloth and how much of everything. And then he said he didn't like me and wouldn't go through with it! It was pathetic. It was cruel." She brushed at her eyes furiously.

Kemen leaned over to look in her face. "Is that it?"

She shook her head, not meeting his gaze. We both waited, and finally she whispered, "He said I didn't have the class to be a merchant's wife. He said I was ugly, and stupid to be reaching so far above my place. I don't have the looks to be so ambitious."

"Oh, Lani." The words were mine, but Kemen was closer to her, and when she buried her face in her hands

82

with a fresh round of tears, he patted her awkwardly on the shoulder.

She sniffed and looked at the floor, embarrassed. "I'm sorry."

"Count yourself lucky. I can't imagine you happy married to a dog." He spoke very seriously.

She almost smiled a little through her tears.

"A stupid one at that. Any fool can see you're beautiful, Lani." There was teasing kindness in his voice. "Besides, he's ancient, isn't he?"

"Thirty-one." She raised her eyebrows. "Younger than you."

He smiled. "Barely. He's ancient. Practically blind, no doubt, and senile. You don't want to be saddled with a doddering old fool, do you?"

She shook her head, smiling now. "He did have a paunch."

HIS HELP WAS more than welcome; there was always plenty of work. He was very kind. When Sayen was sick in the kitchen, he cleaned up the mess while I took her to her room. He took her place. The next morning he was there early to do her work, and when she arrived he told her to take the day to rest. No one would argue with his command, and she did need the rest. Her pregnancy had not been easy.

I didn't exactly take his help for granted, but after a few weeks I'd forgotten how utterly absurd it was. I realized it again when the king himself strode into the kitchen looking for him and he was chopping onions with his sleeves rolled up to his elbows. Like everything else, he did it with excruciating precision. Each onion slice was cut at the same angle, each piece of consistent size.

"What are you doing?" The king was baffled.

"Playing with knives." He was in a strange mood.

"Well, I need you for something else. Could you finish soon?"

"Aye." He washed his hands and smiled at me, a private smile for me alone, as he left. The king was already speaking quietly.

He spent a week interviewing men to choose who would serve as the director of a school that the king established. He had high expectations for it; he and the king had already outlined several courses of study. He questioned the men in great detail. How would they teach? What did they expect in compensation? How quickly would students progress, and when would they be judged ready to work? What assistance would the school provide in helping them find appropriate positions upon completion of their studies? I brought them lunch one day during an interview, and to be honest, I might have cried under the intensity of his questions. He did ultimately choose a man to lead the school, gave him a budget and a schedule for hiring teachers, building the schoolhouse, and other tasks.

I HELPED SARAID in her herb garden, tending rows of basil, mint, garlic, yarrow, a dozen kinds of peppers, chicory, feverfew, lavender, thyme, oregano, saffron, sage, and tarragon. There were more, but I didn't know them all, and some were so finicky that she wouldn't let anyone help with them. We worked in silence most of the time, but it was a warm silence, comfortable.

"Ria, do you know what Sendoa's intentions are toward you?"

I felt my face heat. "I'm sure they're quite honorable."

"I don't doubt that. He's an honorable man. Does he intend to marry you?"

I jerked a weed out of the soil with unnecessary vigor. "I don't know."

"Do you want him to?"

"What do you think, Sari? I turn red every time I see him!" I'd never wanted anything so much.

She nodded quietly and we worked for some time in silence before she spoke again. "You know I was married once."

I looked up in surprise. She'd been alone as long as I'd known her. She must have been nearing sixty, still slim, her hair a beautiful mix of pale gold and bright silvery grey. We'd never been especially close, but I'd always respected her and liked her quiet compassion.

"Yes. I was married." She smiled slightly, keeping her eyes on the plants rather than looking at me. "To a soldier, an officer in the suvari. He died years ago. We were young. He wasn't much like Sendoa, except in one thing. He had the sort of courage that breaks a woman's heart."

She sighed and looked up. "Do you understand me, Riona? A man like Sendoa will break your heart. Not on purpose. But once you've loved him, no one else can ever satisfy you. If he dies, if he goes away to war and doesn't come back, you'll be alone. You're a pretty girl, and you'll have suitors at any age. But you'll never love anyone as you love him. Encourage him if you want, but do it with your eyes open, knowing what you risk."

I swallowed and stared at the ground, my mouth dry. She'd put into words what I most feared. I knew people die. Soldiers die. I wasn't stupid enough to think he'd live forever, nor to think his death wouldn't destroy me. But I pictured my life without him, and I pictured it with him, even for only a limited time, and I had only one answer.

"I don't want anyone else."

TEN

KEMEN

There were dances and banquets I was supposed to attend, but for two months I managed to be conveniently unavailable. I could think of few things I would enjoy less than embarrassing myself among noblemen and ladies by my lack of culture and sophistication. But Hakan finally requested that I begin attending the palace events. As his friend and advisor, it wasn't entirely respectful to miss them all.

I didn't know how to dance, so Kveta taught me. She was a good teacher, patient and kind with my mistakes. When I took her hand at the beginning of our first lesson, I almost expected her to shrink away, though she'd been more than kind the few times I'd seen her since I'd escorted her from Enkotan.

Instead, she gave me a sparkling smile and put her hand in mine, instructing me how to position my arms and where to put my feet. "Relax, Kemen. I'm not a snake. I don't bite."

We moved around and around the room as she taught me different steps. After a week, we had musicians accompany us and provide the tempo.

"You learn quickly. You'll be a superb dancer. Your rhythm is better than mine."

I shook my head, but it did come easily after the first few days. Physical things always do; it's in other areas that I have more difficulty.

"You'll be very popular at the banquet next week."

I raised my eyebrows at her.

"Really. You've been avoiding them, but now you have no excuse."

She was right, though I couldn't have been more surprised. The festivities began with dinner, and I sat at Hakan's right hand, as I was always honored to. After that the dancing began. Hakan and Kveta danced alone first, then the floor was opened to everyone.

I stood back. I enjoyed watching Hakan and Kveta dance, and the music was pleasing and joyful. My clothes were even stiffer and more ridiculous than usual. My old ones had been thrown away, but my new everyday clothes weren't too uncomfortable. But for official functions and special events, I had more ornate clothes of fine fabrics woven with gold and silver. My position apparently required such finery, at least in public. I thought I looked ridiculous in them, but I wasn't used to noble fashions. I had given specific instructions that they were to be as plain as possible, but my idea of plain and the seamstress's idea of plain were apparently quite different.

Riona served wine and refreshments during the dances. In my eyes, she was the most beautiful woman there, though her dress was simple. I smiled at her when I caught her eye, and she blushed most becomingly.

"Would you dance, sir?" Kveta was smiling up at me, one hand out gracefully.

I took her hand but leaned down to speak in her ear. "Now you're being cruel. I thought better of you."

She looked up at me with wide eyes and I smiled to show her I wasn't entirely serious. I was terribly nervous, but I was only teasing her. She couldn't be cruel if she tried.

It felt like everyone watched me, waiting for me to step on her feet, stumble over my own, or turn in the wrong direction. After the song finished, I would have fled to the side, but Kveta kept my hand in hers.

She whispered in my ear, "Ask her," and nodded toward one of her new Erdemen friends, a young lady named Citulali who had come to visit the palace several times.

My heart sank. I didn't want to disappoint Kveta, but neither did I wish to be publicly humiliated by the lady's refusal.

"Go on."

I bowed to Citulali stiffly. "Would you dance?"

She smiled and took my outstretched hand and I blinked in surprise. The dance was pleasant; she smiled as if I were any Tuyet gentleman and not a Dari soldier. After that, Kveta pointed me to another of her friends. I saw a definite flicker of fear in her eyes, but she smiled and nodded. Her hand trembled in mine.

The night was surreal. After that, an older lady asked me to dance, which so startled me that I couldn't find my voice for a moment. Then another. It was almost intoxicating. I didn't imagine that any of them really liked me, but it was a feeling of acceptance, of Tuyetness, that I hadn't expected. The ladies were pleasing. Their hands in mine were small and white and fragile, their lips pink, their eyes all blue or gray, their faces milky white. Their hair was done in fantastic arrangements with feathers and pearls, gemstones and gold.

When the night was drawing to a close, I stood on the side with a glass of wine. Kveta was dancing with Hakan, and I smiled to see them so happy. He would marry her, it was in his eyes, and they would be happy together. I barely noticed the man standing next to me until he spoke.

"Quite a successful night, wasn't it?"

"It was." I smiled even more as the music ended in a rush and Hakan kissed Kveta.

"Who did you choose?"

"What?" I looked down at him for the first time.

"Who did you choose? For the night." His smile looked predatory. "I'd take that one. Her name is Ilara. She has quite a dowry, not that you need it."

"I'll ask you once not to speak of her that way. Or of any of the others. I don't believe they're for sale." My words were clipped in my anger.

"Some of them aren't, you're quite right. But some are. Chenylu Kalyano, there, she's not for sale. But she's generous if you ask." He was looking around the room, but when he glanced up at me his smile faded. "I was just curious."

"I'm not buying."

He shrugged and edged away. My stomach turned with disgust and I made my way to the doors to the garden, with a few stiff smiles for the looks I couldn't avoid. The air was cool and fresh, and I took a few deep breaths, trying to calm my anger. Maybe it was better for a girl to work like a slave on a farm than to be sold like meat in a market.

"Sendoa, is it? I'd hoped to find you here." The voice was smooth and pleasant. She was a little younger than Riona, exquisitely dressed. At my silence, she smiled.

"I'm Melora Grallin." She leaned against the railing next to me and ran one white hand over the feathers in her hairpiece. I was glad Riona didn't put anything silly in her hair. Once, when I helped her across a stream in the forest, my nose was nearly in her hair for a moment; it smelled of sunlight and laundry soap and warmth.

"Beautiful night." She patted at her hair again.

I nodded. There was a long silence, and she glanced at me sideways.

"Are you always this quiet?"

I smiled a little. "Yes."

"Cultivating an air of mystery? It's quite effective. I'm surprised I was the first one out here."

I can't pretend that I didn't know what she meant, but I didn't really believe her. Kveta's kindness and friendship had granted me some measure of acceptance, but I was still a Dari among Tuyets, and a common soldier among nobles.

The door opened behind us, and I turned to see who it was, half-hoping it was Kveta or Hakan to rescue me from the awkward silence. The light streamed out, and the figure turned back almost immediately. "Sorry, sir." It was Riona with a tray of wine glasses and little pastries.

"Wait, please."

She turned back at my voice, her eyes downcast, and offered us the tray with a respectful bob of her head. Lady Grallin took a pastry with careful fingers but no word of thanks to Riona. I traded my empty glass for a full one, though I didn't want any more. She kept her eyes down as she turned away, and I spoke quietly.

"Riona."

After a long moment she looked up to meet my eyes.

91

"Thank you." I was gratified to see a glint of humor in her smile before she ducked her head again.

Lady Grallin watched her go with an odd expression before turning back to me. "I've heard all sorts of fascinating rumors about you. Would you tell me the truth of them?"

"Rumors of what?"

"One of the best is that you were offered the crown and the Hero Song. Is that true?"

"Aye. It was a kind gesture." I turned back to look at the dark garden.

"I doubt that was all it was." She smiled, and I thought she looked much prettier when she didn't try so hard. "What about the skirmish on the border? That gained the respect of the Rikutan king for His Highness?"

I looked down at my hands on the railing. "What about it?"

She put one hand on my wrist. "That you defeated a whole raiding party alone. I can believe it." She ran her hand up my arm.

She smelled of perfume and gold. I licked my lips and stepped away to bow as courteously as I could. "Excuse me. I have business for the king I must attend to."

Eleven

Riona

He stood at a window with a rare smile, quiet and proud.

"What is it?"

"Come see."

I stood beside him to look out the window. He was watching the young king and the princess, who were walking hand in hand in the garden below. They passed a wheelbarrow that one of the groundsmen had left for a moment, and I frowned in confusion when the princess suddenly stopped and emptied the weeds in it onto the ground. She gave it a quick swipe with a handkerchief and then gestured. The two appeared to have a laughing argument and finally to my surprise the king sat in the wheelbarrow, holding his feet up off the ground. The princess grasped the handles and pushed. The two careened over the lawn laughing like children. I looked up in shock to see Kemen's quiet smile broadened almost to a grin.

He glanced down at me, still smiling, his eyes warm. Just then the princess lost control of the wheelbarrow, which overturned and flung the king into a bush, utterly undignified, laughing so hard he simply lay on the ground for a minute.

I was staring in complete shock. A king is dignified, staid, serious. Even when a king laughs, he does it with dignity and royal condescension to those around him. At least the old king, Hakan Emyr, was like that. I had never considered that a king could be different.

"What is it?" Kemen was still smiling.

"I just never expected, I thought..." I couldn't even explain why I was so surprised.

"Why not?" His eyes on my face were disconcerting.

"He's the king. I thought, well, that he would be more..." again words failed me, and I watched as the king stood and brushed the leaves from his hair. He kissed the princess, a sweet smiling kiss, joyous and pure. I felt my face flush and looked away, feeling as though I was intruding although they were in plain sight. I had the distinct feeling that life under the young king Hakan Ithel would be very different than it had been under the old king.

"A king is a man like any other." His voice was quiet as he drew back from the window. "Except that his responsibilities are greater. I'm glad to see him happy."

I looked up at him. He was still smiling slightly. There was a deep, quiet love between them, the love of men who have suffered and triumphed together. I didn't understand it then, but I did later. I also didn't realize then how very happy he must have been to show it so openly.

THE PRINCESS KVETA was excited to see her father again. She was returning to Rikuto after two months at the palace, and I suspected the young king was sending Kemen with a marriage proposal as well. Even a blind man could see their love.

I couldn't blame her for her excitement, but I have to admit I felt the slightest twinge of envy. I wished my father and mother could be there to see me marry. If I ever did.

Kemen was excruciatingly courteous to me, but the contrast between his careful, solemn kindness and the king's laughing joy with Kveta stung me. I wanted him to be happy. I wanted to make him happy, to see him smile and know that it was the thought of me that made him carefree.

In the two months she was at the palace, the king took Kveta riding. They read in the garden together. They sang in the conservatory. Her voice was more than passable, but his was breathtaking, a soaring tenor that could bring tears to your eyes. She glowed with pride in him.

I wanted to hear Kemen sing, but I wasn't bold enough to ask him, and he never volunteered. Once I sang with Sinta when we were in the kitchen. Kemen was cutting peppers beside me and listened with a quiet smile, but he didn't join us.

One afternoon we walked in the garden in the last of the late summer warmth. He showed me a little green and black snake in the grass, and at my gasp he smiled. "It's a grestu. It's not poisonous."

He knelt and caught it with deft fingers. I didn't know a human could move so quickly; the little snake was only as long as my hand and fast as lightning. He held it up so I could touch it, and my fingers brushed his. He was gentle with it as it struggled to escape, and I ran one finger along its cool dry scales. When he put it back in the grass, it disappeared with a flick of its tail faster than I could blink.

"I don't like snakes." Though it had felt oddly pleasant beneath my tentative touch.

"They eat rats and mice."

"That's one point in their favor. But they still frighten me."

He only smiled. I wondered if I'd disappointed him.

"Do you like snakes?" I still felt awkward with him, though he was always so kind. I wanted to know him, to understand him.

"They have their own kind of beauty. Did you feel how strong it was, even though it was small?"

I raised my eyebrows skeptically, and I almost thought I saw a sparkle of laughter in his eyes. I don't know if I'd ever seen him laugh, but I wanted to.

He took Lani riding one morning. She was thrilled, dancing about her work all day. They jumped a small creek, and she said it felt like flying.

Next time he asked me, I would say yes.

TWELVE

KEMEN

I escorted Kveta to Enkotan to see her father the king Ashmu Tafari and delivered a letter from Hakan requesting Kveta's hand in marriage. Kveta rode in her carriage much of the time, but often she rode beside me on a chestnut mare. She asked a thousand questions about the Erdemen countryside. It was cooler than in the carriage; the breeze was warm, carrying the scents of late summer, grass and rotting leaves and cows, smoke from a farmer clearing his field.

The men stayed back a respectful distance. Of course I had scouts ahead to be sure there was no trouble, but none close on the road before us because I didn't want her riding into the dust the horses would kick up.

It would have been polite for Hakan to go ask her father himself, but at the time his crown was still so new that we both thought it risky for him to leave Stonehaven. Kveta was an enjoyable traveling companion. She had a wicked sense of humor. I got more than one look of surprise from the men when I laughed aloud at something she said.

Tafari sent an escort to meet us at the border, and I expected Kveta would retire to her carriage for the sake of propriety. But she lifted her chin and said she preferred the fresh air and my company to sitting alone in the carriage. In a distant way, she reminded me of Lani, with her determined kindness and cheerful heart.

We made the trip in good time, though I didn't push us hard. The Rikutan capital was livelier than it was on my first visit, and our long entourage of Erdemen and Rikutan suvari was greeted with cheering and song.

Tafari met us in the courtyard, and Kveta ran to him like a child. Their love was beautiful, and I wished for a daughter of my own to experience that kind of joy. If Tafari had been welcoming and courteous when I first visited Enkotan, he was twice as welcoming the second time. There was a great banquet that night with music and dancing and all forms of entertainment. Kveta danced with me, and though I was terribly nervous, I managed not to embarrass myself. Her father looked on with a smile.

I delivered the letter to him immediately, but he put it aside and asked to have several days to think on the contents. I'm sure he knew what the letter contained; Kveta had written him many letters over the months she had been in Stonehaven and no doubt had already told of Hakan's affection.

At last, he spoke to me over a quiet luncheon in his beloved garden. "I am pleased to give my consent to my daughter's marriage. Kveta has told me much of your king, and I believe she'll be happy with him." He spoke of the possibility of a pact between our countries, a promise of mutual aid in case of attack. I did not promise anything, but it was heartening that he thought it worthwhile to mention.

She stayed with him, but the wedding was arranged for some two months later, in the golden late autumn. The thought of Hakan's joy at the acceptance of his proposal gave me speed on the journey home, and the thought of Riona's smile made my heart beat faster.

I LEFT THE MAIN company far behind. I pushed Kanti hard, but even so, one horse can only go so fast for so long, and I had to slow my speed near the end, when I was most impatient. I arrived just before midnight after riding all day in an early autumn downpour, drenched from head to toe, my hair dripping, my cloak heavy, and my boots filled with water. It wasn't especially cold, but I was more than ready for a hot fire and some dry clothes.

I wasn't expected for at least another week, so the palace guards were surprised, but they let me in and sent a runner for Hakan. I shook the water from my hair and one of the servants took my cloak as I waited. I dropped to one knee as Hakan entered.

"Where's Kveta?"

"With her father. He gave his consent and his blessing. Here's the letter." It was carefully sealed and double-wrapped in leather to keep it dry. "Seven weeks from now." I smiled, and then grinned when he whooped with joy. He threw his head back and laughed, clasped my elbow and then pulled me into a quick embrace, thumping my back with his other hand. He grinned like a little boy, and I laughed with him.

"You're wet and probably cold and hungry. Go get cleaned up and we can have dinner together." He was still grinning, the front of his robe damp.

"Oh, go back to bed." He looked a little doubtful, but I smiled and clapped him on the shoulder. "I'm boring tonight anyway. I want to change clothes, eat, and go to sleep, and I intend to be done in ten minutes. We can talk tomorrow, but I wanted you to hear the news."

He smiled and flushed, laughed a little and looked down at the floor. "Thanks, Kemen." Then more seriously, "Thank you. Goodnight then."

Riona slipped into the hall as Hakan left, and I smiled at her and bowed.

"You're wet!"

"It's raining." I smiled a little more.

Sinta chuckled and murmured something to Riona that made her blush before she left, leaving only Riona with me in the hall.

"I trust you're well?" I couldn't keep my eyes off her. She held a lamp, and the light caught her hair with a thousand shades of gold.

She blushed and nodded. "Come. I'll get you dinner."

She walked with me to my room. Someone had already started the fire, and she fed it more wood. I stripped off my clothes behind a wooden screen and tried to scrub the mud away with a towel. The new dry breeches felt wonderful, and I ran the towel over my hair.

"Will you want a bath tonight?" Her voice carried over the crackle of the fire. She has a beautiful voice, soft and clear, silvery bright in a dark room.

"Just a basin of water. I should, but I'm tired. I'll bathe in the morning." I wondered whether she'd think I was disgusting if she saw me without my shirt. I was as fit as a man could be, but in the flickering lamplight and the dim glow of the fire, my olive skin looked nearly black. I was afraid, but I would test her. If she didn't re-

100

coil in horror, I would have hope, and in another month or two, if all went well and my courage didn't fail, I would ask her the most terrifying question any man can ask.

When I stepped out from behind the screen, she was lighting another lamp. "I'll bring you some dinner in a moment. There's wine here for you while you wait." Then she looked up and I heard the faintest gasp.

I swallowed and tried to pretend I hadn't noticed, stepping close to the fire and kneeling to poke at one of the logs. I hoped that at least she didn't think me frightening, a dark monster. I tried to steady my breathing, feeling my eyes prick with sudden inconvenient moisture. *Phraa*. I'd been foolish to hope so outrageously.

"Sir? The king had pheasant pie for dinner tonight, if you'd like that. But I can make you anything you want." She knelt beside me. "Are you cold? I can get more wood for the fire."

"I'm fine. Thank you."

Riona stepped away and I sighed, still staring at the fire. I needed a shirt; I didn't want to displease her any more than I already had. I wasn't very hungry after all, but I was a bit sore from the ride. The dry heat of the fire stung my face and I closed my eyes a moment.

I felt a warm touch around my neck, across my shoulders, and I looked up.

"Sir, come sit." She'd put a soft robe around my shoulders, one hand lingering, and was biting her lip. "You must be tired. What can I bring you?"

I stood to sit in the nearest chair, stretching my bare feet toward the fire. I coughed. "Whatever is easy."

"Are you sick?" She looked worried.

"No. Just tired." Riding hard in the rain sometimes gives me a cough, but it's never serious. It would be gone by morning.

She stood by me a moment, then leaned over and tucked the robe closer around my neck. When my eyes met hers, she blushed furiously, and her hand trembled.

Perhaps I was wrong. Perhaps she wasn't disgusted.

The door closed with a quiet click. Obstinate hope had already risen again. Perhaps she was only startled and not disgusted by my color. Perhaps she was only startled because I was a man with no shirt on, and not because of my color at all. Perhaps, I dared hope for one instant, she was actually pleased by what she saw. It was unlikely, but the thought persisted. Even if she wasn't pleased, perhaps she wasn't entirely revolted.

I woke to her gentle touch on my shoulder.

"Sir, I've brought your dinner."

I blinked away sleep and smiled in surprise. She'd brought a spread fit for a king's banquet: fruit, pheasant pie, a lamb tart, cheese, almond pastries, beans with nuts, stuffed tomatoes, and half a dozen other things. I hadn't meant to fall asleep.

"I guess I look hungry." I pulled my robe closer and belted it so she wouldn't have to see more of me than any shirt would reveal.

She smiled and blushed, clasping her hands together. "I wanted to be sure you had something you liked." She bit her lip. "Did you have any trouble on the road?"

"No. The trip was easy enough." I coughed again.

She reached across the table to touch my hand, her fingers cool, slim, and pale against my larger ones. "Have some tea. The lemon might help a little."

I smiled and sipped the hot tea. It was sweet with honey and tart with lemon.

"How long did it take you to get back?"

"Eight days." I think it was a record; I'd been so impatient. My heart was thudding in my chest, and I watched her face as I said, "I wanted to see you again."

"I'm glad you're back." She blushed as she said it. Then carefully, gently, she interlaced her fingers with mine. "I missed you."

I bent to kiss her fingers, and when I raised my eyes to hers, she was smiling.

She'd put hot peppers in the lamb tart for me; she remembered I liked them. We sat in the flickering light and she asked me about Rikuto and about the journey. I reached across to touch her hand again, and she curled her fingers into mine. We stayed up far too late, but every moment felt warm and perfect. When she stood to bid me good night and take the tray to the kitchen, she ran one hand across my shoulders. I caught her hand and kissed it, and she smiled again, her touch lingering.

HAKAN READ KEPA'S latest letter aloud over lunch the next day. The Tarvil raiders were bolder, even venturing south of Fort Kuzeyler at times, and he'd been having problems with morale and with one of his commanders.

"What would you do, if you were there?" Hakan asked.

"If Captain Teretz is shirking, I'd confront him on it. It might solve the issue. If not, I'd court-martial him. But I can't tell enough to judge what's going on from that letter." Kepa was unwilling to make specific accusations in writing, and I couldn't blame him, knowing the letter would be read by the king himself. He didn't want to destroy a man's career unnecessarily, and it sounded like he wasn't entirely sure what was going on anyway.

"And the raiders?"

"I don't think Kepa…" I stopped. Now I was the one about to speak poorly of a man while he couldn't defend himself. I amended my words. "I'm not confident Kepa has the skill to address the challenges he's outlined. I may need to go myself."

Hakan raised his eyebrows. "I can't ask you to do that, Kemen. It's not unreasonable to expect a man of his rank to handle this. Besides, your ribs still hurt, don't they?"

I frowned and shook my head. "Not much. But you're right, I'm not eager to leave."

He glanced at me curiously, but I only smiled.

THIRTEEN

RIONA

The Rikutan king appointed his younger brother regent and was coming himself to see his daughter wed. It should have been a joyful time, and we were happy for the two sweethearts, but for the servants the work was nearly overwhelming. As the wedding approached, we worked frantically. We cleaned the palace from top to bottom. We started preparing food. There would be hundreds of guests for the banquet and maybe seventy requiring rooms, some for up to two weeks.

Kemen sought me out in the kitchen or when I was cleaning, but he had his own preparations that kept him busy. Not only was there to be a royal wedding, but it would be the first visit of Rikuto's king to the Erdemen court in living memory. Kemen would lead the suvari escort that would accompany the king and his entourage from the border.

They departed nearly three weeks before the wedding. He bid me farewell, and I thought he would kiss me. On the lips, I mean, not the properly respectful kisses on my hand he'd given me before. It was a good opportunity, and I would have been glad of it. I was ready. My heart leaped when I saw his tall form ducking under the strings of drying peppers and onions in the kitchen or striding through the halls. When he worked beside me in the kitchen, I snuck glances at his hands, swift and sure, and his face, serious, intense, almost stern.

I hoped the separation would inspire him to be warmer, more demonstrative than usual. He bent to kiss my hand and smiled with his customary reserved courtesy, and then he was gone. I felt myself tingling with frustration, and I pushed it down. Surely, he meant to honor me, rather than snub me. But it was hard to feel desirable, when he had not indicated he was interested in a kiss. Not to mention anything more.

I missed him while he was away, and it hurt that I couldn't imagine him missing me in return. In fact, I had difficulty imagining him ruffled by much of anything. I couldn't envision him emotional or tired at all. Those first few days when he was recovering from Taisto's poison seemed far away. He seemed to have boundless energy, rising before I did to exercise at dawn, working all day and speaking with the king until late at night, sometimes exercising again in the evening coolness. Every morning I found a flower in the handle of the door to my apartment. The gesture was sweet and romantic. Yet it might as well have been left by someone else; I had never seen his eyes unguarded, and rarely had I seen him laugh, though often enough I saw his warmth and kindness.

In contrast, I could feel myself becoming more tightly wound as the wedding approached. We worked to make everything perfect.

THE RIKUTAN KING Ashmu Tafari arrived with a majestic blowing of trumpets and prancing of horses, his entourage a pageant of color. Kemen rode beside him, and it amazed me to think that he was on such good terms with kings of two nations. The Rikutan king smiled at him with genuine friendship when they dismounted; apparently they'd had a pleasant journey. The king Hakan Ithel met the king Ashmu Tafari in the courtyard, a show of warmth and welcome that was both unusual and quite a good start to the visit. They'd never met in person, though numerous messages had been exchanged between them.

I didn't see more of their initial meeting, since I was called away to bring refreshments to the drawing room where they would chat before dinner. They were already prepared, of course, but we waited in the hallway with trays of pastries and cheeses and wine, out of the way until they washed and settled in.

Fourteen

Kemen

I would ask Riona to marry me after the royal wedding. She was busy and tired, as were all the servants. I left a rose at her door every morning, buds for hope, larger blooms for my growing love. Pink for admiration and joy. A pale peach for friendship, my hope to know her better, to see deeper into her heart. Another cream, velvety rich, for her perfection. The deepest burgundy red for her unconscious beauty.

When the roses ceased blooming, I found other flowers, lilies of all colors, blue salvia, golden yarrow. I didn't know what they meant, but I hoped their beauty would make her mornings more joyful.

Lani seemed to be everywhere, running from errand to errand. The day before the wedding I rose especially early to do my exercises, because the day would be very long. When I finished, I wiped the sweat from my face with my shirt and rested a minute against the edge of the well, then went inside. I needed a bath, and then I would entertain Ashmu Tafari and his military liaison for breakfast. I turned a corner in the hallway and Lani ran headlong into me, bouncing off my chest and nearly falling. I caught her arm and steadied her.

"Sorry, sir!" Then she looked up and grinned. "Kemen! How are you?"

"Tired already. How are you?"

She was nearly dancing. "Excited! I've never seen a royal wedding! I hope it's perfect." She rubbed her nose. "You hurt."

"Sorry." I hesitated. "Where will Ria be this afternoon? I want to see her."

She rolled her eyes. "I don't know. She's doing everything. Probably in the kitchen helping supervise the baking. She's the best at it besides Joran, and for a wedding everything has to be perfect."

"Thank you." I wondered whether I should try to help or whether it would be better to stay out of the way. I wanted to see her smile, but the kitchen was already crowded. Perhaps it would be better not to bother her.

She served during lunch, and I smiled at her when I could, though Ashmu Tafari was intent on telling me a story of his campaign against the Tarvil some twenty years before. I caught bits and pieces of it. He'd had a good friend who was Dari, killed near the end of the campaign, but he remembered him fondly as a man of honor, integrity, and a mostly-hidden quirky humor. I wondered if that had helped me in our initial negotiations. Kveta smiled on my other side, speaking across me to her father, and I smiled to see her so happy. Riona reached over my shoulder to put out the plates of nut pastries and sugared fruits, and I tried to catch her eye.

FIFTEEN

RIONA

The kitchen was too crowded as we all worked frantically the day before the wedding. Most of us had barely slept for days, and tempers were short. I was preparing trays of refreshments for the two kings as they watched an afternoon demonstration of Erdemen suvari in the courtyard. Joran backed into me as I was pouring the 317 vintage wine, and I dropped the bottle. It spilled all over the floor and down my one clean dress. I sniffled angrily as I knelt to clean it up. Lani tried to help, but she got called away to do something else. Joran stepped on my fingers and nearly fell over me as I tried to get the last bit behind him.

I gave up. The mess on the floor could wait for later. I finished the trays, my dress sticking to my stomach, and gave them to Sinta to deliver to the royal pavilion. I changed in my tiny apartment, scowling at myself in the mirror. I'd always thought I did a good job, but that day was one clumsy mistake after another.

I hurried back toward the kitchen, wondering if I would get a chance to have my own lunch, and I nearly ran into Kemen as I turned a corner in one hallway. He'd just said something to Lani, who was carrying two trays of refreshments for some of the other guests, and she was laughing.

"Sir, could I speak with you?" I should have known better than to try to speak with him then. His reserve could provoke a rock to anger.

He followed me in to the nearest sitting room and closed the door behind himself.

"Why don't you smile at me more often?"

He blinked at my tone. "What do you mean?"

"You smile at Lani more than you smile at me! I'm glad you like her, but I need to know I mean more to you than a fourteen year old."

He licked his lips. "I'm sorry. I want to honor—"

I should have let him finish. Perhaps his words would have soothed me. But I was upset before I began speaking, and his apology didn't come quickly enough for my emotions.

"You don't tell me what you feel. Or what you think. The king gets to see it. The princess Kveta sees it. Even Lani sees it sometimes. Why don't I? I don't understand how you can love me if you don't share anything with me. *Do* you love me?" I flung the question at him, biting my lip. It was stupid. He had never exactly said it. I assumed, and I pushed farther than I had any right to.

"I do." He stood very still, his eyes on me. Whatever else about him that might frustrate me, I could not deny that he listened with the same single-minded intensity he did everything else.

"Then why don't you show it? Why don't I get to see you smile? Or hear your thoughts? Why don't you ask what I'm feeling?"

111

"I'm sorry. I'd thought you would tell me, if you wanted me to know." He was very quiet.

"I want to know you care about me! And I want to know what you're feeling. You never say! Do you even have feelings?"

His mouth opened a moment and then closed without a sound.

"How can you say you love me if you don't even show me who you really are? If I don't know you, inside where it really counts? I suppose I shouldn't have expected you to understand. I expected you to love me, to show you loved me. Women need love, Kemen. I need love. Love is vulnerable. Love trusts. Love shares its heart. I don't think you even know what I mean by that, much less how to do it." I was crying with frustration.

He stood still for a long moment before speaking. I'd been choked by tears and emotion, and the steadiness of his voice, low and quiet, struck me as a mockery. "I'm sorry to disappoint you. If you would tell me what I might do to—"

What I did next was inexcusable. Rather than listening to him, I was so tired, so frustrated, that I sobbed, "I don't want to speak to you!" and I turned away and ran down the hall to my room.

I cried into my pillow, wishing that he were different, that I were different, that we understood each other. I wanted him to love me, and didn't understand how he already did.

THE WEDDING WAS the most beautiful thing I'd ever seen. The king Hakan Ithel and his bride glowed with the light of their love. Many nobles came for it. The Rikutan king Ashmu Tafari placed the cloth over their heads for the sealing kiss. He had tears in his eyes and he kissed his daughter on the cheek afterwards and whispered something in her ear that made her smile even more.

I'd seen the cloth for two months because Anthea and Sayen worked on it every afternoon. It was deep green silk with the great Erdemen eagle embroidered on it with gold and silver threads. The edge was bordered with the traditional olive branches and grape vines, but in a gesture of friendship the king had ordered the corners accented by the red lilies of Rikuto. Though it was familiar, when I saw it during the ceremony and later hanging on the wall of the banquet hall, its beauty nearly took my breath away.

I served at the banquet, as did nearly everyone. We were all terribly busy, but I managed to serve the royal table a few times. If Kemen's smile was a bit strained, it wasn't too obvious. When I refilled his wine glass, he thanked me as courteously as ever, though he kept his gaze on the table. I thought about bending to whisper something in his ear, an apology or at least a plea to talk with him later in more privacy. But it wasn't appropriate, and of all places to break the rigid rules of protocol, the king's wedding banquet would be the most scandalous. I didn't mind so much for myself, but for Kemen's honor before the royalty and nobility of two nations, I restrained the impulse.

After that, I had to attend to other tables with noble guests, and I could catch only a few glimpses of the royal table. Once I glanced up at him and his eyes were on me. He dropped his gaze immediately and inclined his head a little, as if he were bowing in apology for looking at me at all. I wished I could speak with him, but we had not the time or privacy necessary. Later, in the garden or in a quiet corner of the kitchen, we could talk.

The banquet went long into the night, with hours of dancing after the meal. Kemen danced with the new young queen. I stood still and watched, forgetting entirely that I should have been offering pastries and wine to the guests. He was dazzlingly handsome, broad shouldered, flat-stomached, graceful, athletic and perfect. My heart beat faster every time he turned toward me. He was very solemn, more than was probably proper at a wedding feast, but he smiled at Kveta when they ended the dance and he bowed to kiss her hand. Something about it made me a little uneasy, but I didn't have time to figure out why because there was so much to be done.

Finally, the sweethearts retired to their suite with much cheering and clapping. The nobles who were going to depart did so, and we showed the others to their rooms before beginning the long task of cleaning up. That night we only moved everything to the kitchen and cleaned the great hall. Washing the dishes and dealing with the food would wait for the next day. I fell into bed in absolute exhaustion and slept without dreaming. Servants had to be up early the next day because the guests required food and attention. We were all tired and distracted by the work for some time.

It was two days after the wedding when I realized more clearly how my words must have sounded, how deeply I had cut him. I went searching for him.

If I'd asked I would have found out sooner, but I didn't want anyone to know we had quarreled. I finally asked Sayen after I could not find him after several hours.

He'd departed some hours earlier for the far northern border. The northern commander Yoshiro Kepa badly needed reinforcements to deal with the Tarvil raiders. Some fifty men had gone with him immediately and some three hundred more were to follow within hours. I would have sent him a letter, a message, but I didn't know how to find the men who were leaving. Nor did I realize how long he would be gone.

I confess I thought briefly that it might have been a selfish burst of temper. I misjudged him in that. He was never one for foolish impulse or selfishness of any sort. Neither did he have a quick temper, though I suppose I'd tried him more sorely than I realized.

Later, I understood it as an act of despair.

Sixteen

Kemen

I turned my mind north, devoting myself to the challenge of the northern border, as if work has ever truly eased a man's mind from the sting of a woman's scorn. Distracted, yes, but soothed? Assuredly not.

Fort Kuzeyler was in disarray, and Kepa frustrated and ill-prepared for the challenge. I respected the man, respected his integrity, but I was sorely disappointed in his leadership then. He relinquished command to me with genuine relief, and in his defense, I should also say that he never showed any sign of resentment at the respect I commanded immediately. Another man might have been stung by the way I took control, for in my disappointment and despair I wasn't as kind as I should have been. But he took it well, and served as my deputy with much greater facility than he led.

A few soldiers had been missing for some time. Kepa had finished accounting for casualties in the most recent skirmish, and still some men were missing. Often there are casualties who cannot be accounted for, men who die quietly in the woods alone. My first command was an exhaustive search of the woods for any wounded men who may have been overlooked. We found a few wounded Tarvil who had been unable to flee with their companions, and a few Erdemen soldiers, but still a few remained unaccounted for.

Absent without leave. It is not incomprehensible that men get angry, frustrated, and I, too, would perhaps have chafed under Kepa's inept command. I sent their names and identification numbers to Stonehaven, and after some searching, eight of the men were found back at their homes in rural villages. They would stand before military tribunals for dereliction of duty, but that was out of my hands. As Minister of Military Affairs, the cases might eventually work their way up to me, but for a while I had nothing further to do with the matter.

That left only three men still missing. In the next month, those three would cause me more pain than the rest combined. The Erdemen military is strong for good reason. We have superb discipline. High standards for competence and a command structure that promotes based on merit, not blood. Excellent training, grueling but deliberately so, intelligently designed to produce soldiers with physical expertise, mental strength, initiative, and courage. We do not leave our wounded comrades behind, and in any case I heard that these three had been seen more recently than the last skirmish. In fact, one soldier vowed he had seen them as recently as the day before I arrived, and there had been no action since.

I pondered the matter, but I could think of few good outcomes. The truth proved worse than I imagined. But I did not yet know the truth, so I devoted myself to the immediate tasks. The fort itself was badly in need of repair, and that was my next priority, to give the men a secure place to rest, for we would be driving north hard and fast. Kepa had split his men between worthy tasks, but some tasks were more urgent than others and suffered by the delay.

I pulled them all back to Fort Kuzeyler to finish its repair. I took refuge from my thoughts in the work. A thousand decisions to keep my mind occupied, and a thousand physical tasks to tire my body. Then we left a skeleton crew to hold it and moved the entire battalion southwest to repair the road to Fort Kuzeyler. The road was critical. Messages, food shipments, weapons, armor, reinforcements, and anything else we needed would come over that road. That took over a month, and I pushed the men hard.

SEVENTEEN

RIONA

I knew I had hurt him, and the guilt ate at me, though I tried to hide it. I still stand by my grievance; my frustration was real. A woman does need tenderness, and I wasn't wrong to want it. But I'd been terribly unfair in how I asked it of him, and I hadn't understood how his life made my need seem impossible to satisfy. I thought at the time that he didn't understand how I needed his heart and his trust, but later I realized that he understood it all too well, and felt himself utterly inadequate. It was that realization that brought tears to my eyes suddenly, nearly a month after his departure.

I was brushing the queen Kveta's hair before she retired for the night. My mind was leagues away with him, though I couldn't really picture the wild northern frontier. I don't know why I suddenly understood his hurt. The queen was speaking of something that the king had said, and perhaps that somehow made it real. I do remember that I paused, the brush still in her hair, and she looked at me in the mirror.

"What's wrong?"

I shook my head wordlessly, but she pressed me to answer, and finally I stuttered something about my stupidity, how I had said horrible things to him, though I loved him.

"What did you say?"

I was ashamed of myself, of my words, but by then she was a friend as well as the queen. She turned to me and clasped my hands in hers, and I looked down at the floor as I answered.

"The worst was I asked if he had feelings, and," I faltered. "I said that if he loved me, he didn't show it, and I doubted whether he did at all. I didn't mean it the way it sounded, I just wanted..." I couldn't speak any more, my tears flowing freely.

I saw her stricken face even as she reached to embrace me. She was sweet to me, more than she should have been, but she grieved for his pain more. She understood him better than I did then. Even now it astonishes me how I loved him without understanding him at all.

Eighteen

Kemen

W hen we began work on the road, I sent men to all the villages within five leagues of the border for fifteen leagues in either direction to get names and descriptions of any women taken by the Tarvil. Undoubtedly some had died from ill-treatment, for I couldn't imagine that the Tarvil treated them well, but those who still lived would not remain their prisoners if I had any choice in the matter. The villagers were grateful we were there, but I heard disturbing news. In Ilato, only some three leagues away, the two men I'd sent were greeted with jeers, thrown rocks, and shouted obscenities. They had split, one man coming back to me with the news and the other moving on to more agreeable towns to continue his mission.

I went myself to investigate, taking some thirty men with me. I would not of course turn them on the people under nearly any circumstances, but their numbers would keep the exchange civil. So I hoped, anyway.

The village was quiet when we rode in, the people glaring at us with deep resentment from where they stopped to watch us. No one spoke, and we rode to the small central square. There my questions were answered.

Three bodies hung from a makeshift gallows, their suvari uniforms dirty and damp. One of the soldiers beside me vomited from the side of his horse. There was a stench despite the autumn chill, for the bodies had been there for some time, the skin of their faces black and swollen with rot. I heard muttering behind me from the soldiers, but a quick stern glare silenced them.

I rode to the nearest person, a woman of perhaps my own age, speaking as calmly as I could. I probably sounded as cold as ice, but I didn't feel that way. "Who is responsible for this?"

She shrugged, glaring at me as if daring me to strike her.

"I wish to speak with him. Who is responsible for this?"

"The village. We all did it."

"I wish to speak with your village council then."

She did not reply, her jaw tight with anger.

I dismounted, so that I was not speaking to her from such a great height. "I will speak with them whether you will it or not. If you hate us so much, you'd best gather the council, for I will not leave until I have spoken with them."

She spat at me, the spittle hitting the front of my tunic almost on my stomach since I was so much taller. I could think of no real answer for that, and in truth, I wasn't even angered. No doubt she had a legitimate grievance. Or felt she did. I waited for several heartbeats before repeating my demand. "I will not leave until I have spoken with your village council."

At that she turned and ran, disappearing around a corner. I stood and waited for a moment before returning to gather my horse's reins.

"Sir." One of the men offered me a handkerchief and I dabbed at the wet spot on my tunic. "Now what, sir?" The men were obviously shaken. The army has always been respected, and for good reason. This sudden hatred shocked them, and I had nothing that would ease the pain of it.

"We wait. Someone will eventually speak to us, if only to make us leave." None of the men, so far as I knew, had been personal friends with any of the three, but still I moved them away from the gallows, upwind to avoid the worst of the stench. The rope and wood creaked, and I saw several people dart furtively from one side of the street to the other. We waited. I could feel eyes on us, and I was glad that few civilians have bows.

Finally a man did approach us. "What do you want?"

"I wish to speak to your village council."

"Come then. But only you. The others must stay here."

I nodded and turned to be sure that the men had heard him.

One raised his eyebrows at my nod. "Sir?"

"Wait here. Water the horses if they need it." I handed the reins to Eneko, the young officer nearest me, and followed the man down the street and into one of the buildings. The men were already gathered, and I smiled inside to know that the woman had passed on the message after all.

"Sit there. Who are you, and what do you want?" The room appeared to be part of the inn, and the men sat behind a table all on one side, my seat alone on the other. There were a few men who did not have seats on the other side, and they stood with arms folded behind their fellows rather than sitting nearer to me. The man directly across from me had asked the question.

"I am General Kemen Sendoa, and I wish to speak with you about the soldiers hanging outside."

They had apparently not been expecting that name, and much muttering ensued, with sharp glances at me. I kept my expression as calm and cool as I could. Finally their chosen spokesman turned back to me. "Sendoa, is it?" Most of them did not look nearly so hostile now, but they were still very cautious.

"Aye."

"They deserved what they got. They raped and killed my daughter." The man nearly spat the words. He was off to my right, a man of perhaps forty years.

In truth, I was not entirely surprised. Men, armed, bored, and frustrated, are bound to cause trouble. I couldn't blame the man for his fury. No doubt if I had a daughter who had been so treated, I would have been absolutely irrational in my rage. Yet there was no trial, no judgment, no sentence. I would not say there was no justice, but there was no appeal to the authority of the king, no appeal to the law to bring that justice.

What could I say? I sat for so long in silence partly because I had to consider my words carefully, and partly because even once I had the words in mind, I didn't want them to think I dismissed their grievance, to think I took it lightly. "How do you know those three were the men who did it?"

The man looked down at the table. "My son saw them. He's eight. He ran to me for help, but I was too late. We both saw their faces, and some of the men in the field with me helped catch them."

"You hung them the same day?"

"Yes."

"When?"

"Three weeks ago." Two days after the soldier said he'd seen them last.

"Your daughter died then?"

He merely nodded, looking up at me.

"You should have brought your complaint to Yo-shiro Kepa, the commander at Fort Kuzeyler. He is responsible for the discipline of the men." The words sound harsh, written down, but no one could have heard anything in my voice but sorrow.

"I had no faith in his justice! I don't know him. Mayhap he's a good enough man, but the men under him were not. Who would believe me over a soldier?"

"We asked for the king's help against the Tarvil, not thieving soldiers to rape our daughters!"

"Phraa! What kind of justice would Cyra have then?"

"Better to see them hang than to wait on Stone-haven's whim."

The words poured forth from the men in a violent flood. I sat silent, waiting for their anger to subside, and finally they faded into silence, staring at me.

"Perhaps things are different out here. You haven't seen much good from Stonehaven in quite some time. But you should not doubt the king's justice." I hesitated, staring at my hands before looking around the table to meet each gaze. "I understand your anger well enough, and the deed is done now. Normally it would be murder, but I understand you had no expectation of justice. When a soldier dies, the king's treasury pays one hundred twenty-five golden eagles to his designated heir. The town should pay three hundred seventy five golden ea-gles to the king's treasury to reimburse it for this cost, one hundred twenty-five for each of the three soldiers."

Their eyes widened. It was a brutal fine for such a small village so far from the main trade routes. It would be devastating, better perhaps than seeing the girl's father and others swing, but not by much.

"I will reduce the fine by one half, to one hundred eighty seven golden eagles and one golden hawk. The men were at fault, and the king's purse will pay the other half of the fine. Their families will not suffer for their deed."

It was still quite steep, but no longer impossible, and several men sighed with relief. "I trust that you will bring any further problems to Commander Kepa at Fort Kuzeyler. I understand that the king's peace has not been observed out here for some time, but violations of it will no longer be overlooked. There will be no need for and no tolerance of such vigilante revenge. Is that clear?"

Silent nods. A few careful, grateful smiles.

"We'll take the bodies down and burn them. Bring firewood to the square."

More nods, and I stood. The men filed out behind me into the street and watched as I spoke to the soldiers. "We're going to burn the bodies. Haru, Eder, and Akio, take them down."

It was a gruesome task. I replaced Eder after he vomited, and then Haru, and finally did some of the work myself. I could have ordered some of the others to do it, but I've always believed that an officer's dignity should not be an excuse for shirking unpleasant duties. We stacked wood around the bodies and finally set them alight in the middle of the square. It wasn't ideal, but the bodies were too rotten to move out to a more suitable spot. We stood there for hours. The smoke carried the stench of burning flesh, and as the wind shifted we moved around the square, trying to avoid the worst of it. It was well past dark when we let the fire die. I wanted no remains of the rot to contaminate the square, and the few charred bones could be moved later.

The ride back to Fort Kuzeyler was grim and silent, but we rode through the night. Everyone wanted to pretend the ugly day had never occurred at all.

WE RODE TRIUMPHANT into Stonehaven. Thousands of people cheered us. Great crowds threw flowers under the hooves of our prancing horses. They sang songs of war, victory, and pride. The sun was warm on our backs, the air golden. It was spring, and the ride south had been a ride into perfection.

In the courtyard of the palace, all the sounds fell away. Hakan met me, and I dropped to one knee to give him appropriate honor before the men. There was a crowd of palace servants, and as Hakan bid me rise, I saw Riona, her face the one I had looked for above all others. She ran to me and threw her arms around me, her sweet head tight against my chest. I was laughing, my face buried in her hair. She looked up at me, and her eyes were so blue I lost my breath. She smiled and I bent to kiss her.

I woke with tears in my eyes. I was glad that as the ranking officer I had my own room. I wept alone and muffled the sound in my crumpled blanket.

Nineteen

Riona

Saraid and I attended Sayen at her birthing. It wasn't easy, but she came through it well with a beautiful boy. When I held him, I nearly lost my breath from envy. Eko, her husband, was beside himself with pride. After he kissed Sayen and held the child for a moment, he and all the other men who could get away went to the servants' kitchen for a long night of celebration, pushing the tables to the side for the rophira, the men's dance of triumph and joy, and all the drinking and raucous singing that would accompany it. The king gave them a handsome gift, a beautiful blanket and some gold, as well as a little time off from her work. Her health was fine, but she enjoyed the time with her new son.

Lani said she wanted to be a healer. Saraid said she didn't have the stomach for it, she was too sympathetic and it would upset her too much. But she insisted, and with her father's bemused consent, Saraid began letting her follow along when she saw patients.

Lani confided to me that maybe, if she had a skill like healing, her father wouldn't be in such a hurry to marry her. She liked the idea of helping people. She was softhearted and the thought of helping people in pain pleased her. But when one of the youngest stableboys was kicked by one of the king's new hunters, she had an ugly introduction to what healing is really like.

The boy was her own age, fourteen. He was hysterical with pain, one arm destroyed, the bones crushed and mangled. My job was to comfort him as best I could while the grooms held him down and Saraid worked. His mother was in the city, and someone went to fetch her, but the treatment could not wait.

He lost his arm. Saraid sent Lani out while she cut it, and I held his head with my face turned away and my eyes closed. It was the first time I'd helped with a serious case, and it made me sick. There was so much blood, and it was all I could do to keep from vomiting. Once he was unconscious, it was easier to distance myself from it, see it as a task rather than a little boy.

Saraid called Lani in to help her bandage the stump, and they attended him for days. Lani was teary-eyed and emotional, but Saraid said she did well, and kept her emotions in check when it mattered most. I was proud of her, but I didn't know whether it would keep Joka from wanting her betrothed.

TWENTY

KEMEN

Work finished on the road and we began preparing for the push north. I left Kepa as commander of Fort Kuzeyler and took command of the advance myself. I sent messages back to Hakan detailing our progress. I requisitioned food from Ironcrest, weapons from Rivensworth, and winter gear from Highden. For the bitterly cold winter, the men would need fur-lined boots, thick woolen clothes, thicker cloaks, and gloves. Woolen blankets, and lots of them. Horse blankets; horses suffer terribly in such weather. Saw blades and axes to cut firewood; we'd be needing much more of it.

With Hakan's approval, we began our northern advance. There is a reason kings go to war in spring. It is easier. Supplies are easier to come by. Spirits are high. Men sing in the sunshine as they march to battle. Everything seems glorious, and everything seems possible. Nonetheless, we began our push north just as the first storms of winter hit. Victory is a matter of discipline and organization as well as luck, and we had the first two at least.

We had great success. Most skirmishes were solid victories, though the Tarvil do not stand and fight to the last man. They knew the land up there better, the dangers of the woods, what kind of weather a keening wind foretells, but our Erdemen solders were larger, stronger, better fed, much better trained, and excellently disciplined.

The first real setback came as a message from the main fort. Kepa requested my help urgently, though he specifically stated that they were not under attack. I was forty leagues northeast, camped with some two hundred soldiers after another victory. It had been a brilliant triumph, the Tarvil pincered between the rock of Erdemen kedani and the sweeping speed of our suvari.

I took some twenty men with me and we rode back hotfoot. I didn't want to take many and weaken our attacking force, but I wouldn't be so foolish as to ride alone. I would take my chances in battle and fight face to face with no hesitation, but I wouldn't give the Tarvil an opportunity to remove me by ambush.

A blacksmith, two of his apprentices, and a shopkeeper and his son, were sitting grim and scowling by the fire in Kepa's office. They had caught a soldier forcing himself on a girl behind the forge. They were not from Ilato, but I had sent messages to all the nearby towns about the incident and the reminder, or rather proclamation, that the king's peace still held even out at the border. I had promised that the king's peace would be upheld, and that the army would enforce discipline on its men.

They had been inclined to kill him, and they had bloodied him thoroughly before they brought him to the fort. Now they demanded justice.

The girl had lived. That would have changed things, had it been a civilian trial. But a soldier is subject to the military code. The procedure for trial is set in the military regulations. Trial is by a jury of six soldiers chosen by lot, and the seventh is the highest-ranking military officer assigned to that post.

The penalty for rape is death. If the accused is judged guilty, he may choose to hang or to stand before a squad of archers. There are processes for appeal, of course, which would then go up through the ranks to the Minister of Military Affairs.

It sounds harsh because it is. The military punishes rape by death because it tarnishes not only the individual but the military's reputation, and by extension, the honor of the king.

I recused myself from sitting on his jury. If he wished to appeal, he should have the option. Kepa sat in my place.

The evidence was incontrovertible. He was guilty. The verdict was unanimous, though reluctant.

He appealed, as anyone would have, I suppose. I heard the evidence. I had already made my decision when I spoke to him. His name was Yasu. The name means Peaceful. He was nineteen years old. He was a volunteer and had finished training in Hekku some seven months before. He had been on post for four months. He had a younger brother, but no sisters, and he was from a small village outside Darsten.

"Did you do it?" I could nearly smell his fear, see it in his eyes. Blue, like most Tuyets' eyes. The same blue as Hakan's, a little lighter than Riona's.

He met my eyes and swallowed hard. "Yes, sir." He regretted it. Saying the words was a kind of penance.

For that at least, I respected him. Not for the deed, but for the courage to admit it later, when he was sober and fully aware of the horror. "The verdict stands."

He looked at the floor. "Yes, sir."

He chose to hang. The one to kick to the stool from beneath his feet was chosen by lot from those who had served on the jury. Everyone watched in formation. The five men who had brought him stood close by. Four of them looked grimly satisfied, but one, the storekeeper's son, was very pale and looked like he might be sick.

Yasu was a boy. Nineteen is painfully young. At nineteen, I didn't think it was, but from thirty-four it appeared barely out of childhood. But he committed a man's sin and he would pay the price for it. He stood silently while the branch was selected and tested, the rope tied securely to it. He stood on the stool while the noose was tied, the rope with a bit of slack to give him a drop.

"Do you have any last words?"

He licked his lips, staring at the ground for several minutes. He looked to the blacksmith. "Tell her I'm sorry."

The blacksmith nodded wordlessly.

Then he met my eyes. "I'm sorry, sir. Would you tell my father that, too?"

"I will."

He paused then, and finally nodded. He kept his eyes on mine one more moment, long enough to see me nod, and then looked up at the sky before Taiki kicked the stool from beneath his feet.

He fell, and at the sudden jerk at the end I think we all felt a little sick. But the drop was not nearly long enough. He hung for one long moment before his legs kicked erratically, his face purple.

It was three steps to him, and he kneed me in the stomach as I wrapped my arms about his waist and dropped down with all my weight. I felt the bones in his neck snap. I stepped back, and we watched him twist, a few twitches of his hands bound behind him finally fading.

I had them cut him down just before sunset, and we burned the body that night.

I could not leave the field, so I sent a courier to the boy's father. I did not say what he had done, though perhaps his father could have guessed. There are only so many crimes punishable by death. But I did say that Yasu had faced his execution with regret for his deed and with courage.

I DREAMED ABOUT HIM. The feeling of the bones in his neck disconnecting. The look in his eyes when he told me he was sorry. Regret. Shame. I woke and could not sleep again. I walked through the camp, spoke to the sentries, and returned to sit on the floor of my tent staring at the map. We were forty leagues north of Fort Kuzeyler, and if we wanted we could hold the ground we had taken. Trees were scarce, but there was a copse not far away that would provide enough wood for a small sturdy fort. The rock would also be a good building material, but we would have to bring masons to oversee the work.

But there was nothing to protect. No Erdemen live on the high plateau. The Tarvil tribes have no true settlements. They camp, sometimes for weeks in one place, but it is always a camp. They move on. The soil can't support farming, and I couldn't imagine Erdemen citizens would want to settle there anyway. If anything, it was less protected than the northern frontier we already held. Fewer trees, brutally windy, with no natural barriers to slow Tarvil raiders in the future. Dry, with few streams and hardly any rivers, all of which were frozen nine months of the year anyway. Rare brief squalls in the short summer and blizzards throughout the long winter.

We needed a treaty. Of course we would man the border posts more strongly in the future, but there was no good end to this outside a treaty.

The best way to get a favorable agreement is to make the other side want it. They had Erdemen women who would want to return to their families. The Tarvil would be desperate soon. The most recent skirmishes had shown the colored sashes of five tribes, two of which were from so far north I'd never seen them before. We took a few prisoners, those who were not mortally wounded. I gave the mercy stroke to others, a quick slash across the throat. It is kindness sometimes, but it always makes me sick inside.

I questioned the prisoners who could speak Common. What did they eat? What did they drink? How many children did they have? How many lived to adulthood? What sort of training did they have? It took some effort, but I managed to gain an understanding of their world. I did not yet understand their culture, but I was beginning to. I matched the sashes to the tribes they represented, learned the names of their leaders.

I lost a few men, but not many considering the conditions. I sent many home for rest and got new companies to replace them. We moved our camp close to the trees and began work on the little outpost, which I named Izotz, which means ice. Perhaps it would have been more inspiring for the men if I had named it Fort Courage or something similarly optimistic, but I was in a grim mood and didn't think of changing it later.

We would push the Tarvil, drive them north, until they pled for a settlement. We would be generous, and in return for land we did not want, we would get peace.

THOUGH I'D CAMPAIGNED in the northeast before, I'd never been far onto the high tundra. It astonished me how the winter wind would whip away a man's breath and leave him shuddering with chill, an assault as violent as that of any battle. The campaign slowed with the first blizzard, and both we and Tarvil had to steel ourselves for the winter. Rations were short, since the food shipments had difficulty getting over the snowy roads and in any case winter is always a hard time in the mountains and on the tundra. I didn't want to waste the men's strength on patrol, since the Tarvil were hardly on the offensive. Instead we dug in and hurried our work on Izotz, the smaller, sturdy little post north of Fort Kuzeyler, well onto the plateau that sweeps north to the edge of the world.

In truth, it is a wonder the Tarvil survive there at all. It's a harsh land, rocky, with sharp-edged hills that grow little food for their flocks. They guard their few horses well, better than their children, because they're valuable but ill-suited to the harsh terrain. The horses spend the nights in their tents wearing rich blankets to keep them warm and healthy. There are some small animals that the Tarvil can hunt, little rock achas like short-eared rabbits with strange little paws, and birds that seem to live on air and snow, for I have no idea what they eat. There are carabaa, diminutive, heavily furred deer that travel in small herds, but the Tarvil cannot rely on them for food since they range far across the plateau in search of scarce feed. There are wolves, great wolves of the tundra, larger by far than the wolves I've seen and even hunted in the farthest edges of Erdem's mountains. Heavier in the shoulders, longer in the snout, with lean flanks and hungry eyes, for even they have no easy time of it on the Tarvil plateau.

I dreamed of Riona in the deep quiet nights when snow fell thick and in the screaming wind of winter storms. Nothing important, just simple pleasures. At first, I'd been bitterly hurt, hearing her words as an unfair accusation. I could not give her what she wanted, and she could not ask for it more kindly. But that passed as I rode north, even before I reached Fort Kuzeyler and took over from Kepa.

It was not in her to be cruel, and if I heard her words as a cruelty, it was only my awareness of my own inadequacy that was to blame. She had every right to wish for tenderness; it is the deepest desire of a woman's heart, just as men desperately need respect above all else. I'd failed her, for I couldn't give her that tenderness that she needed. I didn't know how. I didn't even know where to start. I had thought, foolishly perhaps, that the sincerity of my love would teach me. Clearly I had been wrong.

If I had failed her, it was only to be expected that I would similarly fail with any other woman. I was under no illusions that she was some demanding minx with absurd expectations. She was entirely reasonable. Hakan pleased Kveta so much precisely because he could be all those things I could not. Funny. Sweet. Perceptive. Gentle. So my utter despair was not only at my failure to please Riona, but at my realization that she was probably more patient than any other woman would be. That I would not, could not, please a woman was for the simple reason that I was unpleasing, unable to be what a woman desires.

Besides, I did not want another woman. It would be her, or it would be no one.

Is it any wonder then, that I was a bit careless? I didn't expect my men to take stupid chances, but I ceased to have a care for my own life. I'd thought, months before, that I was content, that my life was not one that needed a woman, though I was hardly unaware of their attractions. I was resigned, if not entirely satisfied. But now that I had dreamed of such bliss, almost tasted it, the loss was shattering. It was hardly her fault. She couldn't have known how deeply my heart was lost to her, but nonetheless it was. A man walking about without a heart can hardly be expected to care much for anything else.

We had a vicious battle in a snowstorm just before Izotz was complete. It was just after the new year. If it hadn't been so cold, construction would have been faster, but the temperatures made the wood as hard as iron. We had halted construction for the day. The wind was so frigid that even with gloves the men could barely grasp their tools, and the snow would soon be thick enough to prevent us seeing anything. The walls were complete, but only two of the interior buildings were finished. Some thirty men had been outside the walls bringing in firewood, and we opened the gate to let them in before the blizzard hit. The snow was falling so thickly and the wind so loud that it was a moment before we even realized that we were under attack.

It was a chaotic few minutes, but we managed to get the gates closed, though some twenty Tarvil horsemen were inside when we did. In the lee side of the main building, where the wind was not as strong, we could see a little better and fought the Tarvil on foot. Arrows rained in over the walls. I wondered whether the Tarvil archers realized how many of their own men were inside, or whether they didn't care. Thick layers of clothes protected us somewhat, and most of us wore hardened leather armor under our cloaks. The skirmish was bloody and longer than it should have been.

The snow abated for a few minutes as we were finishing them off. The arrows were a worse challenge than the horsemen, but we had decent cover and soon would be able to send our own archers up to the walk around the wall to return fire. I don't know how it happened, whether Yori was knocked aside by one of the horses or whether he left cover for some other reason. He fell with arrows in his chest and was nearly trampled by a Tarvil horseman before I got to him.

It was stupid, really, if you judge my actions by what is rational. But I saw his face as he fell, and I couldn't be rational. I fought the Tarvil horseman above him and pulled him to cover. An arrow went through my right thigh. It could have been much worse, the wound was clean and through the thick muscle, but it slowed me. The last horseman bore down on us, already off balance with arrows in him as well, but his blade met mine before he fell himself.

Another arrow hit my shoulder as I wrapped my hand around Yori's collar. I nearly fell. I don't know what gave me the strength to jerk the boy under the cover that I had left for him. The arrow in my thigh was angled down and to the outside, and the head slid into the snow by my boot as I knelt beside the boy.

He looked so much like Hakan. I'd seen him before, though we hadn't spoken much. He was eighteen, a volunteer six months out of training. His eyes were the same cool blue as Hakan's. Now he was choking on his own blood, but he tried bravely to smile at me. Four arrows stuck out of his chest. He had only moments to live, but his gratitude made it worthwhile.

We stared at each other. I put one hand on his shoulder, and he clutched at my sleeve. I watched him fade and tried to give him courage as he died.

I was shaking and slightly dizzy with pain. I took off my glove to close his eyes, and I couldn't get my glove back on, clumsy with cold. I thought about trying to rise and walk to the barracks, which would be acting as the infirmary, but I was too dazed to put my mind to it. The snow drifted against my legs, the wind whipping my cloak about. It pulled on the arrow in my shoulder, and I tried to reach it with my right hand. The angle was too difficult, and I could scarcely move my left arm at all. My outstretched fingers barely touched the shaft and succeeded only producing a blinding rush of pain.

Between the gusts of wind, I could see the fog rise from Yori's wounds and from my leg. The blood crimsoned the snow around us, a thin line soaking through my breeches and spreading into the snow, a larger stain around Yori. My mouth tasted of copper, blood, sorrow. The fog of my breath came unevenly, slow and ragged as I focused on it. From Yori's mouth there was no fog, the blood in the corners of his mouth already thick and dark. Inside my leather armor, the sweat of battle was cold and clammy.

The snowstorm drove the Tarvil away, and in the thick flurries, it took the men several minutes to find us. I smiled at Eneko when he stomped up, cursing and shouting. They didn't have a stretcher ready, so Eneko and a young kedani helped me up and half-carried me into the barracks.

It is amazing how much blood the human body needs. I could feel the lack of it in the way I perceived the pain. It was excruciating certainly, but from a far distance, as if it belonged to someone else.

I've felt that hollow coolness, awareness fading, only once before, in that last battle before I was discharged from the army. I'd lain pinned to the ground and watched the blood flow from my chest, slow and steady. It's almost peaceful, though the pain is distracting; if you set your mind past that, put it aside for a moment, there is serenity in the cool touch of death.

I half-leaned against the edge of the table. Eneko, my young deputy, was barking orders, and Amets, the healer, nearly dropped his forceps when he saw me. There would be nothing to dull the pain; Amets had run out of ale, of white willow, of valerian, and almost everything else. He was pale and nervous, I suppose at the thought of me dying on his table. I remember that I smiled at him because I didn't care.

Amets and his assistant cut the head off the arrow and pulled the shaft back through my leg. The shoulder was more of a challenge. Tarvil arrows are viciously barbed, and he'd run out of goose quills to cover the barbs. They cut off my cloak and the leather armor beneath it, and the shirt, tunic, and undershirt beneath that. The point was lodged in my shoulder blade, and he worked it free with quiet, steady cursing. I remember most of it, though not clearly; the darkness faded in and out, the pain a burning fire as the metal grated against bone.

I went north for one reason, to give my life for Hakan's reign. I loved Hakan, love him still, and to die for him was an honor. But I did mean to die, and none of my men could have known that. I had not yet admitted it even to myself. Looking back, I remember that my feeling of satisfaction with the wounds startled me, and no doubt my smile was disconcerting to poor Amets.

HE TWITCHED IN MY ARMS as I dropped my weight. I felt the bones in his neck crack and his sudden limp stillness. I stepped back and watched him twist.

I vomited in the woods. I'd never killed an Erdemen soldier before. I might have trained him myself. Might have led him in battle. Would have died for him without hesitation.

The king's honor demanded it. The honor of an unknown peasant girl demanded it. Which was greater, I cannot say.

I have done many things for Hakan that I am proud of. This was not one of them.

DESPITE MY EXPECTATIONS, I did not die. The first few days were a fog of pain, disjointed memories of reports from scouts and from couriers from the main fort. Eneko listened to them in my room so that I could give my orders, when I was awake enough to have an opinion. The advance was falling apart. Kepa had strengthened the border posts quite capably, but the drive north was stalled.

A military should not depend on one man. It was unconscionable that I had almost left Hakan's army headless, or near to it. Berk Havard was reportedly quite good, but he was stationed on the southern border, not readily available to replace me. There were a few bright young officers serving under me who had the potential to be excellent commanders, but they lacked experience. Kepa clearly could not do it. Eneko, my deputy, was intelligent but inexperienced and clearly petrified at the thought of being left with sole command of our push north. When I determined that I would live at least a while longer, I began planning our next advance.

Eneko, Kudret, Shui, and Akio were the best I'd seen since I'd been there. No doubt there were others who also had potential, but these I had noticed. I called them in to me when I could sit propped up in bed. I questioned them about what they would do and why they would do it. I tried to make them think, and posed questions about possible setbacks and unexpected boons that might change their plans. I made them draw maps of the land from memory and diagram how they would disperse their forces for a given assault. They were respectful, too much so, and I urged them to argue with each other, to question each other's theories. Not in anger, but in useful and challenging exchange.

MY LEG HEALED relatively quickly and well. I was able to ride in a week, though not without pain. My left arm was of no use, but suvari rides with his arms free to handle his sword and shield anyway. Amets treated my shoulder, changing the bandages every evening with clean dry ones, boiled to prevent infection. He did what he could, but the healing supplies were sorely limited. The snow had been so thick that it delayed shipment of everything I'd requisitioned. Replacement boots, additional cloaks, herbs and honey and bandages for treating wounds, blankets, various supplies for the repairs the buildings already needed. Food, of course.

The first time I saw the wound in my shoulder, the reflection bounced from one polished metal mirror to another, I thought it wasn't as impressive as I'd imagined. Barely the length of one finger, a deep gouge through muscle to the bone, not especially wide. But it hurt. It hurt like fire, and it only got worse, despite Amets' efforts. The initial wound had felt clean, painful certainly, but a clean cut that should have healed well. It did heal some, but the pain grew deeper, and Amets lanced an abscess with a hot sharp knife. I nearly screamed at the pain, but it was fast and the next day I felt markedly better.

Amets bound my arm to my side to keep me from moving it. A week went by, and I had another abscess lanced. The flesh around the wound grew swollen and hot, and each night when Amets changed the bandages it was an exercise in discipline to keep silent.

The pain kept me from sleeping at night, though I tried to rest. I caught quick restless naps on horseback or in my room in the afternoons, but most nights I paced uncomfortably or lay on my pallet staring at the wall. When I could sleep, it was hardly restful.

I barely noticed when I stopped eating. We were on short rations anyway, and between the pain and a slight persistent nausea, I didn't feel much like eating. I tried, of course, but most of the time it was easier to pass my rations to whatever soldier looked like he most needed them.

I RECEIVED A LETTER from Kveta in the packet from Hakan that arrived some three and a half weeks after I was wounded. They couldn't know yet, though Eneko had said he'd sent word to Hakan about my injury. Kyosti read it to me.

"It is dated the second of Nalka. Her Royal Highness Kveta Aranila Tafari, *su da* Hakan Ithel, His Royal Highness King of Erdem, Glorious and Free, to the honored Ambassador and General Kemen Sendoa:

"Greetings, dear friend. I write with much gratitude for your great service to Erdem. I hope you are well and look forward to your safe return. We have heard of your astounding success, and I cannot adequately express my appreciation for your skill, courage, and devotion to Erdem. Your valor inspires us all.

144

I write to share our great joy with you. I am with child, and we expect the birth this summer, in Kugatsu. Hakan hopes for a girl, but I hope for a boy with Hakan's eyes. If the child is a boy, Hakan and I request your consent to give him the name Kemen Tahir Hakan, after your noble spirit and your friendship and in hopes that our son has your courage and honor."

I smiled. Kyosti's voice flowed on. Kveta wrote of tea and games by the fire, of riding with Hakan, of banquets, of peace along the Rikutan border. I stared into the fire half-dazed. The pain in my shoulder seemed to come in waves. At night, when I was tired and the fever was worse, the peak of each wave was dizzying; my ears roared and my vision blurred. I thought of Riona, of how she laughed with delight at the little firza chicks. How she smiled at me when I drew water for her. How I wished to take her riding.

"Sir?"

I blinked, and the pain returned.

"Shall I write a reply, sir?"

"Please." I dictated the greeting. "I thank you for your concern and your thought of me. I am well, and the campaign is finding much success due to the courage and perseverance of our soldiers. I will not bore you with the details, though Hakan will have them in a separate letter if you wish to know. I say only that it is an honor to serve with them." I drew a deep breath and tried to focus my thoughts.

"Sir?" He almost stuttered. "You're not well, sir."

"Write it."

IT HAPPENED DURING a meeting with the officers one evening. Kudret and Eneko sat across from me, Teretz to my right, and Kepa and Shui to my left. We were discussing the next advance, whether to wait another three days to give the Tarvil time to consider their losses, or whether we should strike the next morning. Eneko pushed the map closer so Teretz and I could see in the dim light. I lifted my mug.

"How much ale have you had, sir?" Commander Teretz asked.

"This is my second in five days. Is that a problem, Commander?"

He shrugged and bowed a little with a slight, mocking smile. "No, sir. It's only that I thought rations were one mug a week, sir."

I slammed the mug down on the table. "Wounded have always gotten double rations of ale. You wouldn't know that, though, because you've never been wounded in the king's service, have you, Commander?"

He stood so quickly his chair overturned behind him. He flexed his fingers around the hilt of his sword indecisively. "I'll ask you to take that back, sir."

"Why? Isn't it true?" I watched his hand.

"I've never been wounded because I'm not stupid enough to try to get myself killed!" His voice had risen.

Out of the corner of my eye, I saw the others with their hands already on their sword hilts. Tense. My ears thundered with fever.

"You do seem to find yourself conveniently at the back of any battle, though. The last to enter and the first to leave." I'd heard Kepa's report the night before. Teretz was a problem, though his tactics were solid. He'd lost respect among the men.

His eyes flicked to Eneko, who was closest to him, and he hesitated. Then he drew, faster than Eneko, and slashed at me.

I parried with my bootknife, because it was easier to draw from where I sat, and I swept his legs from beneath him as I stood. Eneko's sword was at his throat, and

Teretz was smart enough not to fight any longer, on his back and alone.

Kepa was flushed with rage.

I felt cold and a little shaky, but more with illness than anger or fear. Kepa started to say something, but my voice cut through his and he stopped in respect. "Commander Teretz, you are under arrest. You will surrender your weapons."

His mouth was tight, and he cursed softly under his breath, but he did as I said, laying his sword down on the floor. Kudret pulled his bootknife and the one on his hip from their sheathes, and then they let him stand.

"Where shall we take him, sir?" asked Eneko.

"His quarters." I didn't want him put in with the Tarvil prisoners.

"Yes, sir."

He would be court-martialed later. I could not bring myself to care what happened to him, so long as he was removed from his position.

ONCE, ONLY ONCE, did I consider it. I thought of asking Eneko to return my sword, shield, and bootknife to Riona as my next of kin, my nearest relative, because she possessed my heart. I discarded the idea almost immediately. It would have put a burden of guilt on her that was entirely unjustified. She did not owe me love any more than the sun owes its warmth and light to a blade of grass. The grass might die in shadow, but that is the grass's weakness, not the fault of the sun.

Besides, such melodrama appealed to me only for a moment, a dark moment when I shivered by the dying embers of the fire in my room. My sword and other things would be returned to Hakan, as they should be.

To pass the time in the sleepless nights, I rummaged in my memory for bits of poetry, epic works I could use to take my mind off the pain. I timed the words to my pacing, though I did not speak them aloud. Eneko would have thought I was losing my mind, fevered and mad to pace back and forth talking to myself in the dark each night. I didn't want him to doubt my competence. I was entirely clearheaded and made battle plans with as much lucidity as ever. The third week of Ketsala, I guessed where the Tarvil raiders were hiding after another failed attack on Izotz, and when I sent Kudret at the head of a small squad, he brought back word of a total rout.

The poetry was a distraction, nothing more. It didn't soothe the pain, but it helped me push it to the back of my mind for a few hours every night. I've always had a good memory, I suppose because I've exercised it so much. I've had to, since I can't write information I want for later. I've never read the works I love. I don't have a poetic bent, I could never have been a poet myself, but I've always loved the hypnotic rhythms, the pathos in the great tragedies, the love, the sacrifice, the heroism. I worked my way through all I could remember of Elorsku's Great Moon King, all of Horukan's Plague Chronicles, which was more encouraging than it sounds, all of Kemarda's Sword Brothers, and pieces of my favorite works by Iskanoa, Liraliamu, and Arket.

I preferred poetry to my dreams.

THE SUN BAKES the southern desert. I no longer sweat. This morning we drank the urine of our horses because it was liquid and we needed it. The one man who refused my order fainted by noon, and after that he obeyed. I've lost fifteen horses already, and expect to lose five more by the end of the day. I bled them, and the remaining horses carry their thick blood. We will drink it next. There will be no more urine; the horses have sweated out all they have to offer.

Tonight we reach the Burska ravine. One day to cross it. Then two more days to Olara, provided we make good time. Olara has a well.

I will not lose a man.

ORUKO DID NOT RISE when I started the men again this afternoon. I gave him my hand, and he shook his head, so I waited, my eyes half-closed against the vicious sun. Again I ordered him to rise, and he cursed me in a voice like dry gravel.

"Stand up, for the last time." My voice was no better, but I offered him my hand. The others stood watching, swaying, dried husks of proud soldiers.

He cursed me for my stupid, stubborn pride that would not let him rest.

To rest is to die. We have no water. Olara, with its precious well, is only a day away now. We've crossed the ravine.

He drew his bootknife and slashed at me. I caught his wrist, twisted it until he gasped and groaned. I struck him on the side of the neck and his weak resistance ceased.

"Help me, Yuudai." My throat was so raw the words were a rasp. With much effort, together we got Oruko on my back.

I've been walking for hours. My knees are bloody, though the stain is dark and dry already in this heat. I stumbled twice from weakness, and the other times because the darkness at the edges of my vision overwhelmed me. When the darkness stays at the edges, it is a welcome respite from the blinding sun. My shoulders burn. Oruko's unshaven face scratches my back. Last time I fell, I bit my tongue at the jolt, and the warm tang of blood was a sudden gift of strength. I sucked at it eagerly, but too soon it stopped. I rested on my knees with my head bowed to the dirt, Oruko a crushing weight on my back.

I taste sand, dry dust, the lingering salt of blood, and death.

My tongue is swollen and my mouth is so dry that my orders come out mere croaks. I held my anger at Oruko close to keep my feet moving.

I have run out of anger. I don't care if I die. I am finding it difficult to care if we all die. We could lie down on the burning rocks and dry up, shrivel into desiccated skeletons. It wouldn't take long.

Oruko has not woken yet, though I have felt him twitch a few times. He's not large, but my legs burn and tremble. Everything blurs. I stay at the lead, the men strung out behind me in an uneven line. I hope my dogged, stupid perseverance will inspire them, give them courage to put each foot in front of the other. I put Yuudai at the rear, because he's the strongest and not prone to despair.

Next time I fall, I don't know if I can get up.

I am an officer of the king's kedani, and I will bring my men back.

Twenty-One

Riona

I waited for him. There were banquets and balls, and I wished with all my heart to see his tall form in some corner. The few times I'd seen him dance made my heart swell with pride. It was no wonder he was popular; his athletic grace and easy skill when he danced more than atoned for his dark Dari skin. A few, of course, continued to look down their noses at him privately, and whispered snide comments about a common Dari soldier reaching above his place. I heard them, of course. Servants hear everything, far more than nobles imagine we do. Their arrogant disregard of him stung me, but I didn't imagine he cared what they thought at all. But that was only a few of them; the majority welcomed him into the noble ranks, the social elite. He'd earned their respect, and if he was a bit stern for noble company, he also had courage the noblemen wished to emulate and the ladies nearly swooned for.

Lady Melora Grallin was the most aggressive; I saw her once leaning up as if to speak in his ear and then running her fingers up the lapel of his jacket and touching his hair. He was stiff and painfully polite, and I don't think he saw me as he pulled away, bowed with utmost courtesy, and disappeared from the ball altogether. Lady Grallin pouted in a corner and I heard her whispering later that he was as cold and stupid as a block of wood. Her friend laughed and said she'd tried too hard, that a man like the great Sendoa could only be won with subtler wiles and not such blatant desire.

It made me smile to compare their idea of him to the sweet way he'd come to me in the kitchen to chop peppers, and how he'd comforted Lani after Pireyu's rejection. He wasn't at all as they imagined, and I loved him all the more for it.

Then he was gone traveling before the royal wedding and I didn't see what new tricks they would devise. After my cruelty to him, when he was gone after the wedding, perhaps the deepest pang of guilt was that one of those ladies, even Lady Grallin, noble and cultured, would be kinder to him than I'd been.

I thought of him every morning and all through each day, imagining him leading the men to victory after victory. I couldn't really imagine the far northern border, the high cold tundra where the Tarvil scrape a precarious living, but I knew it was very hard for the men. We heard sporadic reports of battles, mostly victorious. They made good progress and pushed north far past our border.

The messengers brought word of a brutal winter. In Stonehaven we have four seasons. Four months of summer, three of autumn, three of winter, and three of spring. In the far north where the Tarvil live, nine of the thirteen months are called winter. There is one month of a fleeting spring, two of summer, and one of autumn. Even in summer, though, it might snow on a cool day. Deep rivers are frozen all but a month or two out of the whole year. Winter was a great hardship for the soldiers.

In the mornings, when the sun rose clear and bright through the frigid winter air, I was full of hope and pride in him, wishing desperately for him to come back so I could beg his forgiveness.

I started letters to him, writing by candlelight late at night. I must have started at least a hundred and finished maybe some fifteen. I threw them all in the fire, one of them even after it was sealed. I nearly sent it to him, but suddenly I felt it was stupid and presumptuous of me. What right did I have to ask his forgiveness? He owed me nothing. What right did I have to assume that he cared so much about my words anyway? I knew I'd hurt him, but still it seemed unreal. I, a servant girl, should not have the power to so wound someone of his importance. I could hardly believe he'd scrubbed floors just to be near me.

In the evenings, tired from work, alone in my apartment or working during some late banquet, I was not so optimistic. My heart trembled for him, and I imagined all sorts of terrible things. That he was wounded, that he was dead, that he'd been lost in some battle and lay injured and alone in a drift of snow to slowly freeze. I dreamed about it, and woke with a start to write another letter, pages and pages of frantic apologies and vows of my love, before I threw it in the fire in frustration.

A woman, a virtuous woman, doesn't pursue a man like that; at least, my mother would have said so.

I had my doubts since it was I who had thrown vicious words at him and stormed away in the face of his apology. Surely I should make the first move toward reconciliation.

If he even wanted reconciliation. He would have been entirely within his rights to listen to me give my full apology on my knees, and then tell me it was much appreciated but I wasn't worth the trouble of revisiting the episode. There were a hundred noble ladies eager to take my place in his heart, all better educated, better dressed, more cultured, more proper, more beautiful, more fitting for a man of his status.

I would have borne that shame. It would have been right for me to do so; I owed him the apology regardless of whether he could bring himself to forgive me. But I was afraid to ask Kveta to send my letter with her next one and the king's to him, afraid that bringing the king's attention to the matter would betray Kemen's trust, betray the privacy of our relationship. I was afraid he would be shamed by his courtship of me, a servant. And I was stupidly afraid of further insulting him by imagining that he cared as much as I did.

TWENTY-TWO

KEMEN

I fell and Oruko slid off my back with a dry cough. He stood, I stood, and we stared at each other, swaying and grim.

"Walk, soldier." I croaked.

He stared at me a moment more and then turned, shuffling steps following Tarek, who had not stopped.

If I didn't stray off course, we would reach Olara in late afternoon. Without Oruko's weight, my steps came a little more easily.

Then Besar fell. I pulled him to his feet, and with his arm around my shoulders we made it for perhaps half a league before he sagged. I dragged him only a short distance before the darkness rose and I fell again.

I am carrying him. I can't remember how long it's been, but the sun is beginning its descent. It can't be much farther.

Besar is walking again.

Yuudai has fallen at the rear. I might have missed it if I hadn't looked for him. Yuudai, my friend. I stagger back along the ragged line.

"Get up, soldier."

"I am done, sir." He is on his face. He strains to push himself up but raises himself only a handsbreadth before falling.

"Yuudai, that is an order." I pull him to his feet and pull his arm across my shoulders. My throat is too dry to say more.

We stumble together as if we are drunk, and finally his steps strengthen and steady a bit.

"Take the front." My lips crack as I speak. "Four arans north of due east."

He groans as his arm slides from my shoulder, but he obeys. I want him in front of me so I can watch him. I give him the lead because his honor won't let him give in to despair while others depend on him.

ONE NIGHT, I felt the fever spike. I was dizzy and sweating, for once distracted from the ever-present pain. There was a howling blizzard, so I went to speak to the sentries without my cloak, wearing only a shirt and my winter tunic belted over it. The sentries, bundled in their thick cloaks, were nearly frozen within minutes, and we rotated them frequently to minimize casualties to the weather. They would come inside and warm themselves dangerously close to the fire.

When I walked the wall that night with no cloak, Kudret cursed roundly when he saw me and tried to give me his, but I refused. The cold would either bring my fever down or kill me outright, and I didn't really care which.

I don't know how long I stayed out, though I know I spoke to at least four of the sentries. I went inside when my shivering made the pain of the wound unbearable. I expected a chill, a worse fever, a fatal cough, but nothing happened. It did soothe the fever for a time though. Kudret told Eneko, and Eneko came the next morning to plead with me to be reasonable. I was still a bit light-headed, reckless and grimly pleased at the thought of death.

I SEE THE GREEN of Olara from the top of the last hill. Half the men run toward it, the stumbling shuffling gait of men more dead than alive. The others walk, feet dragging. Someone shouts, hoarse and triumphant. I am last so I can be sure they all make it.

I am on my face in the dust, choking on sand. It is gritty and hot on my cheeks. In my mouth. Rasping my throat. The reflected heat of the dust and rocks beats against my face, through my shirt to my chest. Burning. My lips are cracked, and the sand stings the rawness.

My eyes are closed, but I hear them approach. Yuudai, even now I know his steps, and others. A long, fluid string of cursing by someone with a talent for it, obviously not one of my men, because we are all too thirsty to speak so smoothly.

Cool water pours over my neck, trickling into my hair, my right ear. My mouth is open, water so exquisitely blissful it is almost painful, and I am drinking. Too eager. I inhale it, choke, coughing and retching into the sand.

"Every man alive! We counted your company dead a week ago, sir. Help him up."

Someone, not Yuudai, because my sword brother is too weak now, but someone in a uniform helps me up.

"Thank you, soldier." My voice is a broken whisper. I catch Yuudai's eye. Someone hands me a waterskin, and I am drinking again, desperate, dizzy with the coolness.

"GET SOME MORE SNOW. His fever is up again." The voice is not Yuudai's; it is higher, clearer, not raw and hoarse from thirst. My shoulder aches, the pain burning across my back and through my chest.

I am not in the southern desert. I am in Izotz, and heat is the last thing likely to kill me.

TO AMUSE MYSELF, I compared the memory of the dream to the memories of what really happened. In my dream, I entirely skipped the horrendous descent into the Burska Ravine and the grueling climb up the other side, where we lost our remaining horses. I'd also skipped the nights, when we walked in clear chilly darkness, windblown sand stinging our sunburned faces, the stars cold and bright. In reality, I'd lain in the sand at the end until nearly dusk, and my true memory of Yuudai's return with help is more blurry and disjointed. I did choke on the water and someone did help me stand. There was more grit and more despair in my true memories.

Oruko nominated me for the Golden Eagle Regnant, and Yuudai seconded it. I received the award, Erdem's highest honor for valor, from the king Hakan Emyr himself on my twenty-fifth birthday.

I PLANNED THE ATTACK myself, but I asked Eneko, Kudret, Shui, and Akio why they thought I planned certain things. Why I thought the suvari should sweep north at that particular angle. It was because the ground was good, solid and flat with just enough of a downhill slant that it would speed their coming without troubling the horses. There would be a reserve force of suvari off to the northwest on a hill, to reinforce the main body of suvari at need. The suvari archers would come sweeping northwest and then split to flank the Tarvil forces and peel away, leaving the field to the suvari and the kedani behind them. They would join the reserve force on the hill, and be prepared to circle across the northern side of the Tarvil forces shooting south if they had the opportunity. It was a simple plan, but the ground was perfect for it. A frozen creekbed in a shallow ravine would slow their flight north if the Tarvil chose to run.

The Tarvil encampment was quite large, a gathering of their men for an assault against our fort. We had reinforcements from Fort Kuzeyler but even so, our numbers were roughly even. I hadn't known they had so many warriors, and I changed our plan to take better advantage of our archers. The hill was higher than I'd expected, and that helped us too. They were not as well disciplined and were totally unprepared. When we attacked, they fought with courage and fury but no particular plan.

I gave Eneko command, but at the moment of decision he waited for my nod. I took the field myself despite the pain and led the main suvari charge. I couldn't imagine simply watching from the hilltop while men fought and died. War is ugly, but it is one thing at which I am skilled. I believed I owed it to the men I commanded to be on the field.

The charge itself is mostly a blur in my memory. Thundering hooves of lanky, ragged Tarvil mounts and splendid Erdemen chargers. A stunning, nauseating shock on my shield, my shoulder a brilliant fire of pain. The familiar salty tang of blood. The dirtier reek of sweat, Tarvil sweat, Erdemen sweat, and horse sweat. The slash of a sword by my right ear, the hum of arrows, Tarvil blood splattered across my chest. Pain in my right calf, a distant ache, and a sudden burning cut across my thigh. A roaring in my ears, throbbing with my heartbeat. The clash of metal on metal, the crunch of bone, the screams of injured horses and injured men.

I led the first pass, but I watched the second suvari charge from the hill with Eneko. The main body swept around to the southwest with Akio at the head, and I smiled to see both him and Kudret clear again. I heard Eneko speaking through a great roaring in my ears.

"Sir, I am honored to report a sound victory. Shall we pursue them?"

"Only to the ravine."

The archers shifted, a beautiful sweep, and fell back exactly as planned.

"Sir, how is your arm?"

"Fine. What are our losses?"

"Eighteen dead, sir. Seven seriously wounded, thirty or so with lesser wounds. It was a good fight, sir."

It was, indeed.

"And the Tarvil losses?"

"Still counting, sir. I'd guess at least one hundred and forty dead, some two hundred wounded."

I nodded. "Finish the count and fall back. Give the mercy stroke to those who need it. Bring the Tarvil who can be moved back with us." My shoulder burned and ached, and my chest felt tight with the pain. "You did well, Eneko. That was good timing on the suvari archer sweep." My left hand cramped and I flexed my fingers to stretch them. When I didn't think about it, sometimes my whole arm would cramp and tense in rebellion against the pain.

"General Sendoa!" The man came at a gallop.

I didn't hear what he reported. The roaring in my ears was too loud, the blurring spots in my vision too distracting. I heard voices, but I couldn't make out what they said. I have a dim memory of leaning forward holding my shoulder, trying to pull my arm free of the shield grip. I don't remember the return to Izotz. The fever had returned.

It was a definitive battle, though I couldn't be sure of it immediately. When the final count was taken, we had decimated the Tarvil forces and taken many prisoners. We identified the sashes of thirteen different tribes. The man who came at a gallop, whose message I didn't hear until a day later when the fever receded again, brought a bloodied blue sash.

It was blue with gold ends woven with fine red silk threads, blood-stiff near one end. The sash of a high chief, devoid of tribal markings. Not the sash of the highest chief, his would have solid gold ends with no red, but perhaps his heir or an honored deputy.

It would not be long.

Yuudai chokes on his own blood, his throat gaping open. He stumbles to his knees. With his last strength, he brings up his blade to block a strike that would have hamstrung me. My blade meets another, then the sword is in a Tarvil chest, across a throat, into a gut. There is a blur, and then a stunning pain in my right shoulder and I am staring along the length of a javelin up at the sky. My vision fades, gray around the edges, in and out with my heartbeat. Blood in my mouth. I've bitten my tongue, and I swallow the warm coppery taste. From the corner of my eye, I can see Yuudai, facedown in the mud. Beyond him, Mikoto, fallen awkwardly, his sword only half-drawn.

Everything seems quiet, but I think it is only that I am fading. I see the mouth of the Tarvil move; he leans over Yuudai. Then he stares in my eyes. He grins, but it does not reach his eyes, and he pushes the javelin further into the dirt. My head lolls back; I don't have the strength to keep it up. I hear my heart in my ears, and I cannot tell if it is irregular or if it is only my imagination.

I am not frightened.

The javelin pins me to the ground. The pain scatters lucid thought. All I know is the feel of my ribs grinding against the shaft of the javelin, the searing agony of each breath.

It is cold at night.

Morning comes. A magpie cries close by, then another, and a vulture. I smell blood and sweat. Sour, stinking. The men's bodies around me smell. I smell. In my mouth is the taste of death.

I have not drunk water for twenty-four hours.

I am thirsty.

TWENTY-THREE

K emen had been away over three months when a
report came that chilled my heart. He'd been
wounded in what the messenger said was a stupidly heroic attempt to save a wounded soldier under his
command. The young man had died within the hour,
and Kemen looked quick to follow him. The messenger
said he'd taken an arrow in his left shoulder and another
in one leg as he'd pulled the boy to cover.

I went about my work in distracted anguish. I
spilled wine on the queen's lap the afternoon I heard the
news, and when she looked at me I felt as if I weren't
really in the room at all. I was cold and everything
seemed very distant. I started to clean up the mess, and
the king spoke to me three times before I really heard
him.

The queen had kept my confidence. She hadn't told
even her beloved king that I'd driven away his dear
friend and trusted advisor. So only then did he realize

my part in it, when my despair and remorse must have been written all over my face. He stared at me for one long moment. I could hardly think; I was doing everything automatically. I never really knew how much he understood then and how much he realized later, but he must have seen something. He put his head in his hands and told me to leave without worrying about the wine.

I ran into Lani in the hallway. Her eyes were red, as I'm sure mine were too.

"Ria, I want to go to him."

"What would you do?"

"Just be with him! What if he dies?" Her lip was trembling.

I couldn't answer. The lump in my throat almost choked me, and I had no reassuring words.

We heard nothing for a month except one report that the campaign was stalled. Kepa had maintained their recent gains and fortified the new border, but they could make no headway. The blizzards were punishing and rations were short.

The king strode about nervous and twitchy with anxiety for his friend, short-tempered in his worry. He sent reinforcements of course, but reinforcements will not bring a man back to life. None could equal his brilliance either in command or on the field. His death would be a national loss.

Finally a messenger came to tell us that he had cheated death. Lani told me the news, and when I heard it I had to sit down and put my head in my hands. I felt dizzy with relief. For a month I'd imagined him wounded, dying, dead. I blinked back sudden tears at inconvenient times. To know he was still alive, healing, was like coming up for air after nearly drowning.

Lani looked at me very oddly. "Ria?"

I nodded into my hands, not yet ready to face any-one's eyes.

"Did you," she hesitated. "Were you not on good terms when he left?"

"Not the best." My voice shook a little.

"What did you do?" Her tone was accusing. "Did you make him leave?" She was trembling, her hands clenched together.

"Lani, it wasn't like that."

But she was right. I stood up and tried to pull her close, but she drew away from me, shaking her head.

"You almost killed him!"

"I did not, Lani! He's a man, and he makes his own decisions. I didn't make him do anything, and it's none of your business if we argued." I tried to keep my voice low.

She drew in a deep breath and let it out in a rush. She bit her lip as though she wanted to say something, but finally turned away and almost ran down the hall-way.

I had to sit down because I was so dizzy with emo-tion. The accusation hurt and my hands were shaking. Of all people in the world, I loved these two the most, Ke-men, whom I had driven away, and Lani, who hated me for it.

We didn't speak to each other for days. It was hard, avoiding each other in the hallways and sliding silently by each other in the kitchen. She was deeply upset and I didn't want to risk any more accusations. I already felt guilty enough, and seeing her hurt made it worse. I fi-nally gathered my courage and went to her room early one morning.

"Can I come in?"

She nodded.

"I thought you might want me to do your hair."

She shrugged a little and sat down in the chair in front of her desk. I brushed her hair and started the braids, putting golden ribbons in each one before braiding them all together and twining them around her head like a crown. She sighed heavily when I was nearly finished, and I bent over to kiss the top of her head.

"I'm sorry, Lani."

She shrugged, a quick jerk of her shoulders and a duck of her head. She didn't meet my eyes when I looked at her face in the mirror. I kissed the top of her head again, and she turned suddenly. She flung her arms around my waist in a short, tight hug, her face pressed against my stomach, and then she hurried off to her chores.

Twenty-Four

Kemen

B*lood in the snow.*
I woke drenched in sweat and thirsty. Every muscle in my body ached, my shoulder sending hot tongues of fire across my back and through my chest. I thought it was morning, because the room seemed infused with a bright glow. I dressed and walked through the hall and across the courtyard. I think I intended to speak with Eneko, but I didn't make it.

Eneko said later that Kudret found me facedown in the snow some distance from his door. My memory is blurred. Constant thirst, the pain in my shoulder that nearly made me scream, and the dreams.

Once, when I was lucid, Amets explained the infection had deepened, as if I hadn't already noticed. We still hadn't received the supplies I'd ordered, so there was no brandy or even ale for the pain. They held me down and Amets cut away the infected flesh and scraped at the bone, trying to remove the poisonous parts.

HAKAN HAD OBVIOUSLY received Eneko's report. His letter asked about my wound, about the pain and whether I felt strong enough to travel back to Stonehaven for rest. I couldn't blame Eneko for sending it; he'd wanted guidance if I didn't survive. But Hakan and Kveta didn't need to worry about me while Kveta carried the royal child.

I couldn't imagine what Riona would feel if she heard I'd been wounded. She was kind-hearted and would worry about me as about any acquaintance. She might even feel guilty, imagining she had done something wrong when we last spoke. I wished to spare her that. She'd been right, and her frustration more than justified.

I should have been kinder. Warmer. Shown my love better. I should have been different than I was.

A man can change. I know it's possible, and I would have tried. But the opportunity for that had passed. Without her, all that remained was to finish my last task for Hakan. It should have been simple, I could see it almost within reach, but my strength faded every day.

I half-dozed huddled by the fire as I dictated my replies to Hakan and Kveta. Kudret wrote that night because Kyosti was on guard duty. He frowned as he wrote. The sound of his pen on the parchment was pleasantly soothing, a reminder of long evenings with Hakan in his office devising the curriculum for the Common school he started. I wondered how it was doing, and I asked in the letter, although I didn't expect to live long enough to receive his answer.

"I look forward to our next meeting." I stopped. What did I want to say? I was trying not to shiver because the trembling made the pain rise and fogged my mind, but I was so cold. Always cold.

Blood. The snow swirled so thick I barely saw the blade, but instinct saved me. The Tarvil was dead in a moment, then my blade found another. There was a body on the ground, one of many, and I stumbled. Blood in the snow, brilliant red, ruby red against the perfect white. The figure wore a plain servant's dress, and I fell to my knees in sudden terror. Golden hair covered her face, and with trembling fingers I pushed it away.

Riona.

"You already said that, sir." Kudret's voice was worried.

"Said what?"

"That you looked forward to seeing His Royal Highness and Her Royal Highness and celebrating the birth of their child."

I couldn't remember. "Read it to me."

Keeping the words in my head was difficult. Everything was fuzzy and whenever I closed my eyes, I dreamed. I heard Riona's words a thousand times. Once I argued with her, pleaded with her to understand my love, how I would have given everything for her. But she did not want or need the sacrifice I knew how to give.

Kudret reached the end of my letter to Hakan and I still didn't know exactly what I had told him. I dictated the final paragraph with bittersweet affection. Bittersweet, because I dearly wished to see him, to laugh again, to bow before him knowing I had served well. I wished to hold the royal child.

I wished many things.

REVA GALIKOSTA'S SONG of Kardu came easily to mind, and I went through most of it during yet another blizzard that kept everyone except the poor sentries huddled inside close to the fires. But the scenes between Kardu and his lover Ilarminia choked me and I hurried past them. Their romance is only a side-story in the account of Kardu's heroism in the great battles of the war against Ophrano in the Second Age, but the sorrow and joy of their love run through the work like golden threads in a royal tapestry. Kardu was a man of the sword and a man of love, and Ilarminia had one sweet song of lament recorded when she received word that Kardu was wounded in some battle. He lived to see her again, of course, though at the end his death is recorded, as is traditional in all accounts of Erdemen history.

I skipped their scenes together and moved on to Daramenka's Third Royal History, which contains other accounts of the same war. But after three days, I returned to the Song of Kardu. The hero is a model of a perfect man; no doubt his perfection is exaggerated in the poem, but I drew on his example to learn where I had failed. Kardu's love song for Ilarminia is beautiful, but for every one of Ilarminia's perfections, I thought Riona more perfect. Ilarminia's response to Kardu's marriage proposal was more enlightening. She notes his kindness to her, his courage, his masculine beauty. More importantly, she sings of his love for her, how she trusts him with her future, how he is tender, and how she cannot live without him.

Kardu knew how to love a woman, and he received love in return. He deserved it.

We had no action for some time, though the scouts reported frequent sightings of individual Tarvil riders. Then a small skirmish and another lull. It was nearly a month after that last battle that a messenger came. The Tarvil pled for peace.

Their camp was even more barren than I'd expected. Lanky, ragged horses, a few drab tents, a small fire, and one hundred pairs of eyes on me. For my own pride and for the honor of Erdem, I tried to conceal the pain that still tormented me. It had been almost three months since

I'd been wounded. My leg was nearly healed, and the limp would fade soon. But my shoulder might not give me the time.

Otso, their chief, met me at the entrance to his tent. Flanked by some ten or twelve warriors, he bowed to me. His form was bad, but I appreciated the gesture. Tarvil courtesy is different. I attempted to return the honor by bowing and then clasping my hands as his warriors did for their own gesture of respect.

He smiled, a tight cautious smile, and I noted the deep lines of care around his eyes. I did not trust him, and he did not trust me, but now face to face, I could see the desperation that drove their push southward. The Erdemen soldiers with me were tall and healthy, magnificent in comparison despite our short rations. I towered over the chief, whose head didn't even reach my shoulder.

They did not have many formalities. Their purpose, like ours, was a peace treaty as soon as possible. But they did take pains to honor me, bringing a hot spiced drink of horse milk along with some other food. The milk was more than a little soured; the smell made my stomach turn. Otso took a drink first, to show it wasn't poisoned, and I choked some down.

That night and for the next three days I was violently ill; in truth, it nearly killed me. To be fair, even at the time I knew it wasn't poisoned; it was only a testament to their deprivations. Otso drank it with evident enjoyment. It was quite a delicacy, one that I did not fully appreciate then.

The treaty was quite simple, merely a cessation of active attacks by either side while we entered further negotiations. What did the Tarvil need? What did they want? What could they offer? My only fear was that the illness would kill me before I spoke with Hakan, and when I could stomach a bit of water and a few bites of bread on the third day after our parley, I knew I would live at least that long.

Kyosti acted as scribe and drew up the agreement. Otso couldn't read well if his frown of concentration was any indication. I had the terms well enough in mind since I had given Kyosti the words earlier.

"This, at the end. We do not want a treaty in the name of your king. It should be in your name."

"In my name?" My shoulder was paining me so I could barely concentrate.

"I do not know the king. How can I trust a man I have not met? Your reputation is one of honor. We will sign a treaty in your name." He smiled and turned the parchment toward Kyosti.

"I'm honored by your trust, but I have no authority except that which is given to me by the king Hakan Ithel. I serve at his pleasure. The treaty will be in his name, or there will be no treaty at all." If I hadn't been in such pain, I would have bowed to soften my words, to show that I recognized the honor they accorded me, but it was all I could do to speak with a steady voice.

He was silent and finally stood, obviously flustered. "Excuse me." He bowed hastily and retreated to speak with a few of his men.

Kyosti spoke into my ear. "Sir, it may be impossible. Their power is not concentrated in their chief. They have principalities, tribes, roughly united under a chief but still independent. He may not understand or be able to enforce his will even if he agrees."

I shrugged. "They need the peace more than we do. I will not pretend an authority I do not have." My tone was sharper than I'd intended.

"Sorry, sir." He sat back and ducked his head. The pain made me edgy and short, and I put my hand on his

172

shoulder a moment in silent apology. He glanced up and I could see the worry in his eyes. They all worried. I wanted the treaty, and I would get it. But after that, I didn't care if the wound killed me. Every man dies. It is only a matter of timing.

The chief sat down again with a nervous smile. "Your authority comes from the king?"

I nodded.

"But you are a friend of the king, yes?"

I nodded again.

"Then you have influence with him?"

"Perhaps. But he is king, and I serve at his pleasure." My heartbeat was loud in my ears, the fever rising again.

"You serve by choice?"

"I do."

"Then I will sign the treaty in your king's name."

We signed the parchment and in a few moments more we were ready to depart. Kyosti had to steady me when I stood, swaying and nauseated by pain, and even the Tarvil chief looked worried. If I died, I don't know who would have negotiated the final peace. If there was one at all.

TWENTY-FIVE

RIONA

I was serving dinner when the courier arrived with the latest packet of letters from Kemen. The king opened his immediately, skimmed it quickly, then read it again more slowly with a slight frown. The queen read her letter with a smile, and read one section aloud, mostly for my benefit.

"I am recovered, and regret that I have caused you any worry. It will not prevent me from reaching an agreement with the Tarvil soon. It gives me joy to imagine you and Hakan so happy together, and I look forward to our next meeting so that I may share in your joyous expectation of a child."

His words made me smile too, but the king still frowned.

Kveta nodded me out, and I left, but I pressed my ear to the crack by the door. I confess to eavesdropping; I don't do it often but I was desperate to hear what the king's letter contained.

"What's wrong?"

"I don't believe him." The king spoke quietly.

"Why not?"

"As usual, his letter was measured and calm. It tells of advances, losses, everything I could possibly want to know about the war. He's a brilliant strategist; my father should have used him years ago. He predicts a settlement in a month at most. But it reads like a farewell letter! And that one to you; have you ever heard him so affectionate when he's here?"

"He's lonely, Hakan."

"I know. Read mine if you want and tell me if I'm wrong."

"He wouldn't lie to you." There was a very long silence, and then the queen spoke again. "You don't think he's getting better?"

"Do you think he'd tell me if he wasn't?"

"Recall him to Stonehaven then."

The silence was very long before the king spoke so softly that I barely heard it through the door. "I don't know that he'd come."

"You think he'd lie to you and openly defy you? I think you misjudge him."

"If he thought it served me? Or Erdem? Sure, he'd lie, and feel no guilt for it. I don't know, Kveta. I don't know."

Twenty-Six

Kemen

Yori tried to smile as he died, and he looked like Hakan. Noble, brave, young. I tried to give him courage, but he didn't need mine. He only wanted company as he faded.

I loved him. I hardly knew him, but I loved him. He was Erdem's pride, brave, handsome, bright, pure of heart.

Blood in the snow.

I've never questioned whether it's worth it. Perhaps if I were Yori's father or mother, I would. I've spilled my own blood often enough in the king's service. Someone must guard the borders. Someone must enforce the king's peace. Someone must ensure that the king's word is carried out. If the king says, "Here is the border and past this the Tarvil will not come," someone must wield the sword that makes it true.

This time, I have no more blood to give. I have done what I could for you, Hakan. I hope it was enough.

I COULDN'T LEAVE immediately after the ceasefire agreement with Otso because I was so ill I couldn't stand,
much less ride in the biting wind. I sat shuddering by the
fire and vomiting into a bucket at intervals, cursing the
vile Tarvil drink, and when Amets changed the bandages
on my shoulder, I was so dazed I barely noticed the pain.
The second day I began dictating another letter, that one
to Yoshiro Kepa.

After me, he was the ranking officer in the north, but
it was clear he could not direct the men if the peace disin-
tegrated. My letter was an analysis of the strengths and
weaknesses of Eneko and the other young officers under
me and concluded with recommendations of how best to
use them.

Kudret was the best tactician, a suvari, with a sharp,
fast style well suited to the open tundra. But he needed
confidence, and would falter in the face of argument
even when he was right. Eneko was growing as a strategist, and he was the one who had best understood my
feints against the Tarvil and how I pushed them away
from the grazing ground their herds would miss in the
summer. He also needed experience. I expected he
would be pushed into the commander's role sooner than
he wished, but I was confident he would rise to the challenge quickly enough. The truce would give him a little
time.

Kudret wrote the letter for me, waiting patiently as I
tried to sip a little water or diluted ale and then heaved it
back into the bucket again.

"Trust Kudret's instincts, especially when he seems
too aggressive or too willing to risk his men. Question
him and make him think, but don't fetter him too much.
Don't give him too many men; he works best with ten or
twenty. He and Eneko are a good team, stronger when

they work together, but both will need your confidence and support."

He smiled a little as he wrote it.

The letter took me two days, not because it was especially long but because it was so difficult to focus my thoughts into coherent, useful advice. But at last I finished, and Kyosti made a copy of it. The original went to Kepa, of course, and I would carry the copy with me for Hakan on my journey back to Stonehaven. I should have dictated a letter to Hakan about the Tarvil, but I wanted to speak to him myself. Somehow, in my mental fog, it didn't occur to me that if I died on the journey, as I fully expected to, that Hakan would not receive the analysis of the Tarvil that I wished to give him. I suppose I knew, even then, that he didn't need me, but I had the irrational desire to die with my face set toward my king.

Kudret accompanied me with a small escort. We left the fourth day after my meeting with Otso, and Eneko bid me farewell as if he did not expect to see me alive again. I stopped at Fort Kuzeyler only long enough for one of the healers there to change the bandages on my shoulder. It was no longer quite so inflamed, though it hadn't really healed. The infection was deeper and the weakness had worsened. Kepa treated me with grave and solemn courtesy, and when he bid me farewell it was with an air of finality.

The journey south was slow. Kudret seemed to have appointed himself my personal assistant, and though I would have protested at any other time, I was grateful for his help then. During the summer, the journey would have taken about two weeks with good weather, but in the dead of winter it was easily a three-week trek, provided there were no serious obstacles.

The snow was thick around the horses' hooves. The wind blew it into our faces and made it difficult to see the road. For the most part, we huddled within our cloaks, little islands of humanity in the great northern forest. It was too windy to talk most of the time. I don't remember much of the journey, though I do remember that it seemed eternally long, a never-ending ride in wind that cut through our cloaks and whipped away the pathetic warmth of our bodies. I couldn't keep track of the days, but later I heard that it took us a little over a month, slowed by both the weather and my weakness. Sometimes I found myself dozing as we rode, my horse simply following the one in front. I shivered for days, which hurt my shoulder terribly, but finally my body gave up, and I sat a cold still mass atop my horse, only half-aware of those around me.

Once I woke face down in the snow. Hands helped me up a moment later, and someone handed me a cloth. I didn't know why until I saw blood dripping into the snow; my nose was bleeding from the fall. After that, Kudret rode close by my side, and more than once caught me by the shoulder as I slumped to the side and nearly fell again.

The men set up the tents each night, only three, for we slept huddled together for warmth, each body between two others. The men on the end suffered the cold in silence, and they rotated the duty because whoever slept on the end most likely didn't sleep much.

I slept on the end. I wanted no sleeping man's elbow or movement anywhere near my wounded shoulder. Rather, I tried to sleep. I dozed, and probably got more rest than I had in weeks, but I could feel the fever fading in and out, the pain ever present. The men threw thick heavy blankets over the horses; the cold was brutal for them too. One unfortunate horse, a different one every night, went without. Kudret put the horse blanket around my shoulders the second night as I sat by the fire.

I don't normally enjoy luxuries that the rest of the men cannot, but I had neither the strength nor the inclination to argue.

We were over half way to Stonehaven, the wind much abated and the snow drifts much smaller, when Kudret spoke to me one night as I sat huddled morosely near the fire. He brought me dinner, a thick stew and a bit of old bread. The warmth was more welcome than the food; the pain made anything difficult to stomach.

"Sir. We can camp here a few days." He sat by me.

"Why?" The stew was good, and I suspected that he'd picked out a few extra pieces of meat for my bowl.

He shrugged slightly. "To rest. The message can wait a little."

"We would get to Stonehaven in nine or ten days then."

"Yes, sir." He glanced at me with a sudden plea in his eyes. "You must rest."

I stared at the fire. I was weary to my bones, long past the end of my strength. I no longer wished for warmth, to hold Hakan and Kveta's child, barely even for Riona.

I wished only to lie down and not move. I would watch the snow flutter past, stick to my eyelashes and glint like diamonds.

I would close my eyes. My breath could slow and stop. Peace.

But I had to speak with Hakan about the Tarvil. There was hope for them, for us, with a shrewdly made treaty. There was hope for the women they had taken and hope for a peace along the border. They needed it, and we could give it to them. We needed it almost as much as they did. Though the raids cost Erdem little, Hakan's legitimacy would suffer if he could not protect his people.

Someone else could negotiate the details; Hakan was more than competent to set out the parameters without my voice. But I wanted to convey the need, the potential, myself. Later, I realized this was only the reason I used to push myself on, not reality. Hakan did not need me, and Eneko rose to the challenge of leadership in my absence quite capably.

I shook my head. "I may not have that long."

He sighed and leaned forward to put his elbows on his knees. "Sir, you know the king will blame us for your death?" He glanced at me sideways.

I smiled then. "That's a low blow. The king will blame no one but me."

Because I was in command, we did continue, though they were none too pleased about it. The weather warmed suddenly as we approached Stonehaven. The capital is at a lower elevation and it was the beginning of a beautiful spring. It was still chilly, of course, but there were no more snow flurries, though I did see some forlorn patches of old snow in the shade. I was always cold, and even when the rest of the men threw back their hoods to enjoy the brilliant sun I dozed under my hood. In the afternoons, the sun warmed my face and gave me a tentative hope.

I wondered if I would see Riona, whether she would smile at me. I dreamed of that, her smile, her beautiful eyes. I felt more apprehensive that I would see her as we drew closer to Stonehaven. Waking, I expected her disappointment, not knowingly cruel, for she was never that, but disappointment that would cut me more deeply than any intentional unkindness.

Yet in my dreams she smiled, and I was more often in dreams than in reality when we approached the gates of Stonehaven. With some effort, I managed to sit straight and proud as we rode in, and I hoped it wasn't obvious how much it cost me.

THAT FIRST DAY, I pretended, out of pride, that I was stronger than I was, and Hakan pretended, out of compassion, that he believed me. We spoke first of the changes I had made, not the treaty. Hakan asked perceptive questions about Kepa's leadership and lack thereof, and I tried to answer as best I could. Sitting close by the fire, I could almost believe I might live after all. We ate lunch and dinner together, mostly in a companionable silence. He didn't push me to speak much, and I didn't then appreciate his courtesy or kindness. He saw more than I realized of my exhaustion.

I didn't realize how bad I must have looked until I felt his hand on my shoulder.

"We'll talk tomorrow. Go get a hot bath and some sleep."

I'd fallen asleep, or half asleep, my head against the back of the chair. I'd been staring dazedly into the fire, flames dancing, and then, then what? A dream of battle, blood-soaked snow, groans of dying men.

"Right." When I stood, the room spun and everything faded.

Hakan caught my sleeve. I remember stumbling down the hallway to my room. Hakan himself escorted me and ordered a manservant to draw the water for my bath once we arrived. At the time, I was so dazed that I didn't appreciate his concern, but he spoke quietly with the man before he left. I didn't want him to see the wound, so I waited until he'd gone before undressing.

Getting the bandage off was a challenge. After a minute, the servant helped me with quiet fingers and I nodded my thanks. He grimaced at the wound but helped me into the bath without comment. I nearly screamed when the water touched the wound. It felt like fire, and I clutched at my shoulder gasping and shaking with the pain. It bled a little and let out some pus, but after some time it adjusted to the hot water, which pleased me because the rest of my body soaked up the warmth desperately.

I was too tired to really wash, and in any case, the thought of soap entering the wound was more than a little unpleasant. I fell asleep in the water, my head drooping forward until the servant woke me.

I didn't rebandage it, and when the servant asked me if I wanted help, I shook my head. It wasn't worth the trouble. All I wanted was rest.

Clean, dry, and warm, I slept a little, but soon enough the pain woke me. I no longer paced at night when the pain wouldn't let me sleep; I didn't have the strength. I stared at the ceiling for several hours and thought about what else I wanted to tell Hakan. It was hard to concentrate, but I'd turned over the questions so many times in my mind that I was reasonably sure I wouldn't miss anything important.

Eventually I got up and sat at the little table looking out at the darkened courtyard. I fell asleep for a while, waking with an ache in my neck that was almost a welcome distraction from the more familiar agony of my shoulder. I stretched my legs gently because I was badly out of shape. Not that it mattered anymore, but it relaxed me a little.

I met Hakan at his office at dawn. There was no point in pretending I was sleeping. He was grim, more upset than I realized; I was locked in my own small world of pain and fatigue. I spoke to him of the Tarvil, and I was astonished to hear what almost sounded like a defense of them when I said the words aloud. I didn't mean it to sound that way, and I condemned the kid-

nappings of the border women without any excuse. But I
wanted him to understand the barbarians.

When you fight, there is an intimate understanding
of your opponent. Most of all, you understand his fear.
You smell his fear and taste it, hear it like a thrumming
in the air, and you know him in a way no one else ever
can. It's tragic that this understanding so often comes just
before death, but in a way it's also glorious, a meeting of
souls. It's a kind of love, a love that destroys, but love
nonetheless. Hate can never produce the same deep understanding.

The Tarvil were Hakan's opponent. I knew them,
better than he did or any of his other advisors anyway,
and I wanted to tell him everything he needed to know
to defeat them. Not to annihilate them; that wasn't necessary. He could make them no longer a threat, strengthen
the border and protect his people. By protecting his people, he would solidify his own reign. Of course, he understood things about them that I didn't know, and those
things too he would take into account when designing
the treaty.

He heard me out, even taking notes on what I said.
The scratching of his pen on the parchment was soothing, and I found myself staring into the fire for long minutes as I thought. I sat close by the fire, soaking in the
warmth. Hakan fed the fire throughout the morning,
though he kept his sleeves rolled up to his elbows.

I dozed once, waking with a sudden painful jerk
when the door opened. Riona brought our lunch, and I
couldn't bring myself to look at her face. I was ashamed.
I felt like a coward, and I wondered if, in addition to failing her, I had also been unforgivably selfish in my flight
north.

Maybe it looked that way, but I don't think I was,
for I had no expectation she would be hurt by it. Cer-

tainly my departure would have caused her no heart-ache. My heart was lost far more irrevocably than our time together justified, but I'd had no expectation she would feel the same. I thanked her quietly, wishing I had the courage to meet her eyes. I looked after her when she left. Even the way she walks is beautiful, graceful.

It was after lunch that Hakan and I argued. The manservant who helped me the night before with my bath had reported to him about my wound. It was this that had so upset him and made him grim and unsmiling all morning, though he was more than kind.

It began innocently enough.

Hakan said, "Kemen, I would speak to you of another matter."

I nodded.

"I want Saraid to look at your shoulder. Forgive me, I should have had her do it immediately. I didn't know how badly it was paining you."

I shrugged. "To no purpose. There is nothing she can do."

"Do you wish to die?" His jaw was tight.

"I don't much care."

"Are you so unhappy?"

"Does it matter? I've done my duty. I have nothing left for you, Hakan." It grieves me now to remember the bitterness in my voice. It wasn't fair; I had served him in honor and love, not with bitterness.

"I need you. Erdem needs you. You do not have the right to pursue death this way." His voice was low and angry. Later, I realized he had deliberately changed tactics. He wasn't asking anything of me, but he knew me well enough to understand that duty had a stronger call than hope, at least at that moment.

185

If I hadn't been so tired, I would have reacted better. I was blinded by my own frustration and fatigue, and too irrational to recognize his concern.

"You, of all people, ought to thank me! You would have no peace on the northern border if I didn't go. Kepa couldn't do it. He's a good man but a bad commander. The men needed someone they could trust. Who else could lead them now? Who else could have brought you a treaty with the Tarvil?"

"I'm not questioning the value of what you have done!" His voice rose. "I am requesting, nay, ordering if necessary, that you take more care in how you pursue Erdem's interests. You do not have the right to die for one boy, regardless of your own feelings about it. You do more good for Erdem in command than on the field."

"Would you tell me the same if you were on the field? Should I have stood back, the better to command, when you fought Taisto? Or do you deserve life more than Yori did?"

He turned away then. Now it shocks me to realize how unfair I was, but I can plead only my exhaustion. It is no real excuse, but it is the only one I have.

"He was your age, Hakan! Eighteen! He died with four arrows in his chest. Should I have left him to die alone? How many more volunteers would you have then? Even in this I serve you, and you don't see it." I was so angry I could barely breathe. I tried to catch my breath, calm myself, but I was too tired to see clearly, much less rein in my grief.

He stood at the window for some time in silence as I stared at my trembling hands. I had no more words, but I was hardly calm.

Finally he spoke very quietly. "We will speak again tomorrow."

"You won't look at the treaty now?" I stood abruptly, steadying myself against the table at a nauseating rush of pain.

"I will look at it and we will speak on it tomorrow."

"As you wish."

No doubt he heard the anger in my voice, for he turned in time to see me bow. I clenched my jaw at the pain, but I did bow with the respect due to his position. Even in my anger, I did not forget that he was a king. A king I had crowned, but a king nonetheless. The pain in my shoulder was dizzying, and I stumbled as I strode from the room, but I did not fall.

In my room, I found myself too tired even to ready myself for bed, so I sat at the table with my head in my hands. I was too weary to remain angry, but I was also too weary to see the validity of his concern.

Yori had looked much like Hakan, though I couldn't have found the words to tell Hakan that. Tall, thin, more a scholar than a soldier, though he hadn't enjoyed Hakan's exalted education. A volunteer, the fourth son of a poor farmer who had little prospect of advancing any other way. He followed orders, though I'd seen fear in his eyes before the battle began.

Eneko and the others thought I'd been trying to save him, but I knew he'd die before I left cover for him. No, that wasn't it.

He had Hakan's face, and I couldn't bear to see him die alone.

I'd felt I had no choice, though in fairness we all have choices, every moment of every day.

The injustice of Hakan's accusation, his demand, stung me. What difference did it make if I chose to disregard my life? A better cause could not be found. Comforting a dying soldier and securing the border peace were both valid enough causes for sacrifice.

I've never been one to try to hasten my own death, but the past months had, if I was honest with myself, been an attempt to do exactly that. I'd taken chances I never would have before, been more than reckless, though I didn't take the same chances with my men. They wouldn't suffer for my despair. Even in my misery, I wasn't that unjust.

Yet my body and mind could not seem to agree. When I was wounded, my body had clung to life against my own will. Once I realized I would live, I'd pushed on, to make the men's sacrifices worth more than a few leagues of ground, to find a real peace with the Tarvil.

Infection was a slower way to die, but it would do for me. After all the battles I had fought in, it seemed rather anti-climactic but strangely fitting. It wouldn't be the brutality of war that finally killed me, but the slow poison of my own weakness, my own frailty. My inability to do things as they should be done. To speak as gently as I should, stand as straight as I should, understand others as they deserve to be understood.

At least I had time to consider all my failures.

A black mood, certainly, but I was no longer angry, not at anyone besides myself.

TWENTY-SEVEN

RIONA

I saw him when he returned, though he didn't see me. The winter had been harsh even in Stonehaven, and all the men were wrapped in thick cloaks. Everyone else had thrown back their hoods in the sudden spring warmth. His cloak was clasped in three places across his broad chest, the hood pulled low over his eyes. His back was as straight as ever when he rode in, but his exhaustion was evident. Never heavy, now he looked as taut and lean as his sword, hard but brittle with fatigue. When he dismounted he stumbled, and though he steadied himself immediately, he limped slightly as he strode to meet the king.

The king met him near the middle of the courtyard, and Kemen dropped to one knee in deliberately formal respect. I could not hear what they said, since I watched from a window, but the king pulled him to his feet and embraced him. He nearly fell then, and the king steadied him. Even from a distance, I could see the king's worry, but they went inside and I saw no more of him.

He arrived in the late morning, and he and the king were closeted in the king's working office for two days. Sinta brought them their meals, but I convinced her to let me bring them lunch the second day. I don't know what I expected. Kemen glanced up at me when I first entered, but after that stared at the table. I wished I could read his expression, but he has always been opaque. He sat close by the fire, though the room was quite warm. I filled their goblets with wine and he thanked me quietly. I might have been anyone. Neither he nor the king appeared to notice the trembling of my hands while I arranged the plates in front of them.

Sinta relayed bits of information she overheard, swearing me to secrecy. I didn't pass anything along. I've never been one to gossip, and I think she knew I would have gone mad without some news. There had been problems, obviously. Shortages of supplies, weapons, and healers, lack of redundancy in communications, a critical road washed out, an incompetent and untrustworthy company commander. Even if I'd heard it all, I wouldn't have understood it, but I did gather that the challenge had been as much a matter of organization and discipline as of tactics and skill in combat.

The king was grateful, more than grateful, for his skill and leadership. But Kemen had brushed that away. He wanted to explain the agreement, and to Sinta's surprise, she'd heard the beginning of what sounded like a quiet, passionate explanation of Tarvil actions. I wished I could ask him about it, but I didn't have the opportunity. Nor did I believe I had the right anymore.

The second day they finished before dinner. Sinta was to bring Kemen dinner in his room, but she let me do it for her. I knocked quietly, and then louder. When I heard nothing, I opened the door quietly. The windows were open to let in the evening light. He appeared asleep at the table, head resting on his arms and his back to me. I spoke gently before I moved toward the table.

"Sir, I've brought you dinner."

He pushed himself up slowly, as if he were stiff. "Thank you. But I'm not hungry." His voice was hoarse and low.

I put the tray down on the table near him. "Will you not eat anything, sir?" I wanted to be calm, but I was worried, my heart pounding suddenly when I saw the tremor in his hand as he reached for the glass of wine.

He looked at me, and I think it was only then that he realized that it was me standing there, biting my lip in worry. "Thank you, Riona." He looked back down at the table, and for a moment I wondered if I should leave.

"Will you not eat anything?"

He was so still I wondered if he had heard me. Finally the words came, so quietly that I wondered whether he even knew he spoke aloud. "I'm so tired."

Tears sprung in my eyes and I knelt beside him. He closed his eyes as if he could not bear to look at my upturned face. I wished that all the thousands of words of apology that I had thought over the past months would come to me, but my throat closed with my emotion, so I laid my head against his knee. I knew I didn't have the right, I knew I was being scandalous, but it didn't matter.

He flinched when my cheek touched his leg, but he did not recoil more. We sat there in silence for some minutes. Finally I felt him move, slowly, hesitantly. He touched my hair, stroked gently over the back of my head, a comforting gesture more than anything. There could be no desire in it, not after how I had hurt him, but there was forgiveness.

191

I don't know how long we sat there. My heart was full. I wanted to catch his hand, tell him how much I regretted my words, but I couldn't bear to break our tentative peace. Finally his hand rested on my shoulder, still and quiet. The sun was gone by then, though the glow of sunset left a warm light in the room. I waited and finally moved as gently and slowly as I could until I could see his face.

He was slumped over the table, his head resting in the crook of his left arm, his right arm awkwardly angled to reach my shoulder. I waited, but he didn't move, and finally the ache in my legs was so painful that I had to stand. I moved his hand gently to rest on one long lean leg and then stood, grimacing at a sudden cramp.

How had I ever thought him ugly? The strong straight line of his jaw and rich olive tone of his skin had a different kind of beauty, but beauty nonetheless.

I moved the wine glass a bit so if he moved in his sleep he wouldn't upset it. But for all my care, I stumbled into the chair when I turned away. The noise was startlingly loud in the silence, and I looked back at him, expecting him to wake.

He did not move, and I stood a moment. Now that I saw him in repose, the hollowness of his cheeks made my heart twist. I left quietly, biting my lip with worry. I wanted to speak to Saraid.

I saw her in the hallway. She was frowning, hurrying toward me.

"How is he?"

"He's asleep. Why?

"The king told me to treat his wound. But if he's sleeping…" her voice trailed away, but she frowned grimly.

"What? What do you mean?"

She shook her head and knocked softly. There was no answer, and I held my breath as she opened the door. He was just as before, and I watched from the doorway as she spoke to him and then approached.

"Sir?" She put one hand on his shoulder. "Sir?" Her voice was more commanding now, but he remained motionless. She bent to look at him more closely.

"Ria, go get Lani, Joran, and Drokan. *Now.*"

I ran. I found Lani first and sent her to the kitchen for Joran and Drokan while I returned to his room.

He was sitting up, but his back was to me. Saraid's expression as she knelt in front of him was solemn and gentle. I didn't hear her question, but he shook his head slightly.

"It's the king's direct order, sir. You may be able to defy him, but I cannot."

He spoke so quietly that I hardly heard him at all. "I've never defied my king."

"What could I tell him, sir?"

"Whatever you like."

Her eyes flicked to me in desperation. I was before him in a moment, kneeling to look up into his face.

"Sir, please."

He blinked, then closed his eyes and shook his head slightly as if to clear it. "I thought..." he stopped and swallowed. His eyes searched my face.

"Sir, please let Saraid help you." I didn't know what she was going to do; if I'd known, I don't know if I could have begged him so desperately. I took his left hand in both of mine and raised it to my cheek. His hand tightened on mine a moment, and I felt it trembling.

"Please, sir." There were tears in my eyes when I looked up at him.

He held my gaze for a long moment. Then he let his head rest against the back of the chair, his eyes closed.

Saraid looked at me, and then at him, and I caressed his hand again.

His voice was scarcely more than a whisper. "Do as you wish."

"Yes, sir." Saraid stood briskly. "Ria, bring valerian, lavender, and two bottles of brandy. Three or four buckets of water. Lani knows where the bandages and my bag are."

I stood but paused to look down at him a moment.

Saraid spoke to him gently. "Sir, I'm going to help you with your tunic and shirt."

He nodded, and she unbuckled his belt. He bowed his head, still sitting, as she pulled his tunic carefully over his head. I wanted to stay with him, but she shot me an urgent look over his shoulder and I hurried away.

TWENTY-EIGHT

KEMEN

To be honest, I wasn't sure whether Riona's plea was reality or a dream. But even in a dream, I was at her command.

I would have preferred not to endure the pain of the surgery, but Riona had tears in her eyes, and I could not refuse her. The difference between dying that evening during the procedure and dying some days later from the infection was of no real concern. I confess I should have told Hakan; it was unfair of me to give him no warning that I might leave him. Looking back on it, I imagine he knew.

Saraid tried to be reassuring, but her sudden sharp intake of breath when she saw the wound spoke for itself. She had me drink brandy with something in it before she began. I don't know how much it helped. She had Lani assist her, as well as some men. I couldn't remember their names, though I think one of them was the cook. I thought Lani was a bit young for the duty, but from what I remember, she handled it well. For her sake, I didn't curse at the pain, aloud anyway.

"When did this happen? What was it?"

"An arrow. Some three or four months ago." I lay face down on the bed, bare to my waist, with a pillow under my chest. She had spread thick towels beneath me to catch the blood and whatever else might come from the wound.

"Bite on this." A small roll of cloth, to keep me from breaking my own teeth. "Sir, I can't promise," she hesitated. "I can't promise this will help at all. It may not be possible to—" she stopped, as if she thought I had never contemplated the possibility of my death before.

"I don't expect to live."

She looked as if she wanted to say something more, something reassuring, but finally she just nodded.

Lani was very pale, and slipped her hand into mine for a moment as Saraid laid out her instruments. I smiled at her, hoping it was reassuring, and squeezed her hand before Saraid asked her to do something else.

She opened the wound with a sharp knife and flushed it with water. She spoke quietly to Lani, asking for one instrument or another, and finally she said, "Sir, I'm going to have to cut out the infection." Then to the men holding my arms down, "Tightly now."

Twenty-Nine

Riona

I waited outside his room, dizzy and sick with worry. I asked if I could help, and Saraid relayed the question to him. Lani brought the answer.

"He said no." She was white as a sheet, but her voice was steady.

I swallowed. Before he'd touched my hair, I would have thought he was angry. But all I could think when I caught a glimpse of him sitting slumped on the edge of the bed before Lani closed the door was, *he doesn't want me to watch him die.*

I listened outside the door. There was quiet talk, some rustling of fabric and the sound of water, and a bit more talk. I heard his voice several times, but it was so quiet I couldn't make out his words. There was a long silence, then a short strangled cry. My knees wouldn't hold me, and I slid down to sit on the floor, leaning against the wall.

A choked moan, a gasp, then another moan. I could barely breathe. It took me a moment to realize there was someone standing at the closed door.

The king. He glanced down at me before turning to lean against the wall himself.

Then there was only silence, broken sometimes by the low murmur of voices. At length the men came out one by one, each with a respectful bow to the king and a sympathetic glance for me. Joran leaned down to squeeze my shoulder.

Saraid finally came to the door. Her eyes widened when she saw the king, and she curtsied. "Your Royal Highness." She closed the door behind herself and spoke very quietly, her eyes down on the floor. "If he survives the night, he has a chance." She swallowed. "He could recover well, if he lives long enough, but the infection is deep."

She glanced at me, then back at the floor. "It's in the bone. I've cut away what I could, and scraped away the infection I could find, but I can't promise it will help. The herbs should help with healing. But," she licked her lips, "he told me he didn't have the strength to endure the treatment. He might have been right."

The king nodded, his face pale.

"He's sleeping now."

The king nodded again and pushed open the door, though I could tell Saraid would have preferred that he not enter. I followed him in.

When I saw him, tears sprung in my eyes. He'd always been lean, but he'd been strong, tautly muscled and beautiful. Now he lay quiet and still on the bed, on his stomach and bare to his waist aside from the bandage. He was terribly gaunt. Even in sleep, the muscles of his back and arms stood out beneath skin as thin as parchment. The sharp lines of his ribs moved slightly with each shallow breath. If he'd had pale Tuyet skin, I could have traced every blue vein across his body. Even his temples were hollow, his cheeks slightly sunken. I could see his pulse in his temples, his neck, and the crook of his elbow.

The king knelt by Kemen's face and studied him closely, his mouth tightly set. Kemen's head was pillowed more at the back, so the angle of his neck was a bit less; he faced into the mattress rather than at the wall.

Saraid spoke quietly. "He has a fever. Someone will stay with him at all times. He said there was a letter for you in his tunic."

The king nodded as if he wasn't really listening, but finally he nodded again and stood, glancing around the room. Kemen's shirt and tunic were crumpled on a chair, and he picked them up with a strange expression. He pulled them apart, and then pulled another shirt from inside the first. Then another tunic. Four layers. No wonder I hadn't seen how thin he was.

The king pulled a letter from the outer tunic and skimmed the first page by the lamplight, his face tight. Then he stared at his friend again and finally strode out, his steps quick and sharp down the hall.

Saraid said, "Go get dinner, Ria."

"I'm not hungry."

"Then stay with him while I go eat. I'll bring you something. He won't wake for quite some time." She left then, but Lani stayed with me for a while. She sniffled quietly and finally I pulled her close. She was trembling.

"He thanked us, Ria. He knew what we were going to do and he thanked us."

If I had not already forgiven him, more than forgiven him, I would have for that alone.

She pulled away to lean close to him. She slipped one hand into his slack one and studied his face while she rubbed his hand gently. He might have been dead for the response she got, but his breaths, though shallow, remained slow and even, which was reassuring.

It sounds now as though I was calm at the time. Perhaps I looked calm to Lani, but inside I was shaking, weeping, breathless with sorrow and worry. She cried in my arms, trying to stifle her tears. I rubbed her back, but my eyes were always on his face.

The king came to visit him again, pale and tight-lipped in his worry. He sat by the bed for several hours, hardly glancing at me. Kemen did not wake, not even when the king said his name quietly, though he did moan softly once. He looked like death, and the king must have thought so too, because finally he stood abruptly and left the room. I never told anyone, but I saw the gleam of tears in his eyes when he passed me.

The room grew cooler as night drew on and I pulled the blanket up to cover him. Saraid brought dinner for Lani and me, but I was too upset to be very hungry. She said there was little she could do, and she would be resting, but to come get her if his fever worsened.

Saraid came again to check on him in the middle of the night, before the sky had even begun to turn grey. She pressed the back of her hand to his forehead and felt his pulse at his wrist. Then with utmost care she rolled him to his right side, his right arm curled in front of his face, holding his left elbow all the while so that it did not move. She had me help her slip a cloth beneath his waist and bound his left arm against his body. Perhaps what terrified me most was his limp helplessness, the slackness of his strong hands when she moved him. She bent his knees and put a pillow behind him so he could not roll onto his shoulder. The position looked more natural, almost like he was sleeping peacefully, and though I knew he was dancing with death, it reassured me.

Some time after she left, the queen slipped inside, closing the door quietly behind herself. The royal child was due in some two months, and she wore slippers because proper shoes hurt her swollen feet. I moved back from the bed, and she took my place with a quiet thanks. She moved the chair a little closer to the bed and slipped her hand into his. His eyes fluttered open and he blinked for a moment, before turning his head slightly to look at her.

Her voice was very quiet and gentle. "How are you feeling?"

He smiled but his eyes closed for a moment, as if even the smile took more strength than he had.

"Hakan came to visit you."

His lips moved, but I heard nothing. He tried again, his voice low and hoarse. "Tell him I'm sorry."

She pressed his hand to her cheek. If she had been anyone else, I would have been jealous, but her gesture was so sweet and gentle that I couldn't resent it. It was love, but not a kind of love I could begrudge her.

"He wept for you, Kemen. He's afraid to lose you."

I think he would have laughed then, but he didn't have the strength. His words were very low but quite clear. "He doesn't need me." He closed his eyes, as if the words had cost him dearly, but a smile remained on his lips.

She sat by him for some time, but he seemed asleep. Finally she turned to me. "How are you?"

I ducked my head and shrugged, and she pulled her chair closer to me. To my utter shock, she leaned over and embraced me, her arms about my shoulders. Though I'm older, it was such a maternal gesture that I let myself put my head on her shoulder, biting my lip as I tried to control my tears.

Finally I moved away, leaned forward with my elbows on my knees. I hadn't let myself sob as I dearly wished to, but my face felt sticky with tears I couldn't quite hold in. She sat with me in sympathetic silence for some time, one arm around my shoulders. At least she leaned forward to whisper in my ear, "I think he'll live."

I looked at her in surprise. I confess I thought her terribly naive, sweet but unaware of the gravity of his wound.

"Sit by him. Hold his hand. He'll live for you, if he lives at all."

I swallowed and looked down. I didn't even realize I was shaking my head, I suppose in sorrow and despair, until she put her hand on my shoulder again.

"Give him that comfort. It's all he wants." She embraced me again for a moment, then turned and left quietly. I took her place at his side, and though I hesitated, I did finally take his hand in mine.

He didn't wake for hours, and when he finally did, I was asleep myself. I woke to a slight movement, for my hand was still in his, my head bowed forward to rest awkwardly on the covers. I sat up only to groan at the sudden pain in my neck and back. He smiled then, a sweet smile that I couldn't help but return, despite my worry.

"Would you like a drink? Something to eat?"

"Please." In the dim light, his face looked ashen, his lips a leaden grey.

"Wine or water?"

"Water."

I helped him drink, holding the cup and watching his face worriedly. He could scarcely raise his head, and I helped him with one tentative hand while I held the cup with the other. Even that slight effort drained him, and he closed his eyes a moment afterward to struggle with the pain. I let myself brush the back of my fingers across his cheek, push his hair back from his eyes. He smiled faintly, or perhaps it was my imagination, for he was soon asleep.

If we were ever more than tentative suitors, I wanted to ask him many things. How he received the scar on the right side of his chest, an uneven circle faded a pale greenish white. Whether he was ever frightened before battle. What I could do to see his smile more often.

The edges of his collarbones were heartbreakingly sharp. The flickering lamplight cast deep shadows in the lines of strain around his mouth. I laid my head down again after some time, turned to the side so that I could see the slow even pulse in his neck. It was reassuring to see he still lived.

Saraid smiled when she entered just before dawn. "If he still breathes now, I imagine he'll make it. He'll be weak for a long time, but he'll live. Bring him breakfast in a few hours. I'll stay with him for a while."

"I'd rather stay."

"You're no use to him exhausted. I'll be here with him."

I WAS GOING to try to take a nap, but Tanith saw me in the hallway and said the king wanted to speak to me in his working office. I stood outside his door for a moment, smoothing my hair nervously and brushing my hands down the front of my dress in an unsuccessful attempt to look like I hadn't slept in it.

I knocked, and when he bid me enter, I curtsied deeply and closed the door behind myself with trembling fingers.

"You're Riona?" He has a pleasant voice when he speaks, but it is nothing to the beauty when he sings.

"Yes, Your Royal Highness." I kept my eyes on the floor respectfully.

"Look at me, please."

I swallowed and raised my eyes to meet his gaze. There were dark smudges under his solemn, pale blue eyes. He was nearly eight years younger than I was, but he had a natural authority that made it difficult for me to keep my eyes on his.

"Do you love him?"

I couldn't find my voice, and he waited, patient and grave, for my answer. "Yes, Your Royal Highness." I took a deep breath to keep my voice from shaking. "I do love him."

There was a very long silence. "You will attend him then. You're relieved of any other duties. He is to have whatever he wants, whenever he wants it, regardless of expense or inconvenience. Do you understand?"

"Yes, Your Royal Highness."

He gazed at me a moment longer, as if he were evaluating me, and finally nodded. I was dismissed.

SAYEN CAME TO ME in the kitchen as I was making his tray. "Saraid says General Sendoa is awake now and she wants him to eat. She says he's doing better than she would've expected."

I nodded, and she gave me a quick, sudden hug before she hurried away.

He was awake when I brought him breakfast. I fed him, but he didn't want much. A few bites of fresh bread, one of bacon, a few berries, and he closed his eyes in exhaustion. I pushed his hair back from his forehead and he smiled faintly. I thought he slept again immediately, but after a moment he spoke.

"Lani?"

"She's not here. Should I get her?"

"Please." The word was scarcely more than a sigh.

Saraid frowned. "Sir, you ought to rest."

His breathing quickened raggedly and he strained suddenly to push himself up from the pillow. She cried out in alarm, pressing him down with careful hands. "Sir, rest. We'll get her. You can see her. Lie down, please."

I didn't want to leave him, so I asked the first person I saw in the hallway to fetch Lani immediately. She came in a few minutes, wide-eyed and breathless from running halfway across the palace.

She sat beside the bed and clasped his hand in hers, biting her lip.

"How are you?" The question came from his lips, not hers, and his eyes searched her face.

"Better, now that you look like you'll live. How are you?" It was typical of Lani, trying to be cheerful in any situation, but the worry in her voice was obvious.

He smiled and closed his eyes. "I've been better." He lost his breath, but squeezed her hand.

She brought his hand to her cheek with a sigh.

"Brave, helping Saraid." His words were so quiet she leaned in to hear him better. She shook her head and he smiled again and brought her hand to his lips. "Soft heart. Make a younger man very happy."

She made a choked sound halfway between a laugh and a sob and put her head down next to his shoulder on the bed. He let his hand rest on her hair.

It reassured me to see him smile, but when Lani's eyes were not on him I saw his jaw tighten.

"Would you like some wine?" I asked quietly.

"Please."

He smiled again when Lani raised her head. She left still worried but much more light-hearted. When the

205

door closed behind her, I breathed a sigh of relief. I love Lani very much, but my heart twisted to see him spending his last strength on reassuring her. He was utterly drained, so weary and in so much pain he could barely swallow the wine. He slept soon though, and his breathing became more even.

"Go get some rest, Riona. You can bring him lunch if you want."

"I want to stay."

"Go take a nap. I'll stay with him."

She was right. I did go rest and fell asleep quickly, but I dreamed I was working and while I washed dishes, his breath slowed and stopped. Saraid tried everything she knew, but nothing could be done. In the dream, I worked happily for hours, thinking of him healing, until later I heard only by accident that the king's champion had died. I woke with tears on my face.

Saraid would have told me if he'd worsened, but I couldn't sleep again, and so finally I got up and tried to do some of the work I'd neglected.

Saraid found me in the kitchen when I was preparing his lunch. "Ria, he needs sleep more than anything. Go rest and bring him dinner."

"But," I started, but she interrupted me.

"He needs to sleep. If you bring him food, he'll try to eat it to please you. Let the man rest, Ria. He'll be better tonight; the fever is fading." She smiled reassuringly. "You need rest too."

I slept for hours, waking with a start when Lani knocked on my door. "Saraid says you can bring his dinner now."

But when I entered, he was asleep and Saraid was frowning. He muttered quietly into his pillow; I recognized it as Kumar, the warrior tongue, but I couldn't understand it. I tried to remember the sounds of it, so that I could find out what it meant.

"*Waratoshu hani maktai. Hanil amai. Ryuu soktai aka-shni. Hanil rulakshani amai.*" He drew a great breath and let out a shuddering sigh, almost a groan, and turned his face further into the pillow. The rest was muffled, but he frowned in his sleep, flinching away and quieting briefly when Saraid put a damp cloth on his forehead. Then again, "*Hanil amai. Amai. Tavarin suvari, ekanska.*"

He was restless all night, but near dawn the fever seemed to fade, not the dramatic breaking I'd expected, but a quieting that Saraid said was easier on his weakened body.

SARAID CHANGED THE DRESSING on his shoulder twice a day. The first time, she warned me not look at the wound, and I kept my eyes on his face and held his left arm in case he moved. I accidentally caught one brief glimpse of the edge of the wound and the bandage, and it made my stomach turn; blood, some pale slimy substance, dark specks of the herbs Saraid had used, all smeared and crumpled in the bandage. She swabbed out the wound ever so carefully and powdered it with crushed herbs, packed it with honey to draw out the fluid, and bandaged it again. He slept through it without a twitch.

The next time was not so easy. He lay on his stomach, his eyes closed, but he was not asleep. I held his left arm as Saraid instructed, using my weight to push it into the mattress in case he jerked. She spoke softly to him, warning him that she was about to begin. The muscles of his arm twitched and tensed beneath my hands, but he did not strain against my weight, and I gradually let up a little. His breaths came short and fast, and once, at the very end, he muttered something to himself in Kumar, his eyes half-closed. When she finished, he was trembling and I pulled the blanket up over his shoulders. He slept again.

WHEN I ENTERED with his tray for lunch, he was sitting at the table, his eyes closed. He ate a little, though not enough to soothe my worry. It nearly made me cry to see the sharp line of his shoulders beneath the thin fabric of his robe. He was exhausted, letting his eyes close sometimes as he chewed. He took a few bites of bread, a few berries, a little of the rich broth Joran had prepared, but it was all deliberate, as if he knew it had to be done but didn't care much for the job. Too soon he sat back to let his head rest against the back of the chair.

"What can I do, sir?"

He smiled faintly, his eyes closed again. "Just Kemen, please." He paused, as if he were thinking. "A bath. I want a bath."

My face heated.

"I don't need help if you can have the water heated." He had to stop and catch his breath, his eyes still closed, and I blushed even more at how I'd misinterpreted his words.

"I will. Do you want it now?"

He seemed to sag a little in his chair before taking a deep breath. "I want to go outside." He opened his eyes to see my doubtful frown. "I need to see the sky. Please."

I couldn't refuse him. "Now?"

He nodded, his eyes still on my face.

"I'll get a blanket then. I'll be right back." I nearly ran down the hall. It took me several minutes to find Saraid and ask her if it was dangerous for him to move, and she frowned and hurried back with me.

When I returned, he appeared nearly asleep. His robe had fallen open to show the white bandage about the top of his chest and crossing over the top of his left shoulder. The line of his collarbone, the definition of the muscles in his chest, the smooth silk of his skin, made me blush suddenly. He was painfully thin, but still he was beautiful.

"Sir?" Saraid spoke very softly, but he drew a breath and straightened. "I'd rather you not move yet. It's only been three days." Her voice was very gentle.

"Riona will steady me." His eyes met mine. *Please.*

I nodded. "I'll help him. We'll be careful."

She frowned but finally nodded. He wore breeches under his robe, but he was barefoot. I asked him if he wanted his boots, but he said no.

He stood on his own strength, though he kept his hand on the edge of the table to steady himself. I put my left arm around him, holding his hip and waist gingerly, and he rested his right arm across my shoulders. I could feel his every rib, the striations of the muscles in his side, the trembling strain of his steps toward the door.

Saraid followed us out, though she pretended not to because she knew how much he hated for anyone to see his weakness. We paused once when he sagged alarmingly, and I steadied him, but we made it to the garden. He turned toward the roses. He limped a little, a catch in his step each time he put weight on his right leg. When I glanced up at his face in the hallway, his eyes were half-closed, but in the garden when I glanced up again, his mouth was tight, his eyes focused on the ground ahead of him.

I had tears in my eyes when he finally stopped. "Can you stand? I'll lay down the blanket."

He stayed upright, swaying a little, though I'd feared he had no strength even for that. Finally I helped him lay flat on his back; though it must have hurt his shoulder terribly, he made no complaint.

"Thank you." His eyes were half-closed against the afternoon sun. I only nodded, not trusting my voice, and he looked up at me. "What's wrong?"

I blinked back tears and tried to smile. "I'm just glad you're back." Back from war, back from death.

His eyes widened and he reached up to brush the backs of his fingers across my cheek. "Don't cry, Riona."

I caught his hand and held it to my cheek. "Rest, sir." I brushed at my eyes, put his hand down gently, and pulled the edge of the blanket up to cover his bare feet. When I looked back at his face, he was already asleep.

IT WAS EVENING, perhaps five days after his surgery. We came in from the garden and I took Kemen to a small sitting room for dinner. He seemed to be in more pain that day, and I wasn't sure he could even make it the short distance to his room without the rest. It made my heart wrench to see him trying to hide it, how he smiled and shook his head when I asked if he needed anything.

"I'll be back in a few minutes with your dinner." I brushed his hair back from his forehead and caught a pale glint. I looked more closely and saw a strand of iron grey, just one hair, but it stood out from the rest of his blue-black waves.

He nodded. "Thank you."

I sent Lani to sit with him while I made his dinner, and I brought Saraid with me when I returned. I wanted to know if she could give him anything else for the pain, but Lani met us at the door.

"Come see." She looked worried.

I slid the tray of food onto a table and nearly ran to him, Saraid right behind me. He was sitting up, hunched forward and trembling slightly. His breaths were quick and shallow, ragged.

"Sir, what's wrong?" Saraid kept her voice calm.

He muttered something, but I didn't hear it.

"Sir, please. What's wrong? What happened?"

"I'm sorry." His eyes closed. "*Hanil amai.*"

"Sir, what's wrong? Is the pain worse?"

He nodded once, his jaw tight.

"What else? Is there anything else? Are you cold?"

He nodded again. I don't know why I didn't see it until then, but he was rubbing his right foot across the top of his left, and I reached down to touch them. They were cold as ice.

"His feet are freezing."

"Lani, go heat some water." Saraid frowned. "I'd hoped the chills were over. Rub his feet, try to warm him. I'll be back."

She stood and left quickly, stopping only to put another blanket around his shoulders. I sat on the floor in front of him, speaking softly, though I don't know what I said. I put one of his feet in my lap and covered it with my apron, and I rubbed the other between my hands. The bones felt strong and hard beneath my hands, the tendons like lean cords in his ankle. I could feel him shaking.

"*Hanil amai,*" he whispered again.

"Hush, darling." I looked up in his face. His eyes were half-closed and his lips were pressed tightly together as if to keep them steady. He held his arm close, and his left hand was clenched so tightly I feared he would injure himself. "Let me see it."

I rubbed my hand up and down his forearm, trying to relax the muscles. They felt like ribbons of iron be-

neath his thin skin. Lani brought steaming water for his
feet. ~~He caught his breath suddenly when I gently put his~~
feet one by one into the water. After some minutes, he
leaned forward, bowing almost to his knees, and his
breathing slowed.

Saraid spoke to him, and he didn't answer. She
touched his good shoulder, and only then did we realize
he was nearly unconscious, because he slumped to one
side and we both had to catch at his shoulders and ease
him back onto the couch.

"Lani, what happened?" Saraid asked.

Her eyes were wide and her lip trembled. "I think he
just got cold."

"Has he eaten anything?"

I answered that. "Only some berries earlier, and a
little cheese. Hardly anything."

She frowned and nodded, then looked at him again.
He shivered under the thick blankets, murmuring at
times. He switched between Common and Kumar without noticing, but even the Common I couldn't make out
clearly.

Saraid brought the tray closer. "Sir." She touched his
shoulder, and he seemed to wake a little. "Drink this."

His long fingers wrapped around the mug, and he
stared at it a moment, as if he couldn't remember what it
was. He took a sip, and then a long drink, and set the cup
down on the tray. He took a deep, steadying breath and
let it out slowly. He smiled, a wry little quirk as if he
were mocking himself. "I'm sorry. I'm fine. Thank you."

I frowned at him, not believing it at all.

He leaned back with his eyes closed, shivering.

HE SPENT ALMOST a month resting at the palace, regaining strength. It should have been longer, but he had a

212

restless energy, a burning need for activity that drove him north again on the king's business. In that short time though, much changed between us, all for the better.

Saraid insisted that he drink wine laced with valerian and other herbs and when he protested, the king's explicit order prevailed. It helped him sleep through the pain at night and in long naps, forced him to rest.

One afternoon we went to the garden. I brought a book from the king's library, a children's story of sweet and beautiful fairytale love. I spread a blanket on the thick grass behind the rose bushes, mostly out of sight of the windows. He lay on his back, trying to hide his wince of pain at the movement, and I kept my voice quiet and low, hoping he would sleep.

The sun through the leaves dappled the pages. His face looked so peaceful that at last I thought he was asleep, his chest rising and falling with slow even breaths. I put the book aside quietly, marking the page with a blade of grass.

"What happens next?" He spoke with his eyes closed, sleepy and quiet.

"I thought you were asleep."

He smiled and reached for me, resting the back of his hand against my shoe. Such an innocent touch, but it seemed to comfort him. "Almost. What happens?"

"Haven't you heard this story a thousand times?"

"No." He opened his eyes to smile up at me.

"Didn't you read it when you were young?" His smile faded and I felt terribly guilty. "I'm sorry. I'll read the rest if you want me to."

I put the book back in my lap, holding the pages open with one hand. I tucked my other hand into his. He smiled almost sadly, his eyes closing in drowsiness. I read to the end, glancing up now and then to study his face. He looked almost asleep, but he squeezed my hand gently before bringing it to his lips and kissing my fingertips.

"We didn't have stories like that."

"What kind of stories did you have?"

He smiled drowsily. "Stories to make boys wish they were men. Stories of great battles and heroism, kings and quests. Valor. Death. Courage."

"They sound magnificent."

"They are. They are true, and that makes them glorious. But your story is also true."

"It's a fairytale."

He looked up at me, blinking into the sunlight. "It's a story of love. Love is true. Love is real. I wish I'd had more stories like yours. Perhaps I would know better what to do." His eyes closed again.

I moved closer and ran my fingers through his hair. It was black as a raven's wing, with the same bluish sheen, the slightest bit of curl at his temples. He had the long hair of a soldier, long enough to pull back with a bit of leather, though it was loose then. I felt bold, but I said exactly what I was thinking. "You have beautiful hair."

His eyes snapped open and he frowned at me as if he doubted I was serious.

"You do. I like it."

Then he laughed, long, almost silent laughter that shook him and left him breathless.

"What? Why did you laugh?" His lingering smile made me smile through my confusion and worry for him. It might have been the first time I saw him really laugh.

"I always hated it."

"Why?" I couldn't even remember that I, too, had once thought him ugly, a frightening contrast to Tuyet beauty. I saw him as indescribably beautiful, a perfection of the human form, dark skin like silk despite the scars, green eyes dazzling and magnetic, the color of emeralds.

"I wanted to be golden like Tuyets." He smiled, eyes closed against the light, fighting the drowsiness of Saraid's herbs. "Golden hair, skin golden or milky white, like alabaster. Eyes like the summer sky or a stormy sea."

I bent down to kiss his forehead. I wasn't bold enough to kiss his lips, not without some kind of warning, but I wished I was.

He blinked up at me, looking utterly shocked, and I couldn't help but laugh a little in embarrassment.

He licked his lips. "What do your stories say I should do now?"

"What do you mean?"

"I feel like I'm in a fairytale. A man like me isn't kissed by someone like you, not in real life. Did Saraid slip something stronger into the wine?" He was teasing gently, something else I had never seen before. "It is a dream, isn't it?"

He pushed himself up to sit, catching his breath with pain but then turning to me with a shy smile. "Not that I want to wake up." He brought my hand to his lips, more solemn now.

"I don't know how to do this, Riona. I haven't read the stories. I've scarcely even spoken with women at all before you." He bowed his head in quiet apology. "I want to learn. I want to please you. But I will need you to teach me how." He kissed my fingers again, and I felt his lips trembling.

I was bold then, for his sake and for mine. If he was so brave in all other ways, I would be brave for him in this. "We can read the stories together. And you might," I faltered because the words sounded absurdly scandalous, but pressed on, "You might start by kissing me."

His mouth dropped open in shock and then he ~~grinned, laughter in his eyes. He cupped my cheek in~~ one hand, eyes bright, and he bent to kiss me gently. On the lips. We were both shy, awkwardly tender, and afterward he smiled. "It's a good start."

THE NEXT DAY I took him with me to the library. "Have you read this one?"

"No."

"Oh, what about this? *Little Bird and the Raven.* I think I like it better."

"No, I haven't."

"Let's read it then." I picked up the little basket of food and the blanket and started for the door, the book clamped under my arm.

"Let me carry something for you."

"I'm fine." But opening the door with my hands so full was awkward, and he took the blanket and book from me. I looked up at him, worried. He was still terribly weak, and even the effort of our gentle fight over the blanket left him leaning against the wall for a moment in exhaustion.

"I can carry it, Kemen." I reached out my hand, hoping he would let me, but he shook his head.

"Please. Let me."

Finally I did, but I kept a sharp eye on him as we went outside and walked through the garden. Though he was steadier than he had been, it bothered me, and when he was settled on the blanket I asked, "Why wouldn't you let me carry it? You need to rest."

Men are so foolish that way, thinking they have to act immortal, invincible, for us to love them, when we love their weaknesses just as much.

The wine with valerian was already making him sleepy, and he answered with his eyes closed. "I'm tired of being weak and useless. Besides, isn't that what men are for, to serve those they love? Please don't deny me that."

I nearly lost my breath at his quiet plea. "I just—" I had to start again. "You're the last person in all of Erdem who should feel weak!"

His hand found mine though his eyes remained closed, and he sighed as though he were fast falling asleep. I waited, but he did not speak again, and finally I began to read quietly. I thought he slept at one point, so I took a break to stretch my back. He shifted a little and I began again without prompting. He smiled when I took his hand.

The story was finished not long after, and he looked up into the leaves, squinting at the brightness, as though he were thinking very deep and serious thoughts. I touched his hair, ran one tentative finger over his eyebrows, and he smiled with quiet joy such as I'd never seen in him.

Finally he spoke, his smile gone. "You have no idea of my weaknesses, Ria." He looked up at me.

"I have some of my own."

He smiled quickly, appreciating the words but clearly thinking of something else. At last he took a deep breath. "I cannot read." The words were quiet but very clear, and his eyes on my face watched for my reaction.

I sat in stunned silence, and I hesitate to imagine what thoughts went through his head in that eternally long moment. Everyone can read, at least every soldier and certainly every officer. Even servants.

Finally I did the only thing that I could think of. I leaned over and kissed him full on the lips, long and tender.

He was shocked, so surprised he didn't even look happy about our second kiss.

"Thank you, Kemen."

"For what?" Now he was confused, struggling to sit up.

My heart felt nearly bursting with love for him. I moved closer, so that when he did finally sit up with a catch in his breath from the pain, I was there to clasp his hands in mine and smile directly into his eyes. "Thank you for trusting me."

He leaned forward to put his head in his hands, his elbows on his knees. I wanted to see his face, but his hair fell so that I couldn't, and I contented myself with an awkward embrace of his head, one hand rubbing his back in an almost unconscious attempt to comfort him. It was only a few seconds really, but it seemed forever. When he finally looked up at me, he was smiling through tears, one of very few times in my life that I saw him weep.

"I'm sorry." He looked down, brushed at his eyes roughly.

I caught his hand in mine, touched his face so that he looked up at me again. "I love you. I don't care if you can't read. I love who you are." I held his eyes with mine as I kissed his hand, held it to my cheek a moment longer.

He looked down, holding my hand in both of his, then brought it to his lips as he looked up and directly into my eyes. He did not hide his tears, and that too was a great gift.

THIRTY

KEMEN

I didn't see Hakan for over a week. I spent blissful hours with Riona in the garden and by the fire in a small sitting room. I was sleepy, drugged with valerian and whatever else Saraid put in my wine. I slept and ate and slept some more. Waking to Riona's soft voice, her hand in mine, was like paradise. Her fingers in my hair made my heart skip. She kissed me. Everything was worthwhile; I would have walked through fire for one kiss, and she gave me more than one.

It would have been perfect, it was perfect, except for my guilt. I'd been terribly unfair to Hakan, hurt him as only a loved and trusted friend can. It was not until the next Seitsema, ten days after Saraid had opened my shoulder, that I finally went to his office.

Lani was just entering with a tray for Hakan's lunch.

"Lani, please tell His Royal Highness that I request an audience with him. If he has the time." She looked at me very oddly, since I'd never asked so formally before. I didn't even know the correct protocol. He'd never asked it of me, and I had not inquired. I'd presumed much.

She nodded me in a moment later.

Hakan was already up, striding to greet me. I dropped to one knee, but he cut off my apology before I'd even begun.

"Kemen. Sit." He sat across from me and pulled the tray closer. There was a cup already on his desk, and he filled it and the new clean one on the tray, which he slid toward me. "Have some tea. How are you?"

I studied his face a moment before looking down at my hands. He was very serious, kind but solemn. "I'm better." I took a deep breath. "Hakan, I was out of line. It wasn't…" but he shook his head.

"I know. I'm glad to have you back. Consider it over." He smiled, as if he had put it behind him, but I saw the hurt in his eyes.

We drank our tea in silence, and I stared at the floor. Words. They're like a weapon I haven't learned to wield properly, flailing about and wounding those I love most.

"I suppose you'll want to go back?" he glanced up at me, his expression unreadable.

"Aye."

"I've drawn up the terms for a treaty. If you're up to it. We can talk later if you're tired." He studied me seriously.

"Now is fine."

He pulled some papers over and shuffled through them until he found a map, which he spread about before us.

"We will draw the border here, effective upon signing of the agreement."

It was generous, giving them back nearly all the land we had taken.

"We will also give them thirty rams and one hundred and fifty ewes, of good stock."

More than generous.

"They will pay tribute in kind, leather, wool, or livestock equal to the value of twenty lambs per year, due each spring after lambing. This will be used to support the school that will be established in Ironcrest. The school will receive other support, of course, but that's a beginning. Tribute will first be due next year, and renegotiated ten years after that, if not earlier, to be paid as long as the school operates. The school will take twenty students, to start three months after the signing. It may take more students later, but that's a start."

I nodded. "It's more than fair."

"Aye. It is. I doubt they'll argue much. But I'd rather have them grateful and improving their lot than desperate. If they have something to lose, they'll think twice before resorting to raiding."

"What about the women they kidnapped?"

He sighed heavily, then chewed on his lip as he thought. "Do what you can. I can't imagine many of them are even alive. The Tarvil are not kind. But get them back if you can."

"Right."

We said no more about it that day, nor in the days until I left again. We ate together sometimes, and the words hung between us, though we both tried to pretend it had never happened. Hakan did not hold them against me. He was too compassionate, too understanding, for that, always quick to forgive, and he saw clearly enough that I had not been at my best or most rational.

But what comes out when you are pushed beyond endurance is often what lurks inside the rest of the time as well. The hurt remained in his eyes, and I wished with all my heart I could take back the bitter words I had thrown at him.

Aye, I had been bitter, but not at him. At myself and my failures. I had used him, used my service to him as an excuse. I could never have told him that, but perhaps he understood it as well. Once I wished to live, my service to him no longer required that I die. No doubt he noticed that irony too.

I THINK IT WAS in the first week after my return to Stonehaven, but my memory of that time is blurry and disjointed. I'd been in the garden most of the morning, napping intermittently on a blanket in the shade of the willows next to the pond. The breeze blew the warm sweet scent of the roses over me, and the leaves rustled quietly. Riona had been reading to me, but she'd gone inside and Lani stayed with me. Someone was always with me. I wasn't asleep, but my mind felt perpetually foggy.

Lani spoke very quietly, as if she wasn't sure I was awake. "Kemen? I'm not brave."

I smiled a little, too tired to open my eyes.

"Can I hold your hand?"

I nodded, and she slipped her hand into mine. I rubbed my thumb over the fine bones. "You gave me courage, Lani."

She sighed. "I wanted to help. I didn't know what Saraid was going to do. How much it would hurt you." She sounded like she wanted to cry.

I squeezed her hand. "It was brave." I opened my eyes to see her lip trembling.

"I'm sorry." She wiped at her eyes. "I don't think I can be a healer. I almost threw up when you, when…" she stopped, sniffling and trembling almost violently.

I pushed myself up so I could see her better. I was so tired I could barely see straight, and I felt dizzy and stupid with exhaustion. "You did well. A healer's job is difficult."

She shook her head and looked away as she wiped her eyes. Her voice shook a little. "I mostly told my Da I wanted to be a healer so he wouldn't push me so much to get married. He's afraid I'll end up alone if he doesn't take care of it for me. He doesn't want me married yet. He just wants to choose the man and have me sign the papers in case…" she stopped. "He's not doing well." She brushed at her eyes again fiercely.

"Is he sick?" My question sounded inadequate to my own ears, but she nodded.

"He's doing better, I guess. Saraid doesn't know what it is." She shrugged as if she didn't want to talk about it, but she leaned forward and looked down so that I couldn't really see her expression.

I rubbed my thumb over the back of her hand. My shoulder throbbed, and it took all my concentration to form my words. "He wants you married just so you'll be taken care of? That's why you started training with Saraid?"

She nodded. "I do want to help people. But," her voice shook and she sniffed again. "I don't think I can do what Saraid does."

There was a long silence, and despite my best efforts, my eyes closed. "While I'm alive, you will never be without protection." I had to stop and think before I could find the rest of the words. "That may not be worth much. But if you want, I can tell your father that he needn't worry about you being alone."

Riona was there, though I hadn't seen her come. "Kemen, lie down. Please." Her hands were gentle on my back and my good shoulder, supporting me as I leaned back feeling dizzy and sick with pain.

I heard Riona whispering quietly to Lani, then she spoke softly to me. "Do you want any lunch, Kemen? I have it for you here."

I wasn't hungry, but I thanked her anyway. They kept wanting me to eat. The berries were best, fresh and sweet after months of bread, tough meat, and old vegetables. I wanted to say something else, to tell Riona I wanted to speak to Hakan and to Lani's father. I was so tired I couldn't seem to say the words.

But I did not forget.

Thirty-One

Riona

One afternoon I brought him lunch in the garden. He'd been outside most of the morning, dozing in the warmth. With his eyes closed he told me which birds were singing, warblers, tanagers, tiny siskins, vireos, and once the cry of a hawk far above us.

He pushed himself up to sit cross-legged on the blanket when I set the tray down on a little folding table. He was eating more, but he was still terribly thin. He was cold sometimes even when it was warm, and I kept a cloak or a blanket nearby in case he started shivering.

He smiled his thanks and reached for some of the cheese.

"What happened to your hand?"

He glanced at the scar. "I don't remember."

"It looks like it hurt." It was still faintly pink, a thin arc from the top of his wrist to the outside of his forearm, disappearing into his sleeve.

He shrugged slightly. "It happened during battle. I had other things on my mind."

I wanted to hear his voice. Even when I'd thought him ugly, frightening, I'd thought he had a pleasant voice.

"May I ask a question?" I was strangely nervous.

He nodded, pausing to smile at me again. He still looked so tired, but the brightness in his eyes was reassuring.

"I heard something in Kumar and I wondered if you would tell me what it meant." At his nod, I tried to remember the words. The sounds of Kumar are quite different than those in Common, and I wasn't sure I had it right. "*Waratoshu hani maktai. Hanil amai. Ryuu soktai akashni. Hanil rulakshani amai.*"

He stared at me. "Was there more?"

"I didn't hear it all. But I remember *'Hanil amai. Amai. Tavarin suvari, ekanska.'*" I hesitated, but finally asked, "What does it mean?"

He spoke slowly. "It is a quote from Kardanska's account of Stonehaven's founding. It's a poem. Are you sure it wasn't *Ryuu sokti akashnai. Hanil rulakshanai mako amai?*"

It sounded very similar, but finally I shook my head. "I don't think so. What does it mean?"

"The quote is wrong. It's from the death scene of Aitor. It should say, 'Remember me, I gave my honor for your life, beloved lord. Forgive me. Great is the glory I claim for you. I have given all I have; forgive me for my weakness.'" He licked his lips. "The second part is from earlier. It should be, 'Forgive me. Forgive. I have lost the suvari for your crown.'"

He looked down at the table. "But what you said translates to, 'Remember me, I gave my life for your honor, beloved lord. Forgive me. Great is the glory I discard. I have lost all I desired; forgive me.' And the second part, 'Forgive me. Forgive. The suvari is ready, but I won't lead them.'"

We sat in silence, and he stared at his own hands clasped together on the table. I reached out to run my finger over the pale pink line curving over the back of his wrist, wishing to soothe him somehow.

"Where did you hear it?"

"You said it, when you were sleeping and fevered."

He nodded as if he'd expected that answer. I waved at a fly buzzing around the meat, and finally he began to eat a little. Afterwards he lay back with his eyes closed. I read to him, but he slept soon.

The garden hummed with life, bees buzzing and tiny lizards scuttling through the grass. He made me notice those things as I never had before. Lani came out to see if he needed anything and sat with me a while. He murmured in his sleep, and I reached out to touch his shoulder gently. He frowned and shivered, and I pulled the blanket up around his shoulders. He let out a sigh, almost a groan, before shifting and sleeping more easily.

Thirty-Two

Kemen

Those weeks with Riona were balm to my heart. I needed comfort, and she was comforting. I needed rest, and she let me rest. I needed peace, and she was peace to me.

I did nothing. I asked nothing. I had nothing to offer.

But she was there. When I could eat, she sat with me. She touched my hand and was not repulsed by the darkness. She sang to me. When I dozed and jerked awake with dreams of men I had lost, she was there. When I wanted to walk and didn't have the strength, she lent me hers. When I leaned on her, she supported me and did not scorn my weakness.

I had long loved Riona. But in those weeks, I better understood why.

THIRTY-THREE

RIONA

K emen went riding with the king not long before he departed again for the north. The queen was very large with child by then, and we followed in an open summer carriage as the men rode ahead. They kept to an easy pace, more the king's doing than Kemen's.

From a distance, he looked splendid, tall and proud, his shoulders broad and his waist narrow. He wore his sword as he wore his shirt, without thought or effort. But closer, I could see his left arm still bound to his side, the hollowness of his cheeks, the king's careful courtesy and effort not to tire his friend.

Drokan drove the carriage. The royal couple walked with Kemen to the top of a small hill while Drokan and I spread out the blankets and set up the trays of food.

I served during the meal. When I refilled Kemen's goblet, his smile nearly made my heart skip. He let his hand linger on mine a moment. He has beautiful hands, with fine straight bones and lean strong fingers. He didn't talk much, but that was hardly unusual. He didn't seem to be in much pain. The queen Kveta told a Rikutan fairytale, complete with all the dramatic voices she could devise to make the men laugh.

Kemen hardly ate anything, and I wasn't the only one who noticed. The queen glanced at him worriedly several times.

"Won't you eat any more?" she asked.

He shook his head.

She opened her mouth as if she wanted to argue with him, but the king curled his hand around hers and she only frowned at the tablecloth. Kemen didn't seem to notice, leaning forward to rest his head on one hand, eyes closed.

The king spoke quietly. "Kveta and I are going on a walk. We'll be back soon."

Kemen nodded, looking up to smile at them as they rose. The king had to give the queen a hand, and she struggled to her feet, ungainly and beautiful with pregnancy, her cheeks rosy in the warmth. They walked up the hill hand in hand.

"How do you feel?" I reached out to touch his hand.

"Could be worse." He shrugged and smiled a little, but even in the warm sun, he still looked grey with illness and fatigue.

"Will you rest?"

He nodded, and though I wanted to help him, I knew it would hurt his pride if I did, so I waited while he carefully and painfully laid back, his eyes closed against the brilliant sun. I moved closer, so that my shadow fell across his face, and he smiled again.

"Thank you."

I ran one finger down his cheek, tracing the line of his lips. "Are you sure you don't want anything else to eat?"

For a moment he looked like he might be sick. "I'm tired, Ria."

"Darling, I'm sorry. Just rest." I ran my fingers through his hair, hoping to comfort him.

He clasped my hand, held it to his cheek with a sigh, then kissed my fingers. "Your voice is beautiful."

I bent to kiss him and he blinked in pleased surprise. "Shall I sing to you?"

He smiled even more, pressing his cheek against my hand. "Please." His skin was cool and smooth; he'd shaved that morning.

I sang to him softly and watched him doze in the heavy summer warmth. His clothes were too large for him now, and the collar of his shirt was open to show the smooth skin of his neck, the slow pulse of his heartbeat, the sharp angle of his collarbone into the muscles of his chest. If he hadn't needed the rest so desperately, I might have been bold enough to kiss him again. Once he jerked half-awake with a sudden gasp. I shifted a little and he rested his head against my knee with a murmured apology.

The king and queen returned in a little over an hour, flushed from the heat and smiling. They wanted water and wine before we packed everything and started back toward the palace. When the king and Kemen mounted their horses, the king offered Kemen a leg up, but he refused it.

I don't know if Kemen realized that we all stopped to watch him mount, worried that he didn't have the strength yet. Even without using his left arm, and so tired he could barely stand, he mounted in one fluid motion as if it was the most natural thing in the world. I helped the queen into the carriage and we were off again, the pace easy and slow.

I FOUND SARAID in her herb garden. "He's still barely eating."

"What did you expect, Ria?"

"I thought you said he was getting better!" I blinked back sudden tears.

When we returned to the palace, he'd stumbled a bit from exhaustion as he dismounted. He smiled, bowed to the king and queen, kissed the queen's hand. I'd walked with him to his room. Once he'd even stopped to lean against the wall a moment, his hand trembling when I put his arm around my shoulders. When we reached his room, he'd nearly collapsed into the nearest chair. I'd pulled off his boots for him, and when I bent to kiss his cheek, he was so dazed he'd blinked in surprise before smiling apologetically. He was already asleep, or perhaps unconscious, when I draped a blanket over him, his elbow on the arm of the chair and his head braced on his right fist.

She shook her head. "Ria, he's healing, but he's not well yet. It takes time for a body to readjust. He's still in pain. You're not pushing him to eat, are you?"

I shrugged a little guiltily. "Not much."

"Don't. He will when he can."

I knelt to help her pull weeds from around the mint and lemonbalm and threw the torn stalks onto her growing pile. "He's too thin. How can he heal if he won't eat?"

"Ria, it takes time. He's doing better than I'd ever have expected."

I frowned. "I still don't think he should be riding yet."

"He went riding?" She looked up at me suddenly. "Today?"

"With the king. The queen and I followed. They had a picnic."

She yanked up another weed savagely. "Stubborn fool! How far did they go?" She scowled; she'd uprooted a lemonbalm plant along with the weed.

"About an hour at a slow walk; a couple leagues maybe. The king and queen went on a walk and he slept before we came back." I swallowed hard.

"How was he when you got back? Tired, I know, but did he look like the pain was worse?"

"Not really. Just exhausted."

"I should expect so. He shouldn't be riding for another month." She sighed. "I'll speak to him tonight. I did tell you, Ria."

"It wasn't my idea! The queen suggested it, but they wanted him to ride in the carriage. You think he'd consent to that?"

She sighed. "I know it wasn't your idea. I meant that I told you about men like him."

I bit my lip. True. She had.

AS USUAL, I kept my eyes well away from the wound when Saraid changed his bandage. Saraid said I didn't need to hold his arm, because he clenched his jaw and kept still even through the worst of the pain. But I knelt in front of him and watched him, my hand gentle on his arm. I don't know if it comforted him, but it was meant to. His long eyelashes brushed his cheeks, dark and beautiful.

He took a quick, sharp breath, his arm tensing suddenly, and Saraid apologized quietly. Then she said, "Sir, I heard you went riding today."

He made a soft, affirmative sounding grunt.

"I wish you wouldn't. You really shouldn't be riding for at least another month."

The same sound, with a slight quirk of his lips into a faint smile.

"Is the pain worse when you ride?"

"No."

"How's your appetite?"

He made a noncommittal noise and she frowned at his back as she positioned the bandage carefully.

"I'm leaving next week for Fort Kuzeyler." He opened his eyes to look at me.

She scowled even more at his back but kept her voice calm and soothing. "It isn't wise, sir. You can't send a message instead?"

"No." Even facedown on a bed, exhausted, with his eyes closed again and his shoulder opened to the bone, his quiet voice had absolute authority. "I won't take a healer for the journey, but an officer named Kudret Askano will be going with me. Will you show him what to do to change the bandage?"

"As you wish, sir."

I DON'T KNOW why he didn't take a healer. I would have asked, but I wasn't bold enough to question him yet, not about military matters. I took Captain Askano to Kemen's room the morning before he departed again for the north. He was younger than I'd expected and I felt an odd sort of affection for him. Kemen had said he was a good officer, talented and honorable, and I could believe it. He was handsome; he looked like someone's younger brother or someone's sweetheart. If I'd met him before I met Kemen, I might easily have lost my heart to him. I knocked on Kemen's door and he bid me enter, rising to greet the young captain.

"Sir." Captain Askano dropped to one knee as he bowed far more deeply than was proper to anyone but a king. He spoke with solemn courtesy. "I am glad to see you better, General Sendoa."

Kemen bowed to him, and then they both smiled broadly, clasping elbows in the soldier's gesture of friendship.

"Have you met Riona?"

"No, sir." Captain Askano shook his head.

I felt my face heat. Kemen stepped closer to put his hand behind my back, the tips of his fingers just brushing my shoulders. "Kudret, this is Riona. Riona, this is Captain Kudret Askano, a good friend and good soldier."

Captain Askano swallowed, flushing slightly at the compliment. It made him look very young. He bowed to me politely. When he raised his eyes, I was startled by his look. Toward me, there was a flash of... what? Resentment? Anger? Those words are too harsh; it was more of a coolness, as if he knew how I had hurt Kemen. When he glanced back at Kemen, it was with worship in his eyes. Hero worship.

Saraid came then. I untied the cloth that bound Kemen's arm close to his body, a sort of sling that supported it to keep it from pulling his shoulder, while Saraid spoke to Captain Askano about the herbs she used. I didn't have much to do after that, but I stayed and watched.

Kemen pulled off his shirt and Captain Askano seemed to pale a little, though Kemen didn't notice. He lay face down on the bed, and Saraid untied the bandage, peeling the thick cloth back carefully. I kept my eyes on Kemen's face, wondering if he would want me to kneel

235

by him as I usually did. He glanced at me and smiled a little, a warm smile that seemed to say he was fine.

"Thank you for agreeing to do this, Kudret." Kemen spoke mostly into the mattress.

"Aye, sir." He bowed slightly as he said it, as if he was honored by the request.

Captain Askano nodded as Saraid told him what to do. To boil the bandages. To dust the wound with a mixture of herbs that she had already prepared for him. To pack it with honey. She had already told Kemen how to make lavender tea for the pain, but she told Captain Askano how much lavender and white willow could go in how much wine. That oatmeal and boneset tea would be helpful. She showed him how to clean the wound gently and Kemen closed his eyes, his jaw tightening.

Kemen said something in Kumar, and Captain Askano grinned broadly before he followed Saraid's instructions on how to tie the bandage. Then again, quiet banter back and forth, with several grins and one chuckle from Captain Askano. It soothed my worry to see Kemen joking, though I didn't understand his words.

Captain Askano glanced at me and said something very quietly to Kemen in Kumar. It sounded like a question. Kemen spoke sharply, his voice harder than I had ever heard it. Captain Askano swallowed and seemed to apologize even more quietly, with a slight bow toward Kemen's back. He did not look at me again.

I wondered if I should leave. I didn't know what Captain Askano had said, but I could imagine. I was a servant. I had already been more than unfair to Kemen. I didn't deserve him. I couldn't argue with any of that, and I wondered if it wouldn't be better, for his sake, if we had never met. My eyes pricked with tears, and I brushed at them, hoping no one would notice.

Afterwards, Kemen pushed himself up, the muscles in his right arm standing out beneath smooth dark skin. He was still terribly thin, the edges of his collarbones too sharp, but even so, he was beautiful. When he sat up, I could see the hard flat muscles of his stomach, the easy strength and grace of each movement. He'd regained a bit of color, still pale but no longer ashen grey. If Captain Askano and Saraid hadn't been there, perhaps I wouldn't have blushed so fiercely when I realized I was staring. I don't know if anyone noticed. When I handed Kemen his shirt, his fingers brushed mine and he smiled at me.

I looked down at the floor, and he said my name softly. Our eyes met, and his eyes were so warm that I couldn't help smiling a little. I know he saw my damp eyelashes, but he didn't say anything. I didn't want him to make an issue of it. He only bowed his head to kiss my fingers gently.

I wished desperately that he wasn't leaving.

THIRTY-FOUR

KEMEN

Perhaps the most courageous thing I've ever done was leave a rose outside Riona's door the day I departed again for the northern border. It might have been dark pink, which Kveta said symbolized gratitude, for the care she had shown me and for her forgiveness. It might have been yellow, for the joy I found in her smile, for the new beginning we had found, or that I hoped we had found. It might have been red, for the love that grew every day between us. But I chose white, the purest, most flawless white I could find, for the purity of my love for her, for my humility and my hope.

One rose. It was so little to offer, but what I had to say could not be said with words or with flowers.

I wanted to bid her farewell, but for some time I couldn't find her. I finally saw her in a hallway, and she smiled at me, a blushing, almost tearful smile that made my heart skip. I took her hand.

"I leave this afternoon for the north. Otso won't wait forever. He needs Hakan's decision on the treaty." I looked down at my boots, wishing I knew how to speak of more tender things. I wanted to run my fingers through her beautiful hair, touch her lips, her cheeks, but I wasn't bold enough. Instead, I bowed to kiss her hand.

"Kemen?"

Her eyes were like sapphires, blue and perfect, and her lips trembled a little. She drew my hand up to her cheek, biting her lip as if she were trying not to cry. My left arm was finally free of the binding Saraid had insisted on, at least for a few hours each day, and I raised my hand to carefully brush the tips of my fingers over her hair.

"Will you hold me?" Her voice was soft.

She moved into my arms, her hands gentle on my back and carefully avoiding my still-painful shoulder. My cheek was against her hair, and I closed my eyes. She even smells of beauty. She murmured something into my chest.

"What was that?"

"Be careful." She was sniffling fiercely.

I smiled as I grew bolder, using one finger to brush away a tear from her cheek, catching her hand in mine and kissing her fingers one by one.

KUDRET AND SOME twenty suvari accompanied me on the ride north. Hakan insisted on sending a carriage with us, in case I grew too tired to ride. I was pridefully convinced it was unnecessary, but I humored him. He's my king, and a friend, better than I deserve, and if it soothed his worry, I wouldn't argue too strongly.

Of course, I didn't actually ride in the carriage.

The late spring journey was a tour of all the natural beauty Erdem had to offer. The bluebells were blooming, wild roses, bloodroot, and celandine. Lambkill dotted the rocky slopes of the hills, the harsh name at odds with the tiny, geometrically perfect little flowers. On the banks of the Purling River we saw irises, indigo and pale yellow and brilliant red, jumbled together with bleeding hearts and lilies. Once we were far enough east to see them, the Sefu Mountains were silhouetted every morning and the snow glinted vivid red and violet every evening under the sunset.

Saraid and Hakan were right; I should not have been riding so soon. My shoulder didn't hurt too much anymore, though it was stiff and painful when I tried to move it. Kudret changed the bandage for me every morning and night. The wound was healing well, slowly from the bottom, covering the bone first. The scar was so thick I imagined it would be months before I got full use of my arm back, if I ever did.

But the weakness from the long fever and blood loss was deeper than I wanted to admit. The first day I rode for only four hours, and even that took every bit of my strength. The lingering pain was manageable and faded every day, but I was dizzy and sick with exhaustion. Sometimes I rode with my eyes closed, half-dozing in the early summer warmth. Each night I sat by the fire aching and absurdly sore given our easy pace, but each day I pushed myself a little more.

Hakan sent all manner of rich food with us. I felt like I was always eating, but I was tired of looking like an emaciated scarecrow. The few times I'd seen myself in a mirror at the palace, I'd been shocked by my own appearance. The long ugly lines of my face were even more sharply defined. The muscles I'd earned through years of hard training were shrunken and pathetic.

Kudret, and indeed all the men, were more than courteous to me, addressing me with deferential respect and aiding me at every opportunity. They set up and broke down my tent, attended my horse every morning and night, and brought me food and drink at every stop. I appreciated their consideration, but at last I had to insist that I attend my own horse. My arm was still difficult, so I accepted assistance with my tent and saddling Kanti, but I brushed and watered her myself. As I regained strength, we rode longer every day.

We stayed one night at Fort Kuzeyler. Kepa received me with great courtesy, and I was relieved to see that he seemed to bear me no ill will, though he must have read the letter I'd left about leadership in the north in my absence. Another man might have been angry at my terse analysis of his faults, but Kepa was not a man to hold a grudge. I respected him for his character, if not his leadership ability, and I resolved to find a way to use him more effectively. A border conflict was not the place for him.

When we reached Izotz, I could ride all day, though by evening I was nearly staggering with weariness. Riding through the gate brought a rush of emotion that closed my throat, and I merely nodded to the sentry. Last time I'd ridden through that gate, I'd thought I would never see Hakan or Riona again. I was happier, but it brought a pang of guilt. I'd been so unfair to Hakan, who had never been anything but kind to me.

The night we arrived, a courier caught up with us bearing word that the royal child had been born, a boy. Hakan had given him my name.

I SENT SCOUTS to find the Tarvil camp. They had moved, but not too far, and when the scout waved the parley flag, he received an answering wave of Otso's blue and golden sash tied to a long pole.

We were greeted with cheering when we entered their camp. Cautious cheering, but cheering nonetheless, meant to honor and welcome us. Otso was nervous when we settled in to discuss the treaty terms. I brought wine, one of our few bottles from Izotz, to preempt his offer of drink. Horsemilk is not my idea of delicious even when fresh. Rancid, spiced, and served hot, it was positively revolting. Otso was so entranced by the aroma of the wine that he waved away the drink that a boy offered us. I don't know how much he liked the wine, but he was courteous and intrigued by it.

He was more than pleased with Hakan's offer. He pushed half-heartedly for an increase in the number of students, but when I required a corresponding increase in tribute he dropped the matter easily. In any case, the treaty provided for renegotiations at reasonable inter-vals. I knew the last bit would be more contentious.

"There is one final condition. The Erdemen women taken from the border towns will be returned to us."

"It is not possible." He sat back and folded his arms across his chest.

"There will be no treaty without them."

"Why not? They are not badly treated. They are not prisoners. They are guests." He frowned, and I saw a flicker of well-hidden fear in his eyes.

"Then you won't mind handing them over to us, to be returned to their families."

"We need them. It is not a matter of obstinacy. You can see we want the treaty. Increase the tribute if you must, but we cannot survive without women to bear our children. We lost many this winter and last winter too."

"You will not survive if you don't let them go. This demand is direct from the king Hakan Ithel. He is willing to devote the entire Erdemen military to it if necessary." I paused to let my words sink in.

In truth, I could understand his dilemma, and I was beginning to see the difficulty he would have in convincing the tribal chiefs. Representatives from several tribes stood in a silent line several paces behind him. Only one showed open hostility, his eyes flicking from the back of Otso's head to my face and back again. But none were friendly, either with Otso or with each other. Perhaps they were allies of need, but they were hardly an unbroken front.

Yet they needed the treaty desperately. Hakan might be furious with me, and justifiably so, if I ruined this. He'd hardly said what I conveyed to Otso. But I would risk it. The women had no one else to speak for them, and there would be no other chance like this. We could push the Tarvil farther. Even if the truce fell apart, in a matter of weeks they would be desperate again. Nevertheless, it was best to reach an agreement soon, before the Tarvil fled north and took the women even farther from their homes.

"If by chance any of the women would prefer to stay, the king would of course allow them to. But I will personally speak with each one before conveying their decisions to the king."

"You would extend the war for the sake of some thirty women?" He was incredulous. "You would lose many more men than that."

"It isn't a question of numbers. It is a question of principle. The Erdemen army upholds the freedom of Erdemen citizens. We will not compromise on this. You will agree to return the women, unharmed of course, or there will be no treaty."

I did not need to remind him that we held the stronger position. Another company of reinforcements had arrived with me, allowing me to send some three hundred back to their training grounds for rest. The Tarvil were desperately short of food, and we had just received another shipment.

"Excuse me." He stood to speak to the other chiefs. He hid it well, but for one instant I saw a flash of terror and hatred in his eyes, the look of an animal brought to bay. I wondered what price he would pay to get agreement from the chiefs. If he got it at all.

The conversation was quiet. Angry words hushed quickly, and more than one man glanced at me in disbelieving frustration.

"They say they cannot even find the women. They are scattered among the tribes with the men who took them." He leaned over the table, almost pleading.

"That's unfortunate. I'd expect it would take about three weeks to retrieve them, knowing the Tarvil skill as horsemen. But if they will not bring the women, you may tell them to prepare for a resumption of hostilities." I stood and bowed. Kudret and the other Erdemen soldiers followed me out the door of the tent, quick purposeful strides meant to convey my royal authority. We were mounted before I heard a shout behind me. I wheeled my horse about to face him.

"Three weeks? It may be possible in three weeks." He was grim, terribly angry but also afraid we would follow through on my threat. We would have; it was no idle boast. Soon they would accept any terms at all.

"Three weeks then. The women will be unharmed."

"Aye." He nodded grimly.

"We have a list of names, thirty-eight Erdemen women. We will meet you here in three weeks time at noon. We will sign the treaty then."

I SENT A COURIER back with the report to Hakan about the delay and my hope for the agreement. I didn't want to ask anyone to take my dictation for a letter to Riona, so instead I spent several days drawing a rose for her. I threw away several parchments, but at last I had one that was reasonably satisfactory. Of course it was only in black ink, but I smiled to think of it being a white rose.

The edges of the parchment looked empty, so I spent another few evenings drawing a tiny map of Erdem with an arrow pointing to Izotz, then little sketches of the fort, my horse Kanti, and the view east over the wall with the great tundra stretching out like an uneven table backed by the jagged edge of the Sefu mountains. I'm hardly an artist, but it passed the time and it made me smile to imagine her inspecting each one, her blue eyes wide and perfect golden lashes brushing her cheeks.

I was always eating or napping. My shoulder felt stiff and weak, but the pain was mostly gone. I watched the men train every morning. I even began exercising again, though alone because I was barely able to keep up with the group on even the most simple routines. It was high summer, and even that far north we had a few weeks of fickle warmth that brought out an astonishing variety of wildflowers. I filled a second parchment with drawings of northern primroses, tulipvine, hesmanka, and a palesinger nest I found with two eggs and one still-damp chick.

I hoped. I hoped for the sake of thirty-eight Erdemen women that Otso could coerce or cajole his chiefs into cooperation. I hoped for Erdem that we would have peace. And I hoped for myself, that when Riona saw my awkwardly drawn rose she would smile, and that when I returned she would have space in her heart for me.

I LEFT ENEKO in command at Izotz; he could lead the men in combat if things went ill with us. Kepa was a good man, but Eneko would take command if the peace dissolved.

We arrived early on the appointed morning, but Otso and some of his chiefs were already there, along with some fifteen women. I spoke with Otso first, and he said men were bringing the other Erdemen women. Not to worry, they would come. After all this, he hoped it almost as much as I did.

The men set up a mess tent and began cooking lunch. Akio was in charge of the women's comfort. We had brought extra cloaks and horses. I asked him to make sure they got a good lunch, and to let me know if they needed rest. I would prefer to move out immediately, of course. Women are fragile though, and who knew what they had already endured? It might be cruel of me to expect them to travel immediately.

I spoke with each woman for a few minutes. They were uniformly thin and pale. Several were viciously angry at their captors and bore marks to prove they had made their anger known. One had a recently split lip; several had fading bruises on faces and arms. Three said they were not badly treated at all, but they hated the food, the sound of the Tarvil language, the cold, and everything else. One said she'd been given to a young man she rather liked, outside the circumstances of their meeting, but she missed her family. All wanted to go back home.

Akio found their names on the list. One by one, others arrived riding behind Tarvil warriors. Chioma was barely seventeen and badly traumatized. She flinched away even from Kudret's respectful arm when he brought her into my tent. When she saw me, she swayed and nearly fainted, from fright I believe although she hadn't been well-fed either. Kudret helped her to a chair and I knelt to speak with her so that I wouldn't be so terrifying. She kept her eyes on her clenched hands, her eyelashes damp with unshed tears, and I questioned her as gently as I could. Where she was from, where we could take her, if she needed anything. She trembled and shook her head, and I asked one of the other women to care for her.

Men do such horrible things.

Rika was a little older, and kissed the Tarvil warrior who brought her on the cheek before sliding from his horse. She wanted to go back to her family, but she'd clearly had a very different experience.

When I closed the tent door to speak with Asya, from the town of Lirkua, she fell to her knees, weeping quietly. When I tried to lift her, she clung to me, small white hands clutching at the front of my tunic. She thanked me through her tears, and I rubbed her back as she stood leaning against me shuddering.

When the sun was high above, there were only thirty-five women.

I stood in silence with Otso, waiting. Time passed, and we paced about. Otso assured me they were coming. I wanted to believe him; there would be no point in destroying the peace now. But he was not like an Erdemen or Rikutan king with absolute authority. The chiefs might choose to disobey, and he could do little to enforce his wishes.

A rider came at a gallop, speaking quickly to Otso in Tarvil.

"He says two more are coming."

"There should be at least another."

He had no answer.

It was another half hour at least before the two women arrived, riding behind two Tarvil warriors. One of the Tarvil spoke to the chief, who then turned to me. "He says one of the women died. She was sick. It wasn't his doing."

I spoke to the women in the tent, alone where they would not feel intimidated by the Tarvil. "The chief says there was another woman who died. Is that true?"

"She died four months ago. Her name was Sunitha. I didn't know her well, but we spoke a few times."

"How did she die?"

"Their food. The man who had her was nice, not like Jaasku." She cursed, and though I could hardly blame her, the sound of curse words from a woman's lips is somehow more profane.

Thirty-eight were accounted for. None of the thirty-seven alive wished to stay.

I nodded to Otso, and we went inside his tent to sign the final treaty. I'd almost expected something to go wrong at the last moment.

I presented him with wine, but he was eager to honor me now that we were signing the much-desired treaty.

He pressed the vile drink upon me despite my first refusal and drank himself, thinking that I mistrusted him. I finally drank a little to avoid offending him; that would hardly be a good start to negotiations. I didn't fear poison; they had too much to gain through me and too much to lose by my death. I thought perhaps it wouldn't affect me so much, since I was much stronger than the last time.

I expected him to sign with a smile, the quill was in his hand, but he stopped suddenly.

"I would ask a great favor of you before I sign."

"What is it?"

"I ask that you take the first student now. You may choose your price for the cost of his food and lodging and for your trouble from my personal treasure. I ask that you take him to Stonehaven with you and keep him under your personal instruction. He should learn about your government, the structure and working of it, and the military code of honor. Your fighting arts. Whatever else you see fit to teach him. I want him to serve as your *aloka*."

"What is an aloka?" I'd never heard the Tarvil word, but while the chief searched for an explanation in Common, Kyosti whispered in my ear.

"Sir, an aloka is a sort of apprentice, like an apprentice blacksmith or weaver. An aloka serves a Tarvil warrior, who acts as his sponsor and tutor. Competition for the positions serving the most renowned warriors is intense. He's asking a great honor."

I nodded, and addressed my next question to Osto. "Why to me?"

"He may be the next High Chief. His father died some months ago, in battle. He was nearly ready, but Elathlo is young."

"His father was your son?"

"Yes." There was grief in his eyes for only a moment. He was hardened, and sorrow isn't something you show to an opponent. However friendly our exchange now, we were still opponents.

"You are chief. You could choose another who is already prepared." At his sharp glance I added mildly, "It's a lot of pressure for a boy. He may be happier with a simpler life."

He straightened proudly. "He will not shirk his responsibility. He already has much support. His father was well respected, and a strong warrior. Besides, it is an opportunity to build friendship between our two nations."

I wouldn't have called the scattered Tarvil tribes a nation at all, but I nodded. "That may be so. I'd like to speak with him before I decide."

In a few minutes he was ushered inside the tent. Pale, short and stocky, light brown hair with a reddish tint. The cut of his hair and the blue sash about his waist proclaimed his rank. His face was proud, but his eyes showed naked fear when he looked at me.

"How old are you?"

"Thirteen, sir." He didn't bow until Otso prompted him, and then he did hurriedly, as though he'd been so afraid he'd simply forgotten.

"What's your name?"

"Elathlo, sir." His Common was heavily accented but understandable.

"Do you want to go to Stonehaven?" It was unfair of me to ask him that while his grandfather watched. I wasn't used to children then. Now I wouldn't be so cruel.

He hesitated, glancing at the chief before answering almost in a whisper, "I do as Otso-ka wishes, sir."

"He's a good boy. Obedient and hardworking, with a quick mind." His grandfather clapped one hand on his shoulder.

I studied the boy, who dropped his eyes to floor in respect and no little fear. "Look at me." Pale blue eyes, intelligent enough. Terrified, but trying to hide it. If I towered over his grandfather, I must have seemed a giant to him. What would Hakan think of this? What would Riona think?

"How long?"

"I would ask you to take him a year, though if he disappoints you, you could of course send him back earlier."

The boy drew a quick breath and bit his lip. An unpleasant prospect that would be, no doubt.

The silence drew out for a moment before I nodded. "Agreed. I'll take him."

The chief smiled in delight, but the boy bit his lip more fiercely, probably trying not to cry. Kyosti blinked in surprise but quietly added the additional provision to the treaty.

"What price will you take for his food and lodging?"

It was a great gesture of trust not to determine this before the agreement. Perhaps also a measure of his eagerness to have me take the boy.

"You asked it as a personal favor. I will take nothing. He will be my guest."

The boy stared at me a moment from the corner of the tent before he slipped out, and the chief bowed low, though still with bad form.

"If it meets your satisfaction, we will deliver him to you tomorrow. He should have tonight to bid his family farewell."

"Of course."

We took the women back with us that night to our camp. Most of them preferred to ride alone, though at least one was quite terrified of her horse. I think she simply wished to not have a man's body so close to her. I tried to be sensitive to such things. Several rode alone, several rode alone but with soldiers holding the reins of the horses, and a few rode behind suvari I selected. Most of the men were quite trustworthy, but I wanted men who also looked as gentle as possible.

It was not a long ride, but I expected the women were tired. Akio had some of the men construct a sort of privy, a small tent erected over a fresh new latrine for them. Women need privacy, especially in a camp full of soldiers. They were assigned two large tents, with men to stand guard at each corner. It did not need to be mentioned that harassment of them would not be tolerated.

WHEN THE TARVIL arrived the next afternoon, I was contemplating the wisdom of eating a bit of bread with some water to wash it down. Even the thought made me queasy. The Tarvil must have metal-lined stomachs. I'd been vomiting, or trying to anyway, at least twice an hour since the middle of the night. I vowed the education we'd promised them would include how to make a drink from something other than sour horsemilk. Grapes, barley, rice... anything would be preferable.

The boy had his own lanky horse, rawboned and skittish, which he rode well, and a pack on his saddle carrying what little he would bring with him. I thanked the men with him, and they nodded and rode away without a backward glance. The boy looked after them once, though, jaw clenched tightly and blinking a little, as if he was at the edge of tears.

I heard a few grumblings at his presence, but I led him to my tent first. "Make yourself comfortable. We will stay here tonight at least. Let me know if anyone troubles you."

He kept his eyes down and nodded slightly.

"Look at me."

He stared at me wide-eyed.

"You are my guest, and I command these men. You will inform me if anyone bothers you."

He nodded.

"Excuse me." I had to go outside to vomit again. Even water would not stay down for long.

"Sir?" It was Kudret. "Did you want to move out tomorrow?"

"Aye. Have the men get ready. Remind them also that Elathlo is my guest. He is to be treated with all due respect."

He nodded. "Aye, sir."

Elathlo was standing uncomfortably in the middle of the tent when I entered again.

"Don't you have blankets and such?"

He ducked his head. "Yes, sir." He pulled a single blanket from his pack.

"It's a bit cold for one blanket. Is that all you have?"

"Yes, sir."

"Fine. You'll take my bed. It's over there. We'll head south tomorrow morning." I was a terrible host. I wanted to be kinder to the boy, but I didn't really know how. "Are you hungry? Thirsty?"

"No, sir."

"Call me Kemen. We'll be spending a lot of time together. I'd prefer to do it as friends." I smiled at him and took a sip of water. Would it stay down? I wondered for a moment. Then another sip. No, it would not. Even at the time I thought it rather funny. Undignified, but perhaps it helped him see me as I really am, every bit as frail as anyone else. I scarcely made it outside in time, leaning breathless with hands on my knees. I rinsed my mouth and spat out the water.

The boy's eyes were wide. "Are you ill, sir?"

"Aye, a bit. Come, I'll introduce to you to some of the men."

He followed me quietly, bobbing his head in a decent imitation of an Erdemen bow.

"This is Toivo. He cooks for the officers. Stay on his good side and you'll have a more pleasant journey."

Toivo grinned. He has a good sense of humor, but he's also a good man to have at your back in a tight spot. Handy with a sword and reliable. A good combination.

Elathlo's question was so quiet I missed most of it, especially when Toivo shouted with laughter.

"What?" I asked.

The boy dropped his head and bit his lip.

253

"What did you say?"

"I asked if you offended him, sir." He regretted saying it, thinking I was angry, and I smiled as reassuringly as I could and clapped one hand on his shoulder.

"I did not. No, it isn't his doing. When's dinner?"

"Not long. Will you be eating any?" Toivo looked at me dubiously.

"I think not tonight." I had to stop again, lean over and let my stomach determine if it had anything else to give up. It didn't, though it tried valiantly. "You can send Elathlo's dinner to my tent though."

He nodded. "Aye, sir."

"Why are you ill, sir?" Elathlo asked quietly.

"Kemen." I corrected him with my eyes closed, still leaning over. Days without food are manageable, but lack of water affects the body more quickly. If I couldn't keep water down soon, the journey back to Stonehaven would be more challenging. I couldn't imagine how I survived it the first time, weak and sick as I was. Even when I was healing quite well, I was utterly, comically miserable.

"Kemen, sir."

"It seems your chief's idea of a good drink is a bit different than mine."

He followed me back to the tent. I set up the low traveling table and a pallet for him to sit on for dinner, which came soon after.

"You're not going to eat at all?" He poked at his stew cautiously.

"No. I doubt you have to fear the same reaction to our food though. It's cooked well enough."

"What is it?"

"Venison. Maybe some mutton, if there was any left."

"It's good."

254

I grunted, though I didn't mean to be rude. I let myself rest, head in hands and eyes closed. He was pleasant enough, eager to please and respectful. But what would Riona think? What would I do with the boy? Would he just follow me around? What would Hakan think?

"Sir? I mean Kemen. Should I take back the bowl?"

"Aye." I walked him to the mess tent and then back through the fading light.

Kudret was waiting to change the bandage on my shoulder. When he asked if I was ready, he glanced at Elathlo, and I said that he could stay. I stripped off my shirt, sat on the floor of the tent with my legs crossed, and leaned forward with my elbows on my knees. Kudret knelt behind me with the herbs and bandages on the low table beside him, the lantern close by so he could see clearly. I let my head hang down and closed my eyes while he peeled the old bandage away. I opened my eyes a moment and saw the boy's feet move closer as the bandage came off.

Kudret said very quietly in Common, "If you touch him, I'll cut your hand off."

"Kudret!" I spoke in Kumar, my voice sharp. "Elathlo is my guest, and I will not have him threatened."

"Sorry, sir." Out of the corner of my eye, I could see him bow a little as he spoke, in Kumar this time.

I sighed, and I felt Kudret begin to clean the wound, quiet and steady as he always is. "Thank you for your concern. But Elathlo didn't do this."

He hesitated and then said, "Can you be sure he means you no harm, sir? He is a Tarvil. Can you trust him while you sleep?"

"No one can ever be sure. All we can do is trust. If I wake up with a knife in my back, then you may have reason to mistrust him. Until then, I expect him to be treated as my guest. If not for his sake, then for mine."

"Yes, sir." He didn't sound happy about it.

The wound was healing well. I'd spent almost a month in Stonehaven after the surgery, then three and a half weeks riding to Fort Kuzeyler and on to Izotz, then another three weeks between the parley with Otso and the signing of the treaty, for a total of nearly three months since the surgery. I was beginning to feel human again, aside from the illness from the Tarvil drink. My clothes still hung on me and I still couldn't use my arm much, but I no longer used the sling at all.

"Kudret, Otso has no reason to wish me dead now, not by Tarvil hands anyway. They have too much to lose by my death. I don't think you need to worry about him."

"Yes, sir." He spoke calmly, and I felt him relax a little. In a few more minutes, he was finished. I stood to bid him farewell, slightly dizzy with the lack of food and water, and I think he knew that when we clasped arms to bid each other goodnight. He asked me if I needed anything, but there was nothing he could do, and he bowed deeply on his way out.

I pulled the top blanket from my pallet and replaced it with Elathlo's. It would be a bit of familiarity for him at least. Thirteen is very young. I entered the king's service at fourteen, and though my skill was more than adequate, I wouldn't have minded another year of childhood. I couldn't blame the boy for his nerves. At least his Common was good; we wouldn't have too much trouble communicating.

"We'll leave tomorrow morning. I hope you'll forgive me if I turn in early." I spread my blanket on the ground. "Do you need anything? There's water in the canteen there if you get thirsty."

"Thank you, sir. Kemen."

"Blow out the lamp whenever you want." I fell asleep quickly, though I didn't sleep well. I woke from thirst sometime when the moon was high and managed to keep a few sips of water down.

We woke early, and my attempt at breakfast was unsuccessful, though I did manage to keep a bit more water in me at least. Akio looked after the women, made sure they had breakfast and water to wash with if they wanted. I was more than grateful to hand over that duty to him. Soon I'd be riding toward Stonehaven. Riona's smile beckoned, and I dozed in the saddle when my stomach would allow it. They ate lunch still riding, though I decided against it. I was half-dreaming of Riona, how she would smile at me, the way she walked, when Elathlo spoke for nearly the first time all day.

"Was it really the *alamaa* that made you so sick?"

"The drink your grandfather gave me?"

He nodded.

"Aye."

"Why did you drink it?" He seemed utterly baffled. "Didn't you have it last time, when you signed the truce?"

"Aye. I didn't wish to insult your grandfather. The treaty benefits us both too much to cause needless offense."

He bit his lip but ventured, "You might have told him it would make you ill."

I raised my eyebrows. "Would he have believed me?"

He frowned. "Probably not." Then he smiled tentatively. "A high price for a treaty, isn't it? Was it worth it?"

"We'll see. I hope so."

Thirty-Five

Riona

L ani's first time serving refreshments at a ball wasn't going especially well. She was nervous, and had already nearly dropped one tray of pastries when some duke elbowed her accidentally. All the same, I didn't expect what happened.

I carried a tray of wine glasses, and Lani followed me with a tray of cheeses on miniature bread slices as I wove through the crowd. I saw Lady Grallin out of the corner of my eye, speaking to one of her friends, Lady Ilara. I offered her the wine, and she traded her glass for a new one.

Lady Ilara said to Lady Grallin, "It's a shame Sendoa isn't here."

"Why?"

"I thought you liked him."

"I like the way he dances." Lady Grallin's voice was snippily condescending, and I bit my tongue.

Lani smiled sweetly at them and offered the tray of cheeses.

Lady Grallin said, "He's in the north again."

"Pity, isn't it?" Lady Ilara eyed her friend with a bit of what I took to be sympathy.

"Not really. That's what Dari dogs are for. It's what they're good at. The pity is, it's all they're good at." She took a sip of wine.

I barely suppressed the desire to spill the entire tray of wine glasses down her dress.

Lani flushed to the roots of her hair. "Lady Grallin." Her voice was shaking, and I reached for her sleeve.

Lady Grallin's eyes glinted dangerously. "Yes, girl? You wish to say something?"

"He's an honorable man, and - " Lani didn't finish.

"He's a dog. I've turned down five proposals in the past year, and when he was in Stonehaven he didn't even come visit, although I did invite him." She was seething, and even her friend Lady Ilara's eyes widened. "I invited him for tea, and he didn't even send his most humble and respectful regrets. Of course," she sniffed, "I should have known as much. A dog can't be expected to act like a man."

I bit my lip so hard I tasted blood, but I reached for Lani's arm again. She was shaking, and she pulled away from me.

"He's not a dog! He's the best - "

Lady Grallin slapped her hard across the mouth with a resounding crack. Lani's tray clattered to the floor, cheeses flying everywhere. She staggered and then straightened, her eyes wide and her mouth dropping open in shock.

Lady Ilara pulled on her friend's arm. "Come, Melora, let's go."

Everyone in the room was looking at us.

259

"You can have him if you want him, girl. It would be fitting, a servant and a dog." Her mouth twisted. I swallowed hard. That was what I feared most, shaming him before the world when he deserved nothing but honor.

Lani was bright red, the print of Lady Grallin's hand standing out white on her cheek. She glanced at me for one instant, and I knew Lady Grallin had seen what I hadn't. Lani… I should have seen it earlier. I should have known.

I grabbed Lani's sleeve and jerked her toward the door. "Go to the kitchen. Now!"

"But," her eyes were wide, her lips trembling and puffy on one side.

"Go!" I pushed her toward the door.

Lady Grallin was shaking, pulling her arm away from Lady Ilara, who was trying to calm her.

"I believe General Sendoa has the right to chose whomever he wants, Lady Grallin." I tried to keep my voice from trembling, holding my chin high. Servants don't talk back to nobles.

She drew in a quick breath. "I suppose it's you, then." She smiled disdainfully. "You're not even pretty."

The crowd shifted. The king himself was striding toward us through the crowd, and in front of him was Lord Grallin, Lady Melora Grallin's father. She hadn't seen them yet. I didn't mind the insult, but I wanted the incident over. I wanted her gone and I wanted to speak with Lani.

I curtsied. "I don't aim to please you. If General Sendoa is pleased, then I'm pleased. I assure you, I'm just as baffled as you are by his choice."

Her eyes widened. It felt like everyone had fallen silent, though the musicians were still playing; the conversations had all faded and stuttered into a tense silence.

The king was close behind her, and I spoke loudly so he would catch every word. "But it isn't wise to speak against the king's favorite, a man of such standing and honor. Perhaps you set your sights too high, Lady Grallin."

She was white with rage, trembling, and the king paused a few steps behind her to hear what she would say. "He is a dog and a son of a dog! If he spends his life for the kingdom, it is his highest use and no great loss. He was honored by my attention and too stupid to realize it. I gave him a chance, willing even to look past his Dari filth, but I was wrong." Her voice was shaking, and she twitched her shoulder away from Lady Ilara's restraining hand.

The king was almost as pale, his jaw tight, and his gaze flicked to me for one moment.

Lord Grallin reached his daughter's side then. "Come, Melora." He took her arm firmly and began to pull her away.

The king spoke then, his voice falling into the tense hush. "Lord Grallin. Lady Grallin. I would like to see you in my office. Now." He glanced at me and nodded toward the door.

The king might have done any number of things, and from his pale cold anger he appeared to consider them all. Lady Grallin waited for his decision, white and trembling and suddenly tearful, and her father Lord Grallin scowled at the floor and at his daughter alternately. I waited, wondering whether I ought to feel sorry for her. I didn't, although I did feel a bit sorry that her father had been pulled into the issue.

In the end, the king was very lenient, but when he pronounced his decision his voice showed his fury. "Lady Grallin, perhaps you are unaware that Ambassador and General Kemen Sendoa, whom I am very honored to call a friend, was gravely wounded some months ago and is only now recovering. His death would have been a national loss as well as a personal sorrow. I would not suggest wishing for such a tragedy in the future. Such a wish ventures perilously close to treason."

He let his words sink in, and Lady Grallin seemed to sway a moment. Her father closed his eyes and bowed his head. The penalty for treason is death.

"This time I will forgive your unwise and impetuous words. I understand that perhaps you have been disappointed because Ambassador and General Sendoa did not recognize your many charms, and disappointment sometimes results in foolishness. It is the decision of the crown that you will not attend any court events until General Sendoa returns from the north again and personally expresses his wish that you be pardoned."

Lady Grallin gasped. Absent from court, she would not be eligible for marriage by any titled lord. But she didn't understand that Kemen wouldn't care a whit about what she'd said, and so she would be welcome in court again in a matter of weeks or at most a few months, if he were delayed on his way back. The king knew it, and I knew it, and I think Lord Grallin at least guessed.

He knelt and bent his head in quick gratitude. "I thank you, Your Royal Highness. You are exceedingly generous, and I express my most humble appreciation on behalf of my daughter and family."

Lady Grallin curtsied low, though she still frowned in confusion.

The king smiled solemnly. "Lord Grallin, you and the rest of your family are still welcome. Your daughter's foolish tongue does not lessen the honor of your family."

Lord Grallin knelt again.

I smiled inside. Lady Grallin was suitably subdued. Her face was white and she was biting her lip, apparently trying not to cry. When she passed me on the way out of the room, she didn't look at me, and her shoulders were a little slumped. I curtsied to the king when I left, and he met my eyes with a quick, small smile.

Thirty-Six

Kemen

It took a week to get back to Fort Kuzeyler. The men could have gone faster, but the women were tired and ill-fed. I didn't want to push them too hard. The second day I was saddling Kanti when one of the women came to me. She was perhaps twenty-one or twenty-two years old, with a fading greenish bruise over one eye.

"Sir, are you really General Kemen Sendoa?"

"Yes."

"I'm Minu. I wanted to thank you again. I didn't ever expect..." tears welled up in her eyes.

"I'm sorry you had to wait so long. The border should never have been left unprotected." I had to wait for my stomach to settle then. I desperately needed a drink, but I knew it wouldn't stay down long.

"Thank you." She had a nice smile, genuine gratitude lighting her face. "Are you ill, sir?"

"Aye." I couldn't help it, I had to lean over and take a few deep breaths with my hands on my knees. Nothing. There was nothing, had been nothing for two days. "You've a stronger stomach than I if you survived on that food."

"It wasn't good. But they didn't give us that milk drink. They call it *alamaa*, which means drink of gods and kings. It's only for those they want to honor." She smiled, and I nearly laughed.

"I feel honored, and I will feel it for another few days, I imagine."

She grinned. I turned back to finish tightening the girth on Kanti's saddle, and she stood for a minute in silence. Finally, she spoke almost tentatively. "Could I ride with you today, sir?"

I looked at her in surprise, and she dropped her eyes to the ground.

"If you like."

She looked slightly embarrassed. "I just haven't spoken to anyone kind in months. If you'd rather me not?" she looked up at me a little apprehensively.

"'It's no trouble. You're ready?" She nodded, and I boosted her up. I made sure Elathlo was ready to go. He was a good rider, but he had difficulty saddling his horse because he wasn't tall enough to lift the saddle high easily. I helped him and mounted and we were off in a matter of minutes.

I was tired, but I was intensely aware of her arms around me. I wished she was Riona, but I couldn't help but note every innocent touch, every shift of her body. I wondered if I was wrong to ride with her, whether Ria would wish I had not. She was nothing but proper, sometimes only gripping the sides of my tunic. I know now my worry was foolish, that Riona would not begrudge her that small kindness, but at the time I wondered whether I was wrong.

Despite all that, I dozed in the saddle. I've had plenty of practice at it; every suvari learns the trick. She rested her head against my back at times and perhaps she dozed too. I offered her water and drank after her, but it came up again only a few minutes later. When I straightened, I felt a small hand rub between my shoulders gently. Comforting. It was simple human kindness, but it made me smile. When we went over uneven ground, her arms would tighten about me. She was nervous, and I could tell by her seat that she was not an experienced rider.

I dozed again and dreamed she was Ria. I would love to ride with her. I would take her to the edge of the forest to the south. From the top of the hill we could look north over the palace and see the graceful symmetry of the gardens laid out before us like a painting. It would be early autumn there when I arrived again, and not many of the flowers would still be blooming, but the white walls of the castle would shine like pearl in the sun.

My thirst woke me, and again I drank only to heave it up a moment later. It was dizzying, and I blinked at the spots that seemed to fade in and out. I tried again and managed to keep a little bit down. A swallow, only a swallow, but it was a start. Minu leaned against my back again.

We stopped for lunch. Elathlo had ridden beside me all morning, quiet and apparently content. I found a spot a little removed from the group, laid on my back, and pulled the hood of my cloak over my face. It wasn't dignified, but neither would it be dignified to pitch face first from my mount. Elathlo sat by me to eat. "Do you want me to bring you something, sir?"

"No, thank you." A good boy. I wasn't being much of a host.

In the afternoon we crossed rougher ground, and Minu's arms tightened about me again. I shifted uncomfortably, and she pulled back. "What's wrong?"

"My shoulder, on the left."

"I'm sorry. Are you hurt, then?"

"I'm healing."

She adjusted her arms and leaned in to my back carefully. "What happened?"

"It was quite a while ago, an arrow. It's healing well, but slowly."

We rode in silence most of the afternoon, but it was pleasant. I dozed again and dreamed of Ria, and wished fervently that it was her arms around me. Minu was kind, and I liked her, but she was not Ria.

She slept against my back, and once she jerked awake with a small cry.

"What's wrong?"

"A dream. I'm sorry." She sounded very subdued, and I patted her arm around me. After some time, she whispered a quiet thanks into the back of my tunic.

A year before, I would have been breathless at her arms around my waist. I should have been then; Ria and I had hardly been so intimate yet, at least physically. But my heart was with her, and it left only a comfortable companionship between Minu and me. Though we scarcely knew each other, the day felt warm and pleasant, and when I bid her farewell after dinner, I did so with a smile.

We left them at the fort. Kepa would make sure they were conveyed safely back to their homes. Then we were off southwest toward Stonehaven.

WE HAD ONLY ONE incident on the journey back to Stonehaven, the first morning after we left the women at Fort

Kuzeyler. Elathlo had gone out to relieve himself before breakfast one morning. I was speaking to Akio when I heard a sharp crack and a sudden surprised cry followed by some laughter. Normally I would have thought nothing of it. Soldiers tease each other, and they can take care of themselves. But I had a sudden thought that perhaps this was different, and I ran toward the sound, Akio right behind me.

Elathlo had his bootknife in one hand and was trying to buckle his belt with the other, eyes flicking nervously between the three men before him. One had his sword out.

"Attention!" I barked.

They bowed immediately and straightened. The center one sheathed his sword, and all three looked at me with suddenly wide eyes.

"Elathlo, put your knife away."

He complied, eyeing them warily.

"What is going on?" I stalked before them, noting the men swallowing nervously.

"Nothing, sir." The one who had answered was the one who had held the sword. I couldn't remember his name; he hadn't been with us long. None of them had. They were under Shui's command, new recruits not long out of training.

"That is obviously not true. I did not know we taught Erdemen soldiers to lie. Is that a new lesson?" I kept my voice more scornful than angry, though my fury mounted when I saw Elathlo biting his lip in an apparent attempt not to cry.

"No, sir."

"Perhaps you would like another chance to answer my question. Note that I am being lenient. You will not get a third chance. Now, what is going on?" He flinched when I turned to him sharply, meeting his eyes. In times like this, I appreciate the value of my green eyes. They make people sweat, and lose their thought, and often I get the truth.

"We were only teasing him, sir."

"And how were you doing that?"

"I hit him with the flat of my sword, sir. We didn't hurt him."

I glanced at the boy, who stood with a set face, flushed and unhappy. He did not appear injured.

"Apparently you misunderstood my order from a few days ago. I seem to recall making it quite clear that Elathlo is my personal guest. I don't believe this is how Erdemen treat guests. Or did you think I didn't mean it?"

That would be tantamount to calling me a blusterer and a liar, a terrible insult, and all three blanched at the thought.

"All three of you will be docked one week's pay, and you will not ride for three days. Your horses will carry your gear, but you will keep pace on foot."

Again all three paled, and one even seemed to think of protesting, but thought better of it at my stern glance.

"Take note of this. You are volunteers, and recent ones at that. If you had more experience, your punishment would be more severe, but I am lenient today because you are new and young and foolish. Such conduct is not fitting for Erdemen soldiers. I, and you, should hope that I do not hear of such misconduct again."

"Yes, sir." They bowed deeply, thoroughly sobered.

"Akio, tell Shui I'd like to speak with him at my tent."

"Yes, sir." He bowed as well.

"Come, Elathlo." I put my hand on his shoulder as I walked him back to my tent. He was tense and cautious, and I ushered him inside the tent and let the flap fall before speaking to him.

269

"Sit." He sat on the lone folding stool and I knelt in front of him, so that I didn't tower above him. "Did they hurt you?"

He shook his head. "No, sir."

"You're not hurt?"

He shook his head again.

"Have they bothered you before?"

"No, sir."

I studied his face a moment longer. I liked him more than I'd expected to, and I didn't want him to be afraid. I put one hand on his shoulder again. "Tell me if they do, or anyone else does."

He nodded, eyes on the floor. "Thank you." His voice was very quiet. Embarrassed.

I stood. Best to let him have time without eyes on him. Outside I spoke with Shui about his men. He would take care of the necessary reductions in their pay and keep a close eye on them. There would be no grumbling about the punishment; a soldier respects the judgment of his officers. In this case, these three would have little sympathy from the others. Every military has these problems; giving young men weapons does sometimes unveil a streak of cruelty within them. I had seen that already, and I was glad this time it was no worse. But Erdem's strength was not built on barbarism or needless cruelty. Anyone who had served more than a few months would have known that such behavior wouldn't be tolerated.

We were packed in a matter of minutes, the tent broken down and packed on the horses. I had the horn blown to gather the men.

"This morning we had an incident of misconduct. Let me remind everyone that Elathlo is my guest and will be treated with all due courtesy. Consider this a warning. If I hear of further misconduct or discourtesy to my guest, the consequences will be severe."

Rumors would soon enlighten those few who hadn't yet heard what had happened. Most of the men bore no love for Tarvil, but they wouldn't make one boy pay for the deeds of his entire people.

I alternated our pace between a quick walk and a trot, hardly a brutal pace but one guaranteed to tire them quickly. By noon they had been jogging for over four hours, and when we stopped for lunch they collapsed to the ground. I don't think of myself as cold-hearted, but no doubt they felt I was at the time. Endurance is of value in training; it would do them no great harm. A punishment must be unpleasant to be effective.

Elathlo seemed very subdued when he saw them, and I wondered if he thought I was too harsh. I let the group rest for an hour, which I thought was generous. Normally we would stop only long enough to water the horses and let them snatch a quick bite to eat. The men would eat while riding if necessary. After that, I let them walk for an hour before increasing our pace again.

In midafternoon I dismounted and ran. Though I was eating again, my stomach was still rather cautious with any sort of food, but my shoulder was healing well and I missed the exertion. Wounded and ill, I'd been soft on myself for months, and, at least for a while, the emptiness in my stomach made me feel light and strong.

Despite what the three may have thought, I did feel some sympathy for them as they struggled to keep up. I fell back to run with them, but I'm not sure whether it was helpful or not. I meant for it to be encouraging, since I didn't have to share their punishment, but I thought later that perhaps they saw it differently. In any case I enjoyed the run, the pleasant burn in my legs and the feeling of flying over the earth, though my shoulder still bothered me at times.

I called a halt not long before dusk beside the Brightling, which is a tributary of the Silvertongue River. Some of the men set up my tent, one of my favorite perks of being an officer. I stripped and bathed in the river. Most of the men did eventually, though one of the three who had run lay on the ground in exhaustion. I let him rest until it was nearly dark, but when he still didn't move I approached him.

"You'd best go bathe. I don't want you stinking up the camp." The words sound harsh written down, but I didn't say them harshly.

He looked up at me towering over him and groaned as he sat up. I knelt to speak with him face to face.

"Go on. You'll feel better afterwards." I gave him a hand and pulled him to his feet.

"Aye, sir." He nodded and trudged away.

The night air was cool but I did not put on my tunic. I washed it in the river and hung it to dry outside my tent. It would be mostly dry by morning, and the air was pleasant and fresh after my exercise. Elathlo was waiting and I led him to the mess tent. We ate with Akio and a few other officers. Elathlo of course was very quiet, but he listened carefully and watched everything. It was a pleasant dinner, and I was gratified to find that I could stomach most of it. I was glad Elathlo had had no such problems with our food. When we reached my tent, I lit the lamp and spread my blanket on the floor, then sat down to study the map. Elathlo sat down on his pallet and I felt his eyes on me.

"Sir?"

"Hm?"

"Will you really make them run for two more days?" He looked a little worried.

"Yes." I smiled to soften my words. "We've all done it in training. They can do it. It's not supposed to be enjoyable."

"You don't look tired though. My father thought you weren't really human. Are you?"

I blinked in surprise. "Yes, I'm human. I'm Dari."

Maybe he hadn't seen one. But Dari are just as human as Tuyets. Or Tarvil. What a question! I certainly felt tired. I wondered if he thought I was some immortal monster, gifted with superhuman strength and lacking a conscience. No wonder he was terrified to go with me to Stonehaven.

"I'm sorry." He smiled awkwardly. "What happened to your shoulder?"

"It was an arrow last winter. I had surgery on it more recently." It did not need to be said that it was a Tarvil arrow.

He stared at the ground. "My father was an archer." Then he looked up, his eyes sad, a little confused, and quite apprehensive.

I don't know what he expected, whether he thought I would hold it against him. I felt awkward and very ill-equipped to handle a boy's emotions. "I'm sorry. I imagine you miss him."

"Yes." He kept staring at me, as if he expected something else. Finally he asked, "Why did you agree to take me to Stonehaven?"

"You don't want to go, do you?" I reached over to pat his shoulder in sympathy when he shook his head. "If you succeed your grandfather, it will benefit both Erdem and your people for us to be on better terms." He still watched me. "Besides, your grandfather looked as though he wouldn't be particularly happy with you if I'd refused."

"No." He smiled suddenly. "No, he would've been very angry that I'd disappointed you. My father saw you fight once. He said you were a demon or a god, he wasn't sure which. After he died, Otso-ka said you were my best chance to learn *kestan*. If you didn't take me, he would have presumed you judged me incapable of ever learning it."

"What's kestan?" I leaned back on my hands. I had never heard the word, but he spoke of it as if I should know exactly what he meant.

At my question he stared back at me. "Kestan?"

"Yes, what is it?"

Again he stared at me as if he couldn't believe I was asking the question. Finally he licked his lips. "It's the quality of being a leader. A warrior. A king. Strength. Courage. Ferocity. Bloodlust. It comes from the gods and the earth. The alpha wolf has it. A hunger for power and the strength and determination to keep it at all costs."

He looked down then. "I went through the training, but Father said I was still too weak and soft to lead men, that no one would respect me even when I came of age. When Father died, Otso-ka said I was hopelessly soft and would never be fit to rule, but when you offered the peace treaty, he hoped you would take me. If anyone could teach me kestan, it would be you, because you breathe it like air."

We stared at each other in silence. I struggled with the words in my head, discarding them one after another. Finally I said, "It seems your father and grandfather have a very different view of what makes a good leader than I do."

He stared at me, eyes wide in the flickering lamplight.

"Bloodlust does not make a man fit to lead, nor does strength. I serve a king who rules with wisdom, though he's still young, and mercy for his people, not a desire to dominate them. I knew he was fit to rule when I realized he would give up his crown if he thought his people would be best served by another."

"That's stupid!" His exclamation was soft. His eyes widened when he realized what he'd said.

"Is it?" I smiled.

He dropped to both knees, bowing his head to the floor. He spoke clearly, though his voice was muffled by his sleeves. "Sir, I await your just punishment."

I waited a moment, expecting something else, but he remained motionless. "Get up." He raised his head cautiously before jumping to his feet and standing at attention, his eyes on the floor.

"Sit down. Look at me. What was that all about?"

He raised his eyes to mine reluctantly, as if he could not believe I was demanding it of him. "Sir, I am awaiting your just punishment of my unwise and disrespectful words."

"What punishment do you expect?" I was curious, for this was an area of Tarvil culture I knew nothing about. But the boy was clearly very frightened, and I wished I knew how to reassure him.

He dropped his eyes to the floor again. "Whatever you choose, sir."

"I'm not going to punish you. I just want you to answer my questions. If I were Tarvil, what would you expect?"

Again he fell to his knees and bowed his head to the floor. I put a hand on his shoulder and he flinched. "Sit down. Don't be afraid." He sat again, biting his lip. I repeated my question.

His voice was very quiet when he answered. "I would expect at least a beating, sir. But you might choose more."

"Like what?" I wished I looked less frightening.

"An aloka's life is in his sponsor's hands. If I displease you, you have the right to kill me however you choose." He stared at the ground and his voice was a whisper. "The best for the aloka is beheading, because it's fast."

Phraa. No wonder he was terrified of me. "I can't think of anything you could say that would merit death in Erdem. Don't be so afraid. I'm not going to punish you."

He stared at me, his eyes wide and confused in the flickering lamplight.

"No doubt I'm demanding, and I will expect you to work hard. But I've never beaten a thirteen-year-old boy, not since I was one myself, and I don't expect to start now. Neither am I prone to beheading people for nothing more than words. Unless you threaten the life of the king, you have little to fear from me."

He stared back at me, still silent. Finally he nodded, cautiously, as though he didn't quite believe me. I turned my gaze back to the map, more to give him time to think than because I needed to look at the map again. This would be more challenging than I had imagined.

"WOULD YOU LIKE some *imea*, sir?"

"What is that?"

He opened a little packet. "Smell."

The little pile of dried leaves with some brown powder underneath smelled spicy and a little sweet.

"Is it like tea? I'll have some."

He looked at me doubtfully. "I don't think it's like your tea. But you can try it and see."

He took a tiny pot and two small cups from his pack and squatted by the fire outside after putting a little water in it. He boiled the leaves far past what I would have thought ideal, but finally wrapped a cloth around the handle of the pot and brought it inside to sit across from me at the low traveling table. He opened another little packet and carefully poured a lighter powder into the cups.

"What's that?"

"Milk." He was obviously concentrating. He poured the water, now a dark and grainy brown, into the cups and watched the lighter powder swirl around before disappearing.

"It's ready now. It's good luck too. The milk doesn't normally float."

I raised my eyebrows and he returned my gaze very seriously.

"That's what they say. I notice, if you warm the cups first, it always floats, and if you pour the *imea* in while the cups are cool, it doesn't. My grandfather always has good luck when I make his tea."

I laughed and he grinned back. "It's good. What's in it?" It was thick and rich, sweet, spicy, and with a slightly milky undertone, though thankfully not rancid.

"Imea leaves, *sharwan*, and milk. And a little *sosta*. My grandfather doesn't like sosta, so I don't use it normally. But I like it. What do you think?"

I shrugged. "I don't know which flavor it is, so I can't say. It's good though."

He sipped at his cup carefully. It was still very hot. "What is Stonehaven like, sir?" He ducked his head respectfully as he asked the question.

"It has perhaps fifty thousand people in and around it. Maybe thirty thousand are actually in the city proper."

His mouth dropped open. "That many?" his voice was only a whisper.

"More or less. You'll stay with me in the palace. There are servants to help keep the palace beautiful and running smoothly and to care for the horses and dogs." I smiled then, thinking of Ria waiting for me. "I'll probably be quite busy with work for Hakan. Your grandfather wanted you to serve as an aloka. What is that?"

He looked at me as if he thought I was testing him in some way, and answered formally. "It is a time of training to be a warrior. Serving you is a great honor. You might have asked for, and received, his whole treasure if you'd wanted. Serving the most renowned warrior is a great honor, and can be very expensive. An aloka works as a servant in return for tutoring and training. The best warriors have the most skill to offer, and so their alokas serve them diligently in order to earn their training."

"What would you do?"

"Whatever you wanted. Shine your boots. Bring your dinner. Wash your clothes. Clean your weapons." He still looked at me as if he could not believe that I did not know all this.

"Can you write?"

"In my language."

"What weapons have you trained with?"

"The scimitar and the bow."

"Have you done any fighting without weapons?"

He blinked. "Not much."

"We will begin with that first when we get to Stonehaven. You will also need to learn how to bow."

"Yes, sir. What is the penalty for bowing incorrectly?"

"You show a lack of courtesy." He looked a little confused. "There is no penalty, not for someone your age. For a soldier to bow incorrectly to a superior is an insult. I wouldn't recommend it."

"What duties will you expect me to carry out, sir?"

"You can water the horses while we travel and give them their rubdowns at night. Just your horse and mine, not all of them. When we get to the palace things will change. We'll see."

"Yes, sir."

"The proper way to address the king is as Your Royal Highness. I can't say I abide by that very well, but I would recommend that you do so. I doubt Hakan would mind, but it would be better not to antagonize the others in the palace."

He looked slightly confused. "Who is Hakan?"

"The king. Hakan Ithel."

He stared at me. "You call the king by his name?"

I smiled at that. "We were friends before he was king. You will have a tutor to teach you to write in Common. How much arithmetic have you done?"

"Not much."

"You'll learn that as well. You can sit in on some of my meetings with Hakan, though not all of them. And you can ask questions. Things will no doubt be very different than you're accustomed to."

Thirty-Seven

Riona

The next packet of letters for the king and queen contained a letter for me, sealed with a lump of red wax impressed with the tiny sword and shield emblem of his office, Minister of Military Affairs. I'd seen seals before, of course; one couldn't work in the palace without having seen wax seals of many different offices and prominent families. But this one was addressed to me! I wondered if he had dictated a letter, and if so, how personal it would be. He was such a private person I couldn't imagine it.

But what I found inside made me smile more than a letter. He'd drawn the flowers of the north, the fort, the mountains, and a tiny bird's nest. It shouldn't have surprised me, but somehow I had not expected his artistic ability. He was not as practiced as the portrait-makers of the city, and the drawings were only sketches, but he'd captured a distinct feeling of the north. In his sketch, the horse was graceful, mane and tail blowing in the wind, head high and alert. The flowers raised their faces to a pale sky, thin clouds skidding past. The mountains were sharp and harsh as knives, though distant. The tiny birds' nest was more friendly and approachable. One chick with damp feathers nestled against two spotted eggs.

I thought of Kemen, busy with leading the men, training, and whatever other responsibilities he had. I imagined him staying up late, broad shoulders bent over the parchment as he focused on the sketches, the pen nib scratching softly in the lamplight.

I smiled all day.

Thirty-Eight

Kemen

When we arrived in Stonehaven, we were greeted with great cheering throngs and waving banners. I had sent a courier ahead to let Hakan know that we were coming and that Elathlo was with me. We rode triumphant through the crowds. It's an odd feeling. Though I've experienced it several times, it never fails to startle me. I don't like crowds much, but their excitement was catching, and I found myself smiling despite my discomfort.

Elathlo was thoroughly disconcerted, his eyes wide, and he kept his horse close by mine. Everyone noticed him; his dress proclaimed him Tarvil clearly. Most simply ignored him and cheered for us, but I caught a few hostile looks. One man glared ferociously at Elathlo and pushed his way past the woman in front of him to be at the front when Elathlo passed him. I don't know what he was planning to do, if anything, but I kicked Kanti forward a little. I caught his eye and he dropped his gaze to the ground.

At the palace, Hakan met us in the courtyard. It is an unnecessary honor, but he always honored me perhaps more than he should. I appreciate it nonetheless, and I dismounted quickly and strode to meet him. I dropped to one knee to give him appropriate honor before the men. I introduced him to Elathlo, who also dropped to one knee. Hakan smiled and welcomed him kindly. Sinta would show him to his room and help him prepare for the banquet that night.

"We're having a banquet?"

"We are. To celebrate your success, of course, and to welcome Elathlo. If there's anything you want in particular, you'd best tell Joran now. Preparations are well underway." He was in an expansive mood. "I suppose you'll want to wash first."

I did. I was dusty from the road and hardly ready for a banquet, but I had a sudden thought as we walked through the hall toward my room. Bold, perhaps, but Hakan was a friend as well as the king. "I do have one request for the banquet tonight. But it's not about the food."

"Of course. What is it?"

I took a deep breath. "You know I'm courting Riona."

He nodded.

"Well, I would like her to join us. As my guest. Not as a servant. It's awkward having her serve me while we eat."

He nodded. "Invite her then. She won't have a suitable dress, I imagine. Tell her that she may speak with Kveta about that." At my look of confusion he grinned. "Kemen, you will have to learn to think about clothes once in a while if you speak with women. Kveta will lend

283

her a dress. They're not that different in size. But you'd best ask her soon, because Lika will need time for alterations. Go on then."

I laughed and bowed to him before going in search of Riona.

THIRTY-NINE

RIONA

I was watching when he rode in. I couldn't help it, though I knew I should have been working. He was splendid, and the sight of him made me smile with pride. I wanted to speak with him, just to see him, but when they entered the palace, I knew I had to return to work. I was heading toward the kitchen to help with the preparations for the banquet when I saw him in the hallway.

I smiled. I don't know what I expected, but it wasn't what happened. He smiled back, and with his eyes on mine, he kissed my fingers. Then, very tentatively and cautiously, he put his arms around me, as if he wasn't sure I would allow it. I smiled up at him and embraced him in return. He was too tall for me to kiss comfortably, but somehow we would manage. I felt him flinch suddenly.

"I'm sorry!" My hand had brushed across his shoulder. "How is it now?"

"It's fine. Healing well. Could I ask you something?" He looked down at the floor almost shyly, and I nodded. "Would you attend the banquet tonight with me?" His eyes were on mine.

I think I actually stuttered in my confusion. "I can't. I have to serve. I'll be in the kitchen. Besides, it's for you, and the king and queen."

"I already asked Hakan." His voice was very quiet. "If you want to, that is."

"The king said I could go?" I couldn't imagine it, but he nodded, smiling tentatively now. "I don't have anything to wear. Nothing nice enough."

He smiled more broadly. "Hakan said you should borrow a dress from Kveta."

My mouth dropped open in shock. From the queen? The king had said that?

He kissed my fingers again. "Please?"

I nodded wordlessly, and his smile deepened.

I did indeed ask Kveta for a dress. I thought it would be awkward, but the king had already spoken with her, and at my quiet knock on her door, she opened it and drew me in. She had picked out several dresses already and had me try them on right there in front of her mirror. I was a little shy about undressing before her. She is the queen, after all, and not another servant girl. She grinned at me though.

"Riona, you're lovely! You need better dresses than you've been wearing."

I didn't really know what to say. You can't scrub floors in velvets and silks. They're beautiful, but I could never afford them. Like every girl, I wished I had one nice dress of my own, just to have and admire, but I had no use for one.

"Try this one first." It cinched about my waist with a long swath of silk, the sleeves lacy and flowing. Kveta was smiling, as if this was exactly the type of afternoon she had planned for herself. I felt terribly uncomfortable. It wasn't my place to be wearing a queen's dress, much less picking and choosing among them.

"That one is nice, but try this one now." She watched me critically. This was velvet, a deep blue with cream colored lace and a neckline that felt scandalous. I suppose it wasn't really; I'd seen Kveta wear this dress and it was modest enough. It was only that I was used to wearing high necked work dresses. When I caught sight of myself in the mirror, I nearly didn't recognize myself. Work dresses are shapeless things, belted for the sake of convenience but hardly flattering. The woman in the mirror was not me at all; she was glamorous and beautiful, slender-waisted and wide eyed. Only my hair and my hands showed my true self. My hair was up in a practical bun, as it always was, and my hands were rough from work. I don't know whether I was beautiful, but in comparison to how I normally looked, I was positively transformed.

"That one. Wear that one. It's the perfect color! It makes your eyes glow." She was altogether too excited, and I couldn't help but laugh with her.

"Are you sure? This is beautiful. I shouldn't."

"Don't be ridiculous. You're lovely. The dress is perfect. We don't even need Lika to alter anything. We'll have to do your hair." She was grinning. "Kemen will be speechless."

He was. He scarcely took his eyes off me the entire banquet. I was painfully self-conscious. Our table was on the dais looking out over the nobility. It was not a huge banquet, but it was luxurious, and the king had met with several of the men present earlier in the day about various projects. The queen sat at the king's right hand and Kemen at his left. I sat on Kemen's other side, and I watched carefully to see how I should eat and drink, how I should hold the cups and the utensils. The Tarvil boy, Elathlo, sat on my other side, and he too seemed uncomfortable. He sat rigidly upright, glancing across me at Kemen periodically to see what he should be doing.

Finally, I leaned over and whispered in his ear, "I don't know what I'm doing either."

He looked up at me with wide eyes and a tentative smile.

When Tanith filled my wine glass, she smiled and whispered in my ear. "You look beautiful."

The king made an effort to speak with me across Kemen. It was awkward, and I'd never really noticed how that method of seating was good for allowing the king to look over the room, but not particularly good for encouraging conversation at the royal table. He could really only speak with his queen and with Kemen, but he made an effort. We had little to say to each other, but I appreciated the attempt. He had kind eyes, intelligent and perceptive. When I bowed my head with the usual respect, he shook his head. "There's no need for that tonight."

The food was delicious. I'd helped cook it, and servants eat the leftovers of banquets, so I'd had much of it before, but never as it was served, fresh and hot, with the successive types of wine to complement each new dish. The music in the background was stirring and beautiful, plaintive and joyful by turns. It was a beautiful night, and when Kemen quietly clasped my hand under the table, everything was perfect.

Finally the king stood, with a bow to his queen and a lesser one to me, though still more than a king should ever bow to a servant. He whispered something in her ear, and she nodded. Kemen bowed to the queen with a smile, and then to me before whispering in my ear, "Thank you."

FORTY

KEMEN

She was beautiful. Stunning. She took my breath away, and it was all I could do to catch every other sentence that Hakan spoke to me. He knew it, and didn't mind. With the compassion of a man deeply in love, he understood how helpless I was. He asked me to speak with him afterwards, but I don't think he intended to say anything in particular.

We were both a bit tipsy, though not drunk. The room had a low fire, and we sat in companionable silence. Hakan poked at the embers. "Are you going to marry her?"

"If she'll have me."

"You must be blind. She's only waiting for you to ask." He sat back and pulled off his boots before sticking his bare feet toward the fire.

I poured a bit more wine into our glasses. I would ask her, but she deserved a little more courtship. I should not assume her feelings, despite Hakan's confidence.

There was a long, comfortable silence.

"What really happened up there?"

"Where?" I'd been staring at the fire.

"In the battle when you were wounded. I never got a good report. Do you remember?" He was solemn now, and I swallowed.

"There was a blizzard coming. We had the gates open to let in the men who were out cutting wood. None of us knew how fast a storm can hit. The weather at Izotz is unlike anything I've seen, even at Fort Kuzeyler. The Tarvil attacked as the snow hit, and a few were inside the gates by the time we got them closed."

He waited, staring at me, and after a long silence finally asked, "Did you really mean to die?"

I shrugged. "I don't know. Maybe." I stared at the floor and finally drained my glass. "Not consciously, not at first. Later, perhaps. He looked just like you. You might have been twins."

"The boy?" Now he was looking at me very strangely. "The one you pulled to cover and nearly died for it?"

I nodded. "Yori." The name means trust.

"He looked like me?" His voice was rather strangled.

"Aye."

"You might have told me that." He sounded like he wanted to cry, but I don't know why he should have.

"Why? What difference does it make?"

He shook his head.

"You were right. You were rational. You thought like a king. I'm not a king. I'm only a friend, and I couldn't be rational. I couldn't watch him die alone." I poured another glass of wine but didn't drink it.

Perhaps I shouldn't have told him. What difference did it make what Yori had looked like? Did a boy with

291

Hakan's features deserve to live more than a boy with a different nose, a different jaw? Perhaps I burdened Hakan by telling him. It wasn't fair to Yori, either.

He said quietly, "I thought perhaps all this time I was wrong. That we weren't really friends after all. I'd called friendship what I ought to call patriotism." He took a deep breath. "I shouldn't have cared so much whether you do it for Erdem or for me. It shouldn't matter."

"It was love of Erdem when I served your father, Hakan. I was selfish when I sought to die, but what good I did for your throne, I did for you."

EPILOGUE

RIONA

As the king and I had both known, Lady Grallin was again made welcome at court. The king presented Kemen with the question during a small picnic in the royal rose garden. I was again a guest rather than a servant, and though it felt awkward and presumptuous, I was proud to sit next to Kemen. My heart trembled with joy when he reached for my hand, and I intertwined my fingers with his.

When the king described Lady Grallin's punishment, Kemen raised his eyebrows. When the king asked, with a sparkle in his eye, whether Kemen was willing to allow her back at court, he raised my hand to his lips.

"Invite her back. Though I pity the man who weds her." He smiled at me, and my heart nearly burst with love for him. "What do I care what Lady Grallin thinks? I've never been happier."

THE ROYAL CHILD was born that summer while Kemen was away, a boy with wispy blond curls and wide blue eyes filled with laughter. The birth was not especially easy for the queen, but neither was it difficult enough to keep her in bed for more than a day. She and the king glowed.

The boy was given the name Kemen Tahir Hakan, in honor of the man I loved so dearly. He was six weeks old when the queen invited me to come sing with her. I didn't know Kemen and the king would also be there, but the king was more than welcoming and Kemen's smile made me blush with pride in him.

The king himself played the mardosin, his hands brilliantly skillful, and the queen and I stood close to see the music. Kemen sat a few feet away holding his name-sake. The queen had shown him how to hold the baby's head so that the child's neck would not be strained, and Kemen had taken the child as if he were made of the finest crystal, infinitely fragile and precious. Tonight he watched us, and his gaze was so warm on my face I kept looking up to smile at him and losing my place in the music.

He was still very thin and quickly tired, though he was regaining strength. The slow recovery frustrated him, and he pushed himself harder than he should have. He'd begun early morning training sessions with the Tarvil boy almost immediately on his return. They drained him, though he tried not to show it. The one time I asked him to take things more gently, he smiled and said it was not entirely out of pride, but for Elathlo's benefit; the boy needed a challenge.

The last song was one of my favorites, but I barely sang. The king's voice soared, effortlessly beautiful, and the queen's lighter one wove around it like a golden thread. I closed my eyes, my lips barely moving. It was a love song, as all great songs are, and I smiled to hear it so perfectly sung.

When the song ended and I opened my eyes, the king was smiling gently, but not at the queen as I expected. His gaze went past her shoulder to Kemen. He was asleep slumped in the chair, long legs stretched out, with the infant cradled against his chest. One elbow was braced on the arm of the chair to support the child, and the other curled across the baby's back protectively. He was smiling slightly in his sleep and his cheek brushed the baby's fluffy curls.

Kemen

"I don't know how to dance." She kept her voice low, but she sounded on the verge of panic.

"Stand on my feet."

She almost giggled, and my heart leapt at her beauty. "They'll all laugh."

"I can't see anyone but you." I pulled her close with my right arm. She looked down for a moment and placed her dainty feet on my boots, and slipped her right hand into my left.

"Left. Right. Left." Then she had the rhythm, and she trusted me, lifting each foot in time with the music. She smiled up at me, and everything was perfect. I barely noticed when that song ended and another began.

I leaned down to speak in her ear. "I love you, Riona."

She kissed my cheek. "I don't know why." Her eyes were so blue I nearly lost my breath. "I love you too."

My heart was pounding so hard I was dizzy, and my voice shook a little when I whispered in her ear. "Will you marry me?"

She had tears in her eyes, a smile that lit the room, when she nodded. She slipped her other arm around me and in the middle of the dance floor, I kissed her.

THE ERDEMEN HONOR SERIES

CONTINUES IN

HONOR'S HEIR

Back in the Erdemen royal palace, Kemen begins training Elathlo, the young Tarvil heir. His own life and love are finally peaceful. Elathlo, however, is terrified of Kemen and his future on the tundra, making him the perfect target to pressure in a plot against Hakan. Because of a boy's fear and a traitor's anger, Kemen may lose everything he loves.

Elathlo must face his fears and defy the traditions of his people if he hopes to be the leader his people need.

C. J. Brightley

C. J. Brightley lives in Northern Virginia with her husband and young daughter. She holds degrees from Clemson University and Texas A&M. She welcomes visitors and messages at her website, www.cjbrightley.com.

Made in the USA
San Bernardino, CA
08 April 2014